HUNTER'S FIND

By

June Kramin

Pau Hana Books

Hunter's Find
By June Kramin
Copyright © 2012 by June Kramin
...

Published by Pau Hana Books
February 2014
Third edition March 2020
First published with Musa Publishing 2012

ISBN: 978-1310988530

Published in the United States of America
Cover Art by Valerie Kramin
Stock images: Shutterstock

For my BFF Jeanne ~

I know it will be years before you have the time to read it,
but I had to give you one of them.
Love you, Buddy

CHAPTER ONE

Hunt was walking the few blocks home from the Ace Bar. He'd had a few too many beers, but still held himself well. It was too convenient that he could walk home from the bar without worry of driving while drinking.

A police car stopped and rolled down the window. "How you doing tonight, Hunt?"

"Just a little unwinding after a long shift."

"You going to make it home?"

"I'm not that bad off. I only had a few. And you know I only have a block to go, jerkweed."

"Jerkweed? Don't make me go all police brutality on your ass, Blaine."

Hunt laughed. "Aren't you off duty yet?"

"Had a late bust. You know how I love doing paperwork."

"You want to go back to my place for a drink?"

"You trying to pick me up? Your luck would be better on Third and Market in the city."

"Har de har har. Is that where you're heading?"

"Been too long of a day. I'm on my way home."

Hunt slapped the side of the police cruiser. "Good night, Roy."

The officer slowly pulled away from the curb and flashed his lights as a goodbye. With the brief flash of red, Hunt saw something at the base of the hedge he hadn't noticed before and rushed over.

A young woman was lying there unconscious. There was blood trickling from her lip and her shirt was torn badly enough, he could see her lacy bra fully exposed. He quickly stood and whistled loudly. Hunt was grateful Roy heard him. The brake lights flashed immediately and within seconds, the officer was reversing toward him.

"She had a pretty good blow to the back of her head. That's our best guess as to why she was out when you found her. She wasn't raped, and there's no sign of roofies in her system. Must have had a fight with her boyfriend or pimp, or whatever the case may be," the doctor explained.

"She wasn't dressed like a hooker. You don't often see them outside the Ace Bar anyway," Hunt replied. "That shit tends to stay in the city."

"Well, whatever or whoever she is has yet to be determined. There was no ID on her whatsoever and no one here knows her. You want me to call for prints on her?"

"Let's wait till she wakes up and try asking her first. There's no reason to jump straight into a worst case scenario. You read too many detective novels, Doc."

"We're not so far out of the cities that we don't see some weird things happen here. You of all people should know, Hunt."

"Is it okay if I go wait in her room? Maybe if I'm there when she wakes up, I'll start off on the right foot."

"Knight in shining armor syndrome?"

Hunt grinned. "Something like that."

"She is a looker."

"This is professional."

"Of course it is. Go on in. Holler for a nurse when she wakes up."

Hunt fell asleep in the chair while he waited in her room. The adrenaline finally wore off, and the beers kicked in. He startled awake when he heard, "Excuse me." Hurrying to his feet, he tried to appear as awake as possible. It was starting to get light out; he was surprised he'd slept as long as he had.

"Who are you and where am I?" the woman asked as she pulled the sheet higher on her chest.

"Montgomery Hospital. I found you last night on Main Street and brought you here."

She stared at him blankly.

"I'm sorry." He approached her with his hand out. "Hunter Blaine. Friends call me Hunt."

Shyly, she accepted his hand and shook it. "Does this hospital make it a habit of letting strange men stay in the room with patients?"

"Um…no, I suppose not. But I'm—"

"Oh good. You're up." A large woman, too perky for this time of morning, came strolling in and interrupted them.

"I would have come for you, Mona. She just got up."

"Hunter Blaine! You stayed in here all night?"

"Doc said it was okay."

"Get yourself outta here this instant. You look a fright and probably scared the poor darlin' half to death."

"I'm all right, really," the woman said, softly. "I don't understand why you're here."

"I found you last night and brought you in."

"Found me?" Her expression changed, as if memories were finally returning. Hunt was anxious to ask her questions before she fell asleep again.

"Do you know—"

"Not now, Hunt. Scoot, you brute. I'll allow you back in after rounds."

"Yes, ma'am." Hunt headed for the door but then stopped. "Can I at least get your name?"

"I'll fill out the paperwork, Hunt. Beat it."

He ignored the nurse and kept his attention on the woman. She rested her head back on the pillow. Her gaze met Hunt's.

"Amanda. Amanda Gentry."

"You from around here?"

She shook her head. "Iowa." Her eyes closed and he left.

Hunt checked his watch and decided he had time to go to the gym before he went to work. He could shower there. A few beers after work were all Hunt allowed for a vice. He didn't smoke and didn't care for fast food. He prided himself on his cooking abilities. Well, he could grill anyway. It was trickier in the winter in Vermont, but he made do for himself.

His friends' wives were always trying to set him up, but at twenty-seven he was far from ready to settle down. His high school and college sweetheart took his heart for a ride a couple years back, and he didn't care to relive that any time soon.

Sex was easy enough to come by when he wanted it. A nice hotel room and a night in the big city held him over for a while. Hunt never paid for hookers. His natural charm and good looks melted anyone of his choosing in any bar. At six feet five inches with a perfectly sculpted body, he was impossible to resist. Hunt never spoke of what he did for a living. The intrigue of his silence made him that much more irresistible.

Keeping his private life was important, that's why he went out of town. Everyone in his small town knew him; they didn't need to know his personal business, too.

As Hunt worked out, his thoughts drifted to Amanda. He said her name out loud then glanced around to see if anyone else in the gym had heard him. Her age had been almost impossible to guess. Her tiny frame could have easily made her in her late teens. In the police car, he kept glancing at her as they went past streetlights. He had cradled her in his lap, protectively, as Roy sped to the hospital.

Once they were there, too many hands were on her as she was taken away. As she slept, her tanned face, which was now void of all blood and makeup, gave nothing away. This morning when she spoke, he wanted to place her in her early twenties. Even with what little she said, she had more confidence than a teenager would have. *Amanda.*

"Stop it, Hunt." He left the treadmill and headed for the shower.

Amanda lay still in the hospital bed, feigning sleep. She had given them a false name and nothing else. Well, she told that Hunt character she was from Iowa, but that was also a lie. She was waiting for a break in the rounds and nurses popping in checking on her so she could make a run for it. The last thing she needed was cops showing up and asking her questions about what had happened.

It was ten o'clock, and it had been a half hour since anyone had bothered her. When the last nurse was there, she complained her head hurt and her arm was itchy from the IV. The doctor gave permission for it to be removed and prescribed something for her headache.

"It will make you sleepy, so don't try to get up without help, okay?" the doctor suggested.

"All right. Thank you."

"If you're sleeping when the police arrive, we'll just ask them to come back. Your health comes first."

"I appreciate it. I do want to help them catch whoever did this to me, but I'm afraid my head hurts too much to be of any good right now."

"I understand. I'll check on you in a few hours."

"Thank you so much, doctor." She conjured up a few fake tears to blink away then accepted the pill, but never took it.

After she figured the coast should be clear, Mandy slipped on her shoes and managed to tie her torn shirt enough so the fact it was torn wasn't so obvious. The pattern was busy enough, the dried blood wasn't noticeable. Carefully slipping out the door, she hurried down the hall unnoticed. After she took the corner, she caught sight of a policeman approaching her. *Don't panic! He has no idea who you are. Keep walking!*

She tried to keep looking straight ahead as the officer passed, but she had to smile and nod when he tipped his hat to her. After she passed him he called out, "Amanda?"

Not thinking fast enough, she spun around at the sound of her name. "Shit. You're a cop?"

"Are you supposed to be leaving already?" Hunt asked her.

She froze, not knowing what to do. Fear finally took over and she ran. She shoved an empty gurney and a wheeled shelving unit into the hall trying to block his way, but Hunt caught up to her before the next turn of the hallway. He pinned her to the wall with his body, reached for her hand, and held it behind her back.

"Stop it! You're hurting me!"

"You promise not to take off and I'll let go."

"All right," she grunted.

He let her go and she spun out of his grasp. She only took a step before she knocked down a large chair outside of a room, trying to block his way again. He tripped on it and dove for her, knocking her down in a tackle.

Amanda was unmoving as Hunt sat up. He reached for his handcuffs, but became worried he'd hurt her. Kneeling at her side, he assessed she was fine after a brief moment.

"If you're going to fake being knocked out, you need to watch your eye movement better, sweetheart."

Her eyes opened. "You hurt me."

"You tripped me. I merely fell with style."

"Fell with style? Who the hell are you? Buzz Lightyear? Your lard ass probably broke a rib." She rolled to her back and held her side.

"Lard ass?" Hunt grinned. "Zero body fat, doll face." He removed his cuffs from his utility belt, trying too hard to flex his arm in the process. Why he felt the need to impress her was beyond him.

"Don't you dare cuff me! I'm the victim here!"

He put one cuff on her arm and the other on his. "This should keep you safe until we get back to your room, victim." He held his hand out and helped her up.

When she stood, she bent over and held her side.

Hunt stood in front of her and leaned in. "You okay?" She took a swing at him, but he ducked the blow then took her hand. "Where do you think that is going to get you?"

"Go to hell," she said, then began to sway.

"I'm falling for that again. Not." He gave her arm a tug. "Come on. Back to your room."

She didn't take a step. Her expression had glazed over.

"I don't need this shit before my second cup of coffee, lady. Come on."

Her eyes rolled back and she fell into him.

"Ah, shit."

Amanda woke up in her hospital room again. This time her hands were fastened to the bed. "Goddammit!" she shouted as she pounded her head backward into the pillow. Even that hurt her lump from last night and she let out a slight cry. She was less than thrilled when Hunt entered the room.

"You all right?"

"If I'm not, you here to beat me again?"

"Beat you? That's the second time I carried your ass to safety in twenty-four hours. You blacked out, princess. You shouldn't have tried to sneak out of a hospital with a concussion."

She turned her head away from him. "Leave me alone."

"Like it or not, you're my case. Finders keepers, as they say. I'm supposed to get some answers out of you. I suppose that isn't going to come easy."

"You don't have any right to keep me against my will. I didn't do anything wrong."

"Well...that's what I'm trying to understand." Hunt pulled up a chair and sat next to her bed. "I assumed you were attacked and hurt. But it doesn't make sense that you tried to escape the hospital."

"Maybe I don't have insurance."

"Still not buying it. You ran from an officer of the law, then you tried to deck me. I think there's more to the story."

"An officer of the law? You do really take this cops and robbers stuff seriously, don't you? You practice your big bad cop moves in front of the mirror, pretty boy?" Despite the restraints, she tried to sit up then winced at the pain in her side.

Hunt got to his feet. "I did hurt you."

She scoffed. "Don't flatter yourself. Bennett's kick—" she immediately regretted what she'd said.

Hunt took a step closer. "Who is this Bennett?"

"Shit." She dropped hard back on the bed. The jarring hurt her and she cried out again.

Hurrying to the door, Hunt bellowed for a nurse. One rushed right over, leaving the nursing station a few feet away. "Were her ribs x-rayed last night?" he asked.

"I just got here. Let me look at her chart." The nurse walked over to the chart at the end of the bed. "No. They didn't see any reason to, I guess. Their immediate concern was her concussion and the lacerations on her face." She approached the bed; Hunt was at her side. "Turn around please."

He did as he was told.

The nurse lifted up her gown and gasped. "Oh, sweetie." She dropped the gown and hit the call button. When another nurse came in she said, "Get Doc Miller to rush some x-rays. Looks like she's been kicked in the side." She turned to Hunt. "I don't know how they missed that gowning her up last night. I'm sorry."

Hunt waited while Amanda was x-rayed, since they had to undo the restraints to take the shots. The doctor explained she would be sedated for the pain, but Hunt didn't care. From what he'd seen of her already, no sedation was enough. He wasn't going to let her escape. If he had done his last set at the gym, she would have been gone.

He couldn't explain what drew him to her. She could be a prostitute crack-head for all he knew, but something about her intrigued him, and not just her looks.

The name she had given was false. The only Amanda Gentry in Iowa was eighty-six years old. She had turned when he called her name in the hall, maybe only the last name was false. Trying to pass the time, he ran over a few scenarios of what he could do to find out more about her. He hadn't seen her in the bar; that ruled out a lot of witnesses. He didn't know any Bennett from the area so he was back at square one within a minute of trying to think things through. He needed to search the place where he'd found her and look for any clues.

He was so caught up in his thoughts, he was startled by the swinging doors. "How is she, Doc?"

"Two ribs have hairline fractures, but she'll be fine. She needs some rest, that's all."

"How long will she be out?"

"I'd say another couple hours, easy. We went light on the anesthetic, but she's really out hard. My guess is she's exhausted."

"She needs to remain in the restraints regardless."

"No problem, Hunt."

"No bathroom breaks. Give her a bedpan if she whines to use the bathroom."

"Got it. I'll want her up and about tomorrow though, for exercise."

"I'll be here for it. She doesn't leave that bed without me here. Understand?"

"I'll let everyone know. Seems like a lot of fuss for a teeny buck-ten brunette."

"She's a slippery one and I don't know her story. I'm not letting her go before I get it."

"We'll do what we can."

Hunt came back at six. He tipped his hat at the nurse's station and they waved him over.

"You may want a cup, Hunt. She's a feisty cuss. Pretty pissed off about the restraints."

"So, I've noticed. Why the cup?"

"She got Darin pretty good. Sent her dinner flying, too."

"She hasn't eaten?"

"Can't get her to. She refuses to let us feed her. I told her we couldn't take the restraints off. Can't get an IV back in her either. Hate to drug her up again to do it."

"Bring me a tray."

"Lord help you."

He entered her room, but she didn't turn her gaze from the window. "Mandy?"

She quickly turned her head to him then frowned.

"So that is your real name."

"They should promote you to detective. Fancy work there, cop."

"There's no Amanda Gentry in Iowa. I was curious if your first name was even real."

"Did I say Iowa? I meant Idaho. You know...I get so confused with those 'I' states."

He tossed his hat on her nightstand and sat in the chair again. "I need answers so I can get back to my job. As much as I love babysitting you, I do prefer real police work."

"Afraid some speeders are going to go crazy down Main Street with you missing?"

He held up a gold locket on a chain and she instantly grew still.

"Where did you find that?"

"Where do you think I found it? It was in the grass where I found you."

"Give it back."

"I'll give it back when you start talking."

"There's nothing to tell you. I got jumped and beat up. Did you find a purse? No. That's because the shithead who beat me took that, too. Is this some kind of sick, twisted Vermont custom? Women who get mugged and beaten get shackled to hospital beds while they heal? That'll teach me to leave Ohio."

"I thought it was Idaho."

"Fuck." She closed her eyes and rested her head back on her pillow again.

"Muggers don't usually give their names. You said Bennett, and I want to know who that is."

The nurse came in with the dinner tray. Her expression revealed she knew she was interrupting. She placed the tray on the rolling table then walked out of the room as suddenly as she had entered it.

Mandy hadn't turned back to Hunt to answer him, nor did she acknowledge the nurse's presence while she was there. She glanced over at Hunt when he unbuckled her restraint.

"You need to eat something. Then we're going to talk."

"I'm not hungry."

"You eat or I'll stick a needle in your ass myself and practice my IV skills and cram it through the tube. *Capiche?*"

"I eat—you give me my necklace back."

He opened the locket up. The picture was of her and a little girl around three years old. "Who's the kid?"

"Who do you think it is?"

"Your daughter would be my guess. Where is she?"

"Not in Vermont. I didn't care for the hospital plan your Blue Plus offered."

Hunt allowed himself a grin. He stood and wheeled her dinner tray and table over to her. "You eat. I'm right outside. I'll be back in a bit and give you the necklace, and we'll talk. You try to fling the tray at me and I'll be right back with that needle."

She sneered at the plate. "What? No Jell-O?"

"You have fifteen minutes of peace. Enjoy it."

Hunt was surprised to find Amanda still in bed when he came back. She had eaten almost everything and pushed the rolling table aside.

"How was dinner?"

"Do you really want to talk about the shitty food?"

"How about we try again with your name?"

"Jane Doe."

"I thought we already determined you name was Amanda."

"That's right. Last name is Hug-n-kiss."

"Amanda Hug-n-kiss. Clever." He reached for her hand to get it back in the restraint but she pulled it away. "Fighting me isn't going to get you anywhere."

"Let me go to the bathroom at least. They won't let me go."

"Didn't they offer you a bedpan?"

"Do you like to do your business with company?"

"I'm a dude. I don't care."

"Well, I'm not. Just give me three minutes. I don't do the male ritual of reading a novel while I sit."

"Sports section fan myself."

"Would you knock off the sarcasm?"

"You first."

"Look." She let out a heavy sigh. "Please? Afraid I'll beat you with a toilet paper tube?"

He gave her a hard stare, then walked to the bathroom and gave it a good once over. He came back, reached for her other restraint and undid it. "I'm waiting in the room by the door. You have three minutes and you leave the bathroom door cracked open."

She hopped out of bed and ran for the door, closing it as much as he asked, without saying thanks.

Hunt stood quietly as she flushed then washed her hands. After turning the light off, she walked back to the bed and climbed in. Hunt approached her and again reached for her arm.

"Is that really necessary?"

"If you were me, would you trust you?"

"I won't be able to sleep like this." She finally gave in and gave him her arm.

"You should have thought about that. A few well-placed lies and you could have been out of here by now."

"You mean a well-placed kick."

"That, too." He finished fastening her other arm and sat back down. "I believe we were at your name."

"Smith."

"Husband John?"

"How did you know?"

"Nice." He kicked his feet out in front of him. "Despite what you may think, I can do this all night."

"What did you do with my necklace?" Amanda asked, after giving up on her silent standoff with Hunt.

He dug into his shirt pocket and pulled it out, then opened up the locket and held it in front of her. "I'll ask you again. What is your name and who is the kid?"

She looked up at him as if she wanted to say something, but she never opened her mouth.

"Who beat you, Amanda?"

She closed her eyes for a minute and sighed heavily, then opened them back up with a frightened expression.

"You were right. She's my daughter. Her father kidnapped her and I'm trying to get her back."

"Bennett is the father?"

"Sure."

"Sure?"

"I mean yes."

"He kidnapped her? Why haven't you involved the police?"

"I tried. You pricks wouldn't listen."

"Here?"

"Not here. Home. I only tracked him to here."

"Ohio?"

"You think I'm stupid enough to blurt it out? Give me some credit."

"Where then?"

"New York."

"You chased him from New York to Vermont?" he said in a tone that clearly stated he didn't believe a word she was saying.

"I didn't chase him. I did a lot of tracking around. She's been gone for two weeks."

"Why wouldn't the authorities help you?"

"Because he's her father. We're not divorced. We're not going through a custody battle. They said there isn't anything they could do. They say he's probably taken her on a vacation and will come back."

"And you don't believe this?"

"He's already tried to kill me twice. Why should I believe something as stupid as that?"

"Tried to kill you?"

"Did you or did you not find me left for dead?"

"A concussion is hardly life threatening."

"I was dead for all he knew."

"Where does he have her now?"

"I don't know."

"How did you end up by the Ace Bar?"

"He grabbed me by the strip mall and got rough in the car. I escaped the car when he slowed down. I guess I hit my head when I jumped out."

"And rolled onto the grass by the hedge?"

"Look...I don't know. I was unconscious."

Hunt took a notepad out of his pocket and flipped it open. "From the top. Your name."

"Amanda Smith." He raised an eyebrow at her. "I'm serious. No more games. Smith is really my last name."

"Where in New York?"

"Brooklyn."

He put the book down. "You don't have an east coast accent. In fact, you sound more like you're from Iowa."

"I was born in Iowa. Moved to New York after college. Look...are you going to help me get my daughter back, Barney Fife, or do you want to play the state capital game next?"

He stood and placed the necklace back in his pocket. "I'm running out to my car to make a call. I'll be back in a minute. If you even think about trying anything funny, concussion or not, you'll be spending the night in a cell. Got it?"

"Try your intimidation technique on someone else, Kojak. Where am I going to go?" She gave the restraints a pull to make her point.

Amanda didn't really have to go to the bathroom; it just was nice to be free. She could probably take that stupid oaf cop, but she wasn't ready to risk it. The drugs had finally worn off and even though she wouldn't admit it, she was starving. The meal was horrible, but it helped calm her growling stomach.

She went through the bathroom drawers as quietly as she could. All she found was a bobby pin and an emery board. A real nail file might have helped—this wouldn't. She threw it back in the drawer and shut the light off.

As soon as Hunt left her room, the orderly came in again. She immediately gave her shoulder a jerk, which helped to produce some tears. A car accident in high school and too many years of abuse had left her with a trick shoulder. Her right shoulder popped in and out slightly with ease and minimal pain. The trick worked great in bars when she was younger, now it was about to get her something other than a shot of tequila bought for her on a bet.

"What happened?" Darin asked.

"My shoulder hurts!"

He felt the front then the back and let out a whistle. "Feels dislocated. I know how to get it back in for you. I'm actually in physical therapy rotation right now." He reached for her, but then hesitated. "I shouldn't be doing you any favors after that nut shot."

"I'm sorry." She conjured up more tears. "Please. The pain is unbearable. I don't know how I did this. Will you please help me?"

He unfastened her left arm and reached for her shoulder. As soon as he had a hand on each side, she brought her leg up and kneed him hard in the skull. He went down and she hurried to unfasten her other arm. As he sat up, she picked up the small lamp on the nightstand and crashed it on his head.

He was out cold.

Fifteen minutes later, Hunt was walking toward her room and was surprised at all the commotion going on. "What happened?" he asked as he rushed in. An orderly was on the floor with a nurse kneeling next to him. Another one was looking out a window, but turned and answered him.

"She clocked Darin again. Got him in the head with a lamp this time."

"How did she get free?"

Darin sat up. "She was hollering her shoulder hurt. I was sure it was dislocated, so I unhooked her to try to pop it back in. I thought maybe she was pulling too hard on the restraints or something and hurt herself good."

"Dammit! I told you not to take them off for anything! Did anyone see which way she ran?"

"The only way she could get past us would be down the west wing past maternity. Security was called right away. She can't have gotten out."

"You'd better hope not." Hunt took off toward the west wing.

Swiftly gathering her clothes, Mandy ran out the door, not looking back to see if anyone saw her. There were no shouts; she was home free until they found the orderly.

She made it down the two flights of stairs and snuck into the laundry room when she found security at a nurse's station. Rather than changing into her clothes, she tossed them in the trash can and took a set of clean scrubs off a shelf. She crawled out a window and was crouched behind a hedge when someone came running her way. Sitting as still as possible, she peeked through the bushes. A police car was parked right in front of her, along with the man who was, without a doubt, Hunter.

CHAPTER TWO

Hunt reached his car and continued to search for any sign of Amanda. He was about to call the station for backup when an ambulance came screeching beside him. Deciding to wait for it to pass, he was startled by a tugging at his utility belt. His gun was slipped from his holster and as he spun to seize it, stared into its barrel.

"Give me your keys."

"Amanda, this isn't going to get you anywhere."

"I say otherwise. Hand over your fucking keys!"

"They're in the ignition."

Mandy glanced through the window then turned back to him. "That's not so bright."

"We have that small town trust thing going on."

Two doctors approached. Mandy grumbled, "Shit!" She lowered the gun. "Get in the back."

"Excuse me?"

"You heard me. Get in back! I won't have you calling for help the second I leave." She clicked the safety off of the gun to let him know she meant business.

Hunt opened the back door and got in.

Before he closed it she said, "Toss your radio in the bushes."

He unclipped the portable radio and again did as he was told.

"Your mace and nightstick too."

He reluctantly added them to the hedge.

She kicked the door closed. "Try to open it."

He pulled the lever and leaned into the door. It didn't budge. The inside locks were set. Hunt cursed to himself for leaving it that way. Amanda hurried to the driver's door and got in. It started up and she took off, squealing the tires as she left the curb.

"You mind telling me how you think this is going to help your situation?"

"Shut up! I need to think."

"I'll say. You sure as hell haven't done much of that since I found you. Do you want me to name off all the laws you are breaking?"

"How about you exercise my right to remain silent?"

"You don't have that right."

"I don't?"

"You haven't been officially placed under arrest."

"Oh. I'm sorry. You want to get right on that?"

"Sure. You can pull over anywhere."

Amanda laughed. "If you are the best your town has to offer, this is pretty pathetic."

"The fat lady ain't singing yet, sweetheart."

"Just shut up. I need to figure out where I am and get to my car."

"Black BMW four-door?"

"How did you know that?"

"It was reported last night for being in a private lot. Got towed to impound this morning. I got the message before you decked poor Darin again."

"Shit! I suppose there's no way to get it."

"Well shucks, ma'am. Us here rednecks only got us four of them there cops and one of 'em is watching the bad guy vehicles. You could try clubbing Otis with a lamp, but I don't think he'd take kindly to it."

"A simple no would have done."

"It had Pennsylvania plates. This is a lucky guess, but I take it New York was a lie, too."

"Guess so, genius."

Hunt took the necklace out of his pocket and opened it up again. "Quite a cutie pie."

"Put that away. As soon as we get out of here, I want that back."

"The kid isn't so bad either."

"Knock it off. Is this a new approach I'm unaware of? Try to pick up the prisoner?"

"I'm pretty sure I'm the one playing prisoner right now."

"Just leave that alone and put it away."

He refused to do as he was told. "She part Italian?"

"I said put it away."

"Striking eyes. Must be her dad's."

She slammed on the brakes, causing him to sail into the partition Plexiglas with a thud.

"Sonofabitch!"

Just as rapidly as she had stopped, she hit the gas and accelerated forward, causing his body to be thrown backward this time.

"Drive much?"

"I said to put it away," she demanded.

Hunt did as he was told. He was quiet for a few minutes, but couldn't take the silence. He was curious about this woman. "So, is this abuse thing new, or have you always put up with it?"

"From cops or my ex-husband-to-be?"

"Your husband. You know I only did what I had to. If you hadn't run, none of this would be happening."

She shrugged. "No. It wasn't a habit of his to beat me."

"Why did he take off with her?"

"Because he found out I was going to."

"Can I ask why?"

"You can ask, but I don't need to tell you anything. It's none of your fucking business."

"Does everyone have such a grand vocabulary where you live?"

"I didn't realize I was in the Bible belt."

"You're not. We have a lot of sweet little old ladies heavy in the church scene, and we tend to watch our mouths. Never been much for swearing."

"Too fucking bad for you."

"You kiss your kid with that mouth?"

Again she slammed the brakes, causing him to go flying forward. She picked the gun up and pointed it at him. "You mention my daughter one more time and I'll blow your face off. You got me?"

"Loud and clear," he said with no emotion.

Amanda was looking for a way out of town. She didn't want to be seen behind the wheel in the police cruiser. No doubt the whole town knew every cop car and every policeman that belonged in it. As if Hunt read her mind, he spoke up.

"If you stay on this road, someone is going to see you and realize you don't belong."

"I'm working on it," she shouted. "I don't suppose if I asked you, you'd tell me how to get on a county road."

"Take the next left. There will be nothing but farm houses in about a mile."

"And why should I believe you?"

"Do you have a choice?"

She took the next left. The road turned to gravel after a few blocks, but she had no problem maneuvering the car on it. Either it had been graded not long ago or it wasn't used that much.

"Do you have a plan, or are you just going to drive until you run out of gas?"

"Why don't you have a GPS in this thing?"

"I don't need one. I know my town. I've been in Vermont all my life and know how to get anywhere three different ways."

"Typical man."

"This would go faster if you let me know where you're going."

"You're not coming with me. I need to find a nice quiet place to dump you and get another set of wheels."

"Grand larceny a past profession of yours?"

"Look. Shut up with the cop shit. I don't expect you to understand. I don't see a ring, so there's no wife and probably no kid."

"No and probably not," he agreed, but arrogantly.

"You wouldn't understand what a parent would do for their child."

"I do understand you aren't doing her any favors by breaking a dozen laws. There would have been a way to deal with this properly."

"Bullshit! You and your law courses. You think you know it all, but you don't. You've probably never left your small town. Probably never missed a Sunday sermon and sat there like a good little Catholic in your suit and tie."

"I'm Protestant."

"Whatever! There's a whole life out there, and people don't behave like a fifties sitcom. He never would have come home with her. I'm not giving her up to him. That bastard is not raising my daughter."

Hunt let out a loud sigh. "Just tell me where you're aiming for. You'll get stuck going in circles for hours here if you don't let me help you."

"I need to get to West Bolton."

He scooted forward to get his bearings. "In about five miles you'll hit tar. Head North. It's a straight shot and paved, although it's not the smoothest anymore."

"Is it a main road? You sending me into a trap?"

"It's not. I use this road so I can speed getting to Newport. No one ever patrols it."

She laughed loudly. "I'm supposed to believe you speed."

"I have a '78 Challenger. Of course I speed. I just don't do it in my own town."

"What's in Newport?"

"My sister and my niece. I do understand what a parent will do for their kids so don't sell me short."

"Don't try to tell me you're going to help me."

"I never said that, I said I understand."

She was silent for a minute. "How long do we have till West Bolton?"

"About an hour."

"Let's play the 'How long can we ride without talking' game."

Hunt waited ten minutes before he said, "Are we there yet?"

"Are you four, for crying out loud?"

"It's not my job to make your kidnapping of me a pleasant experience."

"Mission accomplished. Now shut the hell up." She picked up the gun and tapped it on the Plexiglas wall that separated them, trying to show him she meant business.

As she tapped the Plexiglas, the door moved slightly. He hadn't fastened it after using it last. Amanda hadn't made an attempt to fasten it. She hadn't noticed it. Hunt grinned at his luck. He'd wait for her guard to drop and reach through and gain control of the vehicle again. She wasn't as smart as she thought. Hunt grinned at his cleverness. Deciding to distract her and not give her an opportunity to see it, he tried to spark up conversation again.

"So, what makes you think he's in West Bolton?"

"I never said he was in West Bolton. I said I needed to head *toward* West Bolton."

"He have a fishing cabin up there?"

"And I'd tell you this if he did?"

"There are some gorgeous lakes up there. A friend of mine owns a resort off Sunny Lake."

"Intrigued. Really."

"You always such a cold-hearted bitch, or is this a new attitude to go with the kidnapping persona?"

"Careful there, Barney. You used the B-word."

Hunt waited another few miles. When Mandy's concentration was elsewhere as she frequently glanced between the road and the gauges, he made his move. He thrust his arm through the small window and wrapped his arm around her neck. Amanda screamed and clawed at his arm with one hand while she struggled to steer with the other.

"Let go of me! You're going to make me crash!"

"Then hit the brakes and we won't."

She hit the gas instead of the brake, accepting his challenge, but found it hard to keep control of the car. She let go of his arm for a second to try to snatch the gun, but he stole the opportunity to take hold of her arm and used it to wrap around her own neck. He held it there firmly with his. Amanda gasped for air and tried grabbing at his arm with the hand she was using to steer. The car hit a pothole and jerked hard to the right. It effortlessly went through an old wooden railing and plunged into a small lake.

Amanda screamed and Hunt let go. As soon as the car hit the water, she opened her door. She knew enough to know she wouldn't be able to if it went under. The open door allowed water to come in much faster and it began to sink immediately. Almost before she could take a deep breath, the car was under water.

The lake wasn't terribly deep. The car hit the bottom almost as soon as it was completely under water. Amanda swam to Hunt's door and tried pulling it open. He was franticly kicking at the window, but it was doing no good. She swam back into the front seat and found the gun on the floor. She rushed to Hunt's door again and motioned to him to back up. He moved as far as he could to the opposite end of the car. She placed the gun on the window and fired.

The shot was slowed down by the water, but it did the trick. The glass remained intact but fractured. Hunt swam over and kicked at the glass with both feet. After two hearty kicks, the glass finally broke free. Amanda waited as Hunt made it through the window, then she swam for the surface.

She let out a loud gasp as she reached fresh air, anxious to fill her lungs. Hunt was just a second behind her. He swam over to her and she panicked. She expected him to be furious and try to take hold of her. But when he reached for her, the look in his eyes was concern.

"Are you okay?"

"I'm fine," she said as she took another deep breath.

"Nice thinking with the gun. Thanks."

"You're welcome, I guess. Kidnapping you wasn't a part of the plan. Killing you certainly wasn't. Just what the hell were you thinking, you idiot?" She swam for shore and could hear him close behind.

"What was I thinking? I was thinking you'd play it smart and know when someone had the best of you and give up."

Within a few yards the lake was shallow enough for her to stand. She brought herself to her feet and tromped her way toward shore on the lake's muddy bottom.

"The best of me? I told you I am not stopping until I get my daughter. We'd be there by now if you hadn't pulled your macho stronghold bullshit!" She made it up to the shore and flopped down onto the grass on her knees. She dropped to her butt then lay down on her back, still trying to catch her breath. That he had tried to be nice to her had thrown her off for a second. Now she was frustrated and pissed even more so at their situation.

Hunt dropped himself next to her. She sat up, suddenly realizing the tables could easily be turned. The gun was still in her hand, but he could have taken it if he tried. She wasn't about to get in a one-on-one fight with him. She wouldn't come out victorious, he was too built. She might be able to outrun him, but the ordeal had left her exhausted. Besides, run to where?

"So, what now, genius?"

He sat up and pointed at a small light not too far away. "We'll have to head to that farmhouse and ask for a phone. This is the end of the line for you. You do realize that, right?"

"I don't think so."

"Where do you think you'll get out here? There's not a town for another twenty minutes. You're not walking, and I know you're not thinking about stealing a car."

"Then you still don't know me."

"Are you seriously telling a police officer you intend on stealing a car?"

"I'm not telling you anything." She got to her feet and walked away.

Quickly catching up to her, he took hold of her arm. "I'm not letting you walk away. Are you insane?"

She shook herself free. "You owe me. I could have let your ass drown."

"Thanks for reminding me." He held his hand out. "I'll take my gun back any time now, sweetheart."

"Just leave me alone and let me do what I need to do."

"After you totaled my car and presume to walk away with my gun? Again, I don't think so." He grasped her arm again. This time, she pulled the gun out and pointed it at him.

He let go of her and put his hands up, but then he surprised her when he stepped toward her so his chest was up against the gun.

"You're not going to shoot me, Mandy."

She dropped the gun down and tucked it into the front of her pants. "I don't recall telling you it was okay to call me that. As a matter of fact, you don't need to call me anything. Here's where we part ways." She turned again but only got two steps away before he took hold of her arm again. As soon as she spun around, he fastened a handcuff on her wrist.

"What the hell are you doing?" she screamed as he clicked it.

"What do you think I'm doing? It's what I've been doing since we met, besides carrying your unconscious ass to safety."

"Take it off." She reached for the gun, but he beat her to it and tucked it in its soaking wet holster.

He attached the other band of the handcuffs to his wrist. "I don't put it past you to try to take off again, cuffed or not."

"You can't be serious."

"As cancer. Let's head for that farmhouse and see what we can do from there."

"You bastard. You know why I'm doing what I'm doing."

"And I'm going to say again, there are better ways to get it done. A dozen legal things are popping into my head without even trying to think about it."

"You don't understand my situation."

"So, make me understand."

She huffed. "You still wouldn't understand. Let's just go." She turned to walk to the farmhouse, and he kept in step with her.

They walked in silence and were about halfway there before he spoke. "I'm really dying to hear how you think your situation is so damn special. I've been a cop for a long time. If you think I haven't seen it all—"

She cut him off. "Cop? Don't you mean law enforcement officer?"

"Quit busting my balls. I could have hog tied your ass in the water, but I chose to give you the benefit of the doubt. I'm surprised you didn't run for it."

"I'm desperate, not stupid."

"I beg to differ there."

"Do you ever know when to shut up?"

"Apparently not."

"Gee. I can't imagine why you're not married."

"My choice, princess. Don't think I'm not having a hard time staying single."

She laughed. "My God, you keep yourself in high regards, don't you? Not just as a cop, but now you're the town stud?"

"I'm saying it's my choice. You can lay off the stud shit. I'm really not that tough of a guy to get along with."

"Obviously not with someone you've been handcuffed to before."

"I've never had to handcuff myself to someone before. Haven't had to pull my gun out too many times either—or tackle someone, for that matter. You are a first in more ways than one, I'll give you that much. How are your ribs by the way?"

Again he'd surprised her. "I'm fine," is all she would say. She was feeling sore, but she wasn't about to let him know it. She didn't need or want his pity.

Hunt and Amanda stood in front of the old farmhouse, disappointed at what it had turned out to be. Instead of a functioning home, it appeared as if had been abandoned for years.

"It doesn't look too bad. Maybe it still has a phone," Hunt said.

"That's a stretch."

"The service light still works, so that's a good sign there's probably electricity anyway. We don't have anything better to do than check it out. There's not another place for miles. You're starting to shiver. Maybe we'll be able to start a fire and at least get dry."

"I'm fine."

"Yeah, I know. You keep saying that, but your shivering is about rattling my fillings."

"So un-cuff me."

"Good one. Come on." He gave the cuffs a tug as they headed toward the porch stairs.

Hunt knocked, even though he thought it probably wasn't necessary. He opened the door with no resistance, it wasn't locked. Hunt called out "hello" as he walked in and waited only a moment before hitting the switch he found beside the door. He was thrilled to find the lights working.

"It doesn't look as bad inside as it does from the outside," he said as he scanned the room. There was a couch and a few chairs covered with sheets. There was a heavy amount of dust on a coffee table. "Doesn't look like anyone has been around for a while, but it looks like they plan on coming back at some point."

"They didn't even lock the door."

"We never locked the door at the house I grew up in. Farm folk are a little more relaxed about that stuff."

"Even if you're gone for months or, by the looks of it, years?"

"Probably nothing worth stealing anyway. If someone wants to burn it down, it's worth more insured than in this condition." He walked them through to the kitchen and over to an old rotary phone on the wall and picked up the receiver. "No dial tone."

"Color me surprised."

Ignoring her, he opened up the refrigerator. It was empty and unplugged. "They really don't plan on being back for a while. We're lucky for the lights." He wandered around until he found the thermostat. He moved the dial up to seventy, but it never kicked on. "Probably have to light the pilot."

"I said I was fine."

He sighed. "I know." They entered the living room where they found a fireplace. There was wood in it and a stack along the side. A paper grocery bag was there filled with newspapers. He found a box of matches on the mantle. "I need two hands for this. What are my chances you'll stay put?"

"You really want me to answer?"

"That's what I thought." He walked them over to the couch and pulled off the sheet. It was a futon couch and had a wooden frame. Hunt unlocked his side of the cuff and told her to sit, then attached it to the armrest.

He got a fire going and turned back to Amanda. "I'm going to go light the hot water heater and furnace."

"Water heater."

"Right. And furnace."

"No. It's just a water heater, not a hot water heater. Why would you need to heat hot water?"

Again he sighed. "Now you're an appliance salesman?"

"Salesperson."

"Is that really what you do?"

She laughed. "No. I suppose if I properly name the engine size in your car, that makes me a mechanic."

He stood and shook his head. "I'll go light the *water heater*. You should be able to take a hot shower in twenty minutes or so." He didn't give her time for a response and headed for what appeared to be the basement door. He was back up in a couple of minutes.

"It was electric and on. Very odd. That's a big electricity sucker."

"Why don't you scold them after telling them we were breaking and entering, officer?"

He had no response for her as he unlocked her handcuff and stood her up then led her to the bathroom. After seeing there was no escape for her, he opened up the small closet and was glad to see towels. He turned on the water and waited until it ran hot.

"You're good to go. Get in there and get warmed up." She stared at him blankly. "Look, Mandy. If you think I'm going to try anything...don't flatter yourself with such a thought. And don't even think about coming out and trying to clobber me with anything. We are no longer in a situation that I'm tolerating anymore screwing around.

I've had it up to here with your shit." After raising his hand over his head to make his point, he took a towel for himself off a shelf and slammed the bathroom door closed.

A few minutes later, the water stopped. Hunt gently knocked on the door.

"What?"

"I found a robe. It smells like old people, but it'll keep you warm till we get your clothes dry. Correction. Until we get the scrubs you stole dry."

She opened the door and reached her hand out without looking at him, but did say thank you as she pulled it back in.

When Amanda opened up the door, Hunt came walking over to her. He had removed his wet clothes and was wearing a towel, secured around his waist. She swallowed and had to try hard not to stare at his perfect chest. She hated to admit he was handsome. She knew he had a nice body, since he had filled out his uniform so flawlessly. But she had no idea he was this perfectly built, and she hated herself for caring.

"You always waltz around your prisoners half naked?"

"I didn't get as lucky with another robe. Must have been an elderly widow who lived here alone. There are no guy clothes at all. Anything I found beside the robe wouldn't interest you. You'd look like Omar the tent maker dressed you."

"I hung my clothes up to dry."

"They'll dry quicker by the fire. I'll go get them."

"I got it," she said as she turned around. "I don't need you handling my underthings."

When she came back out, he had four chairs lined up by the fire. His clothes were spread across two of them. He also had a mattress on the floor. "What's with the mattress?"

"Phones are dead and it's late. I'm not hoofing around out there in a towel at this time of night in the cold. I'll check the outbuildings tomorrow. Maybe there's an old truck I can get going. If not, we'll walk to the next place."

"I'll take the couch."

"The hell you will. You're on here with me."

"What? I'm not sleeping with you on that smelly thing."

"You're not sleeping even a foot away from me. I don't trust you as far as I can throw my cruiser. Oh wait, I don't have to worry about that. You totaled it."

"Excuse me, but I do believe that was *your* fault!"

"I wasn't the one driving."

"No, just the one trying to kill the one driving. If you had let me—"

He cut her off. "I'm not going into this with you again. I'm tired and we're sleeping on the bed. End of story. You pick a side and I'm cuffing us together."

"The hell you are!" She turned to walk away, but he took hold of her wrist and promptly slapped the handcuff on it.

"I gave you a choice. Now you get to sleep on the right side, princess."

"Stop it with those names already."

"Oh, because I like being called Barney and Kojak?"

"Truce already. Just let me sleep. Where am I going to run in a robe?"

Hunt laughed. "You? Forget it." He walked to the bed and sat down.

"You're sleeping like that?"

"I don't have a choice. Don't go getting excited, *he* certainly isn't."

CHAPTER THREE

Amanda had no choice but to join him on the bed. After a few minutes of silence, she finally couldn't take it anymore.

"That's disgusting, you know."

"I didn't do anything."

"The fact you called it 'he.' Why do men do that?"

"And you don't call your breasts 'the girls'?"

"I..." She couldn't even argue the fact. She did. "Well, when I'm with my friends maybe, but not in mixed company."

"Please. With that mouth of yours, you're pretending to be a prude? Just relax and go to sleep already. You've had your panties in a bunch all day."

"I'm a prisoner. What do you want? Me to hop up and bake a cake?"

"Hate to sound four again, but you started it."

"Oh, for crying out loud." Amanda flipped over as best as she could without wrenching her arm. "Good night."

In a few hours, it began to get light out and Amanda was slowly waking up. She gasped when she found herself face to face with Hunt. His arm was around her, and her hand was flat to his chest. She jerked up and startled him in the process.

"What's wrong?" he asked, as he bolted upright as well.

"What's wrong? You were fondling me in my sleep!"

"Get over yourself. You must have been cold and snuggled into me. It's one of the primal instincts for men to take care of women. Apparently, I was merely responding to your needs."

"Nice textbook answer. And that?" she said as she lowered her gaze to his towel.

Hunt grinned. "It's morning. You were married. Don't flatter yourself."

"You're a pig."

"And you're still hostile. I was hoping a night's sleep would help your attitude."

She leaned over to the chairs and checked her clothes. "They're dry. I want to get dressed. Un-cuff me."

"I need to take a leak first."

"You're not going to while we're attached!"

He laughed. "I meant I'm going in the bathroom first. I don't know if I can trust you at the couch for even that long. Maybe I should have you come in there with me. I do get stage fright though. You any good at singing?"

"You're an ass. I'm not going in there with you."

"I could whistle Lee Oskar's 'Before the Rain' if you don't want to sing."

Her expression softened. "You know that one?"

"Of course. Awesome tune. You want to hear it?"

Again her expression turned sour. "No. Just do your business so I can get dressed." She pulled the robe tighter with her free hand, pulled him toward the couch, and sat down.

"I love a woman who assumes the position on her own."

She stood and tried to slap him but he caught her hand. "You've gotten the best of me for the last time a few tricks ago. You can lay off anytime."

"Then knock off the talk."

"Oh please." He un-cuffed himself and fastened it to the couch. He picked up his clothes on the way to the bathroom. After hesitating a minute at the door, he went back and got hers as well.

Hunt expected to hear the sound of wood splintering while he hurried through getting dressed. He was pleasantly surprised to see Amanda sitting there when he came out of the bathroom.

"I didn't expect you to not try to get away."

"What makes you think I didn't try?"

"The couch is still in one piece, for starters."

"I'm wearing a robe, dick."

He made a "tsk tsk" sound. "You really need to try some stress relief."

"I guess it would be too much to ask for some coffee?"

"I could go for some myself. Too bad the kitchen is cleaned out. I checked them when you were in the shower last night." Hunt undid the restraints and walked her to the bathroom. "You've got three minutes, then I'm busting the door down."

"You're all heart." Mandy was out in a little over two minutes. Hunt was separating the logs, making sure the fire would burn itself out after they left. He got up and returned to her with the cuffs in hand when the door opened.

"Are those really necessary?" She crossed her arms.

"Yup," was all he would offer for an answer as he clasped it on her. "Let's see if we can get lucky in one of the old outbuildings." He hesitated. "And by 'get lucky' I mean find an old vehicle."

"I knew what you meant."

He grinned. "I know. I don't know what it is about you, but it's so much fun to bust your chops. I've never met someone wound so tight before."

"Screw with a mother trying to get her child back more often. I'd bet you'd get your fill."

He stood staring at her. "Honestly, I'm not so sure I'm buying what you're selling."

"That's your prerogative, I suppose. You're the one in charge."

"Glad to see you're finally admitting it."

She held up her arm with the handcuff. "Like I have a choice."

Her stomach grumbled and Hunt grinned. "Let's get going. I'm getting hungry myself."

"I'm fine."

"Of course you are." Hunt led them toward the kitchen. He'd noticed a door last night that should take them to the garage. Cupping his hand to the dirty glass, he strained to see in the dark garage. "We're in luck. Maybe. There's an old truck in there."

"Fat chance it works if they left it."

"Let's find out." He tried the door but it was locked.

"That's stupid," Mandy said. "Leave the house unlocked but lock the garage?"

"Maybe the house was an oversight."

"Or maybe someone broke in before."

Hunt moved his hand along the top of the door trim, and a key fell to the floor. "Definitely not the smartest people on the planet." He opened the door and hit the fluorescent lights, which protested, but sluggishly flickered to life. The truck was an old brown eighties model

Ford. With Mandy reluctantly in tow, Hunt opened up the driver's door.

"If the keys are in it I'm going to shit an eggroll," Mandy scoffed.

Hunt reached in by the steering wheel and pulled out a key. "Pork or beef?" He climbed into the driver's seat and gave the key a turn. The engine didn't even click. "Maybe our luck isn't as great as we think."

"Think again," Mandy said as she pointed to the far corner, past the door.

Hunt stuck his head out and smiled. "I like a woman who knows what a battery charger is."

"Seems like you like a lot of things about women."

"Hmmm." Hunt rubbed his chin as if in deep thought. "I think you're right."

"Can we cut the crap and plug this thing in and get going?"

"You that anxious to sit in a jail cell?"

"As long as you're not cuffed in it with me."

"That, sweetheart, is affirmative. Trust me. You're no picnic to be attached to, either."

Together they walked to the charger and each took a side. They carried it to the front of the truck and Hunt popped the hood. After helping him brace it, Mandy reached back and plugged the charger into the wall. She gave Hunt the black cord first, then the red one. After he got them connected, she turned it on.

"Scoot over," Mandy said as she tried to move him out of the way.

"Why?"

"I want to check the oil. If it's been here for a while, it's probably low or thick as hell."

He gave her a hard stare. "And you're going to do an oil change right here?"

"Try adding a can if it needs it, Barney." She pointed to a row of oil cans on a shelf behind him.

"What exactly are you?"

"A mother who wants her kid back, but will settle for some coffee first. I don't want to get stranded on the side of the road because you let the engine seize up after we were lucky enough to find a vehicle."

"Don't get ahead of yourself. It hasn't turned over yet."

"May I?" she asked as she pointed to the dipstick.

"Would I like your hand on my dipstick? Be my guest."

Ignoring his comment, she simply said, "Hand me a rag," as she motioned to the shelves.

He reached for an old shirt and handed it to her. He cooperated with the arm that was secured to her as best as he could, and watched as she wiped the dipstick then checked the oil.

"It actually looks fine, or would you like to give it a second opinion?"

"If you think you know that much, I suppose I can let it go." After she was done, he walked them around and climbed back in the driver's side and tried again. The truck started right up. "Let's leave it run to charge for a bit. I'll leave a note and number to contact me in case someone comes home and finds it missing."

Mandy followed him in and stood patiently while he composed the note, much to Hunt's surprise. When he tried to go back out the door, she planted her feet.

"What now?"

"Can't you just let me go?"

"Are you off your nut?"

"There has to be a hint of compassion in there somewhere. You can't be all sexual innuendo as you claim."

"I find it helps calm situations somewhat."

"I hate to break it to you, but it doesn't. Look...I saved your life. You owe me this."

"You were also the one who put me in that situation in the first place."

"You did that all by yourself!"

"I kidnapped myself? You owe the city for a new police cruiser, too. I'm not taking the blame here and being made a laughing stock. You're coming with me."

"You bastard."

"That's Sherriff bastard to you. Come on."

Amanda climbed in the truck and Hunt fastened his handcuff to the door pull. He gave it a few tugs to make sure it wasn't going to come off easily. He'd hear and see her trying anything if she got rough with it, which she would have to do. He opened the garage door, drove through, got out to close it again and they were on their way.

"You have brothers who were into cars?" he asked her.

"Excuse me?"

"I'm just wondering where this car knowledge is coming from."

"Car knowledge? I checked the oil, for crying out loud. I didn't clean out the carburetor."

"I'm only trying to make conversation. You're one tough cookie to get to open up."

"I'm not accustomed to making conversation with people who keep me prisoner."

"I'm not that bad of a guy. You're just on the wrong side of the law right now."

"So, you're telling me when this is all said and done, you'd like to be friends?"

"Don't be silly. I'd settle for sex." Hunt grinned.

"Would a blow job be out of the question?"

Hunt glanced over at her then had to correct his driving when a car horn honked. He had veered over into their lane.

"It's not so fun having that shit thrown at you constantly, is it?"

"I wouldn't say that. I accept. Should I pull over?"

"Go to hell."

Realizing he wasn't going to get anywhere for conversation, Hunt remained quiet until they hit the main road. "I know where we are. I'm getting off the dirt roads."

She was still quiet.

Within a couple of miles, they reached a small town. He pulled up to a small convenience store and removed the keys. "I'm going to phone in and pick up some coffee. How do you like yours? Assuming I can trust you to drink it and not throw it on me."

"Cream and sugar. I wouldn't waste something like coffee on the likes of you."

"Danish?"

"I'm not much for sweets. Coffee will be fine."

Hunt stood at the counter and used the phone where he could see her through the window. Waiting for her to spot him, he waved. After promptly being flipped off, he grinned. She wasn't going to learn her attitude oddly turned him on. He was able to get some coffee and food on credit. You have to love small town hospitality.

He climbed back in the truck and offered her a coffee then an egg and cheese biscuit. "I know you're hungry. You don't need to play tough on my account. I had one, they aren't that bad."

"I thought cops ate doughnuts."

"Only the ones not fit enough to be on the force."

"Oh, that's right. Mister zero body fat."

"You're welcome," was all he replied before slamming the door. She was starting to get on his nerves after all. He didn't even try to spark conversation the rest of the way back to the station. He let her mope over her coffee and untouched biscuit.

Amanda could hear laughter from her cell. Hunt was probably taking quite a razzing from his fellow officers about her and the car. She didn't care. All she could concentrate on was trying to figure out her next plan of attack. One of these bozos had to let her out sooner or later, and she had to get away. Shouldn't be too hard. With a little luck, Hunt would leave and she could pull a fainting spell or something. The two "Barney Fifes" didn't look too bright. One had to be right out of high school and didn't weigh much more than her. She'd be able to take him easily. The other she could probably outrun at a fast paced walk.

After surveying the room, she only found the one way out. The place was pretty rinky-dink, but there was no key hanging on the wall by her cell, much to her surprise. Hunt barged through the door and over to her cell. She stood.

"Leaving me, dear?" she said, snidely.

"I need a shower and a change of clothes. No worries, I'll be back in a few minutes, cupcake." He slipped a pair of jeans, a tank top advertising a local bait shop, and a long sleeve blouse through the bars. "These were in an unclaimed box out front. Looks close enough in size for you. Probably belonged to some anorexic teenage girl."

"Are you telling me I'm too skinny?"

"If the shoe fits, lady."

"The charm just never ends with you. Am I supposed to get dressed in here?"

"Yup. Change or not. Totally up to you. I'll let you shower if you want, but not until I get back."

"Like I'm showering with you gawking over me. Pass. Thanks."

"Suit yourself. No funny business while I'm gone. I mean it, dammit. When I get back, I want some answers. No more of this damn bullshit. I've had it."

She sat back down on the cot. "I've said all I'm going to say."

"Then you'd better get comfortable, sweetheart." As Hunt walked away, she flipped the bird at his back.

Mandy watched the small window in the door, but was careful not to let it be known she was paying attention to the two other deputies. They had to be curious about her. After Hunt's story, she guessed they were expecting her to be some kind of Houdini. *Can't disappoint now, can I?*

Waiting until she could see one of them peeking through again, Mandy made a show about changing into the clothes. She was sure one or both of them were glued to the small window, drooling. *Too skinny my ass.* She had zero body fat as well, but she was certainly muscular enough in all the right places.

Mandy turned to face the door and watched them back away. She waited until one of them peered through the window again and let herself fall to ground as if she'd fainted. Allowing her head to hit harder than she would have cared for made her silently curse, but she wanted it to look real.

The younger of the two came busting through the door and over to the cell. "Hey? You okay, lady?" He waited for a moment before asking again. "You all right? Don't mess with me. Hunt said you're a handful." After waiting another few moments, he cursed and unlocked the door. He fell to her side and placed his hand on her neck. "Damn it. I don't feel shit. Roy!" He shouted toward the door. "Get your ass in here! Something is wr—"

He didn't get to finish his sentence. Mandy had kneed him in the head hard enough to knock him out cold.

She went for his gun first and tucked it in the back of her jeans then removed his nightstick. He had left the keys in the cell door so she locked him in then ran for the only exit.

Just as she got there, the large officer came through holding a jelly doughnut and was licking his lips from the filling. *How cliché.* Mandy almost hated to clobber him. Almost.

"What are you hollering—" He stopped talking when he discovered her standing out of the cell.

She held the nightstick like a pro and he dropped his doughnut. He motioned for his gun and she took a step closer. "Don't even think about it, Burford."

"Name's Roy."

"You too stupid to know...never mind. Hands above your head." When he did so, she took his gun. "Get in the cell next to your friend there."

"Aw maaaaan. Hunt is gonna have our hide."

"I don't see how that's my problem. Move. Don't make me knock you out. I'm pretty sure I couldn't drag you to the cell."

He started to walk past her, but then turned quicker than she would have thought he was capable of and seized the arm holding the nightstick. She kneed him in the groin and he hit the ground. She pulled out the gun and touched it to his forehead.

"Get in that cell, or your head will look like the doughnut you were eating."

After inquiring where to find Roy's truck keys, Amanda sped away in it, taking a different route than she had with Hunt. She hated that she had said she wanted to go toward West Bolton, but he knew she was lying about everything else—maybe he would assume she was lying about that, too. She would probably add some time to the drive, but it didn't really matter. The way Hunt kept interfering was slowing her down badly enough. What was another hour? At least she was out of the jail cell. She really thought it would be much worse.

"At least you didn't have to shoot anyone," she said to herself as she turned on the radio. Roy had it set to country, so she hit the scan button. It took a while to find another station. She was pretty much in the middle of nowhere. "It's not nowhere, but you can see it from here," she mumbled.

After making two full passes around, the radio finally stopped at a classical station. Lee Oskar's "Before the Rain" was playing. She hit the button again so it wouldn't continue to seek. Amanda's mind went to Hunt's comment about whistling that song in the bathroom. It was odd he knew it, let alone mentioned it to her. It had been a favorite of hers for as long as she could remember. It had been playing in the garage just about every time she went out to visit her dad when he was tinkering with the '57 Chevy he was taking his time restoring. No one else had ever heard of it, and she didn't ever recall listening to it over the radio before. She got chills, but chastised herself to get a grip. "It's only a song, dummy."

Her stomach flip-flopped as she imagined Hunt standing there in just a towel. She cursed at her reaction to the memory. He was handsome and had a great body, but she wanted nothing to do with him. "Shake it, Mandy. He's too arrogant and conceited for you. Not to mention the whole cop thing." She shook her head. "Since when did you start talking to yourself, you stupid bitch." She hit her palm hard on the radio's power button and turned the music off. Jamming her foot a little heavier on the gas, she continued down the gravel road in silence.

"What the fu—" Just seeing the condition his deputies were in caused Hunt to stop talking mid-sentence. He ran to his office for the cell key and rushed back into the room.

"What the hell happened?" he said angrily as he unlocked Roy's cell.

"She got the upper hand on Cool Hand Luke there."

"And that's why you're locked up, too?" Hunt turned to let Luke out as well. "What happened, kid?"

"Don't call me that! You're barely older than I am, Sheriff."

"Just spill it, dammit!"

"She was sprawled out and unconscious."

"You mean you thought she was unconscious."

"I suppose I did. I watched her fall to the ground. It seemed like she hit her head pretty hard. She wasn't moving, man."

"But she moved fast enough when you went to check on her, right? Dammit, Luke! I told you not to go near her!"

"Right! And if you came back and she was dead, who would you blame then? The doughnut king over there?"

Roy grasped Luke's shirt and slammed him into the cell's gate. "Suck it, Junior!"

"Both of you knock it off!" Hunt hollered. "I don't suppose she's getting far on foot. Both of you get your asses out there and start looking. Keep your ears on your radio for reports on stolen cars."

Roy let go of Luke and turned away in shame.

"What?" Hunt asked.

"She took my truck keys."

"Perfect. Just fucking perfect." Hunt stormed out of the back room. His men were close behind. Picking up a duffle bag, Hunt haphazardly stuffed weapons and ammo into it.

He added enough magazines for the rifle to take down a small army. He threw in every pair of handcuffs sitting in the locker and a handful of zip ties.

"Just who are you expecting to—"

A glare from Hunt cut off Luke's question in a hurry. "You two bozos will pick up the slack in the shifts while I'm away. Figure it out." He turned to leave, but Roy stopped him.

"When you coming back?"

"Not until I have her again. I'm so pissed off at you two idiots I can't even speak." Again he stormed toward the door. Again Roy stopped him.

"But, Boss..."

"Don't 'but boss' me. She already has too much of a lead."

"You know where she's goin'?"

"I have an idea." He turned to the door, but was stopped again by what Roy said.

"I've got a tracker in my truck."

Hunt spun back around. "Like OnStar?"

"Hell no. A thief would see that. She won't even know this is there."

Hunt dropped the heavy duffle bag to the floor. "How do I track her?"

"I'll get you the GPS device from my locker." He was back in less than a minute and offered it to Hunt. He gave him a quick explanation of it. "That's all there is to it."

Hunt put it in his pocket. "You're still on my list."

"I know, Boss. I'll pull doubles till you get back."

"Split the shifts with Junior here and call in Ole if you have to."

"He ain't gonna be too happy about coming out of retirement."

"He ain't gonna be too happy with my foot up his ass, either."

"Yes, Boss," was said to a closed door. Hunt was gone too fast to wait for a response.

After tossing the bag of weapons in the lockbox bolted to the truck, Hunt climbed in and booted up the GPS. "Who would have thought the doughnut king would have had the brains and foresight for this?"

Hunt didn't usually talk to himself either, but his nerves were on edge. He'd never come across a criminal as slippery as Amanda before, and it drove him crazy he couldn't figure her out. His nerves were about as shot as they'd ever been. "Bitch thinks she's fucking Rambo, for crying out loud." When the red bleep finally popped up on the screen, he smiled from ear to ear. "Gotcha."

He recognized the road she was on, but remembered what she said about going to West Bolton. If he stuck to the main road, he'd get there when she did. "Get ready to pucker up and kiss my ass, sweetheart."

CHAPTER FOUR

Hunt was surprised when he hit West Bolton an hour later and had to keep going. He was sure he would have beaten her to it. She must have been driving like a maniac on the county roads. It had crossed his mind to call the local authorities, but that thought was driven out of his head. He wanted her for himself. Also, not wanting to explain her escape was a big factor. Being made a fool of with his deputies was one thing. Involving another county's department was another altogether.

He was certain she still had the truck. There was no way she knew about the device. She was sure to keep the truck as long as she could. He didn't put grand theft auto above her, but the fact she was taking side roads led Hunt to believe she felt she was fairly safe. When the red dot started to head east, Hunt switched to dirt roads as well. He grew angrier as the miles ticked by. He no longer cared about sneaking up on her. If the truck wasn't Roy's, he'd ram her and drive her off the road on sight.

The light stopped moving and he began closing in on it fast. Judging from the road they were on, Hunt expected to find the truck parked at someone's summer cabin. Instead, he found a bar a lot larger than the area called for, with more than its share of neon lights, advertising various beers.

Hunt circled the building and spotted Roy's truck parked in the back. He was on his last nerve and didn't hesitate for one second before putting his truck behind it, blocking her in. He was glad no one was in the parking lot to smart off at him. He was ready to plug the first person who looked at him wrong.

As usual, Hunt was allowing his temper to take over. Rather than walk in quietly and try to be inconspicuous about locating her, he pulled the door open with all his force and about ripped it off its hinges. There was no automatic closer on the door and it pulled a lot more freely than he had expected.

A few people at the bar glanced his way for a brief moment then simply returned to their beers. One man's expression was that of fear, as if to say, *"Whoa. I hope that wasn't his wife I was just hitting on."*

Hunt scanned the bar area and didn't find her. He hurried up a small flight of stairs to the dining area and caught sight of her in the far corner right as she spotted him. She was sitting next to a man built pretty much like he was, but his skin was much darker. Hunt couldn't place his nationality from this distance, nor did he care. Closing the gap, he took long strides toward them.

A waitress passed with a tray full of beers. Hunt took one off and threw a ten dollar bill on her tray. "Keep the change." She wasn't going to complain about him shorting her a customer's drink. She returned to the bar to replace it.

When he reached the table where Amanda sat, he spun the chair backward, sat down, and took a long draw from the beer. "Hey, doll face. Come here often?"

Amanda's eyes had been wide from the moment she'd spotted him. He expected that. She had to be nothing short of shocked to see him. What he didn't expect was her to not try to flee. She sat next to the man as if in fear of him, not Hunt.

The man, whom Hunt decided was Italian, wrapped his arm around Mandy's shoulder. "Can we help you with something, friend?"

Calmly, Hunt took another long draw of beer. "You? No. Her? Most certainly. Your arm is around something that's mine right now, and I intend on taking it back."

The man glared at Mandy. "New boyfriend? So soon? Tsk tsk, Amanda. What will Gerard say?"

"I'm not her boyfriend, and I don't give a fuck who Gerard is. The lady is leaving with me."

The man held his hand out as if he were trying to calm Hunt down. "I'm afraid as she's just found her way back to us. I can't let you take her."

"Us? Are you one of those intellectual types who insists on referring to yourself in the third person?"

"Turn around and meet Bennett," he said with a smile.

Hunt turned around and took in the figure walking toward them. He was roughly the size of a small house, and the bulge in his jacket was unmistakable. The dude was packing. It wasn't illegal to have a concealed weapon in Vermont, but Hunt was now especially intrigued by his new "friends." With the stories Mandy had given him, he couldn't imagine what her connection was to them.

Hunt turned back around and smiled at the man. "Is that all you got, Guido?" He turned his attention to Mandy, who was shaking her head. He still didn't like the fact she was acting so afraid. Not that he cared if she were lying in a pool of sweat, he just didn't understand why she fought so hard to break free of him and find these men if she was only going to sit here afraid of them.

The name finally registered with him. Mandy had said Bennett was the name of the man who had kicked her. The father of her child. Something was seriously wrong. Making no secret of what he was doing, Hunt bent down. Sure enough, he found a gun pointed at Amanda's side. It was the gun she'd taken from Roy. When he sat upright, the man he called Guido smiled wide.

"Just go about your business, friend. There's nothing to see here."

Hunt got to his feet and moved his jacket aside, revealing his own gun in its holster. He hadn't attached his badge on purpose and was glad he didn't. He sensed in this case, it would have only made matters worse.

"I'm not your friend. I can't tell you how much I need the company of this lady with me back to my hometown. I'd appreciate it if your interference stopped here."

Guido laughed. "You hear that, Bennett? Pretty boy would appreciate it if your interference stopped here." He glared at Hunt. "And I can't tell *you* how much I'd appreciate your company, outside."

Hunt glanced to Amanda, who had been silent since he'd gotten there. *Is she really worth this?* he thought to himself as he headed toward the back door.

Once everyone was outside, Bennett pointed toward a large black SUV and Hunt walked over. The man finally introduced himself, saving Hunt from calling him Guido again.

"The name is Tony and you're leaving here alone."

"I'm afraid I've got a problem with that," Hunt replied.

"I'll say you do." Bennett pulled out his gun and pointed it at Hunt, but Hunt was on his just as fast. It was a standoff.

Mandy finally found her voice. "Leave him out of this, Bennett. Your beef is with me. Barney here will leave without any trouble. Won't you, Barney?"

Hunt didn't drop his stance with the gun, but turned to Mandy with an angry glare. "Sweetheart, if you call me Barney one more time..."

The fight they pretended to start was enough of a distraction. Hunt was able to knock the gun out of Bennett's hand and knock him in the chin hard enough with the butt of his gun, it sent him to the ground with a solid thud. He was out cold.

As soon as Hunt had knocked the gun free, Mandy rammed Tony in the gut with her elbow. When he bent down, she kneed him in the chin as well. Hunt shot out one of the tires to the SUV then took Mandy by the hand and ran for his truck. He figured he could take them one-on-one in a street fight, but two on one with semi-automatic guns kind of screamed, *Just grab the girl and get the hell outta here, idiot.*

Hunt unlocked his door with his fob as they ran. He shoved Mandy in just as a sharp stinging hit his side. Fighting the urge to cry out in pain, he climbed in and pulled his door closed, ducking as bullets hit the side of the truck. His tires squealed as he sped away.

"You're hit!" Mandy screamed as she watched him pull his hand away from his side. It was covered with blood.

"Just grazed me."

She leaned over his lap. "I want to look at it."

"I'm fine!" he shouted as he shoved her away. "I want to put some distance between us and your goons first." He took the first gravel road they came across. "Turn my GPS on. I need to get us outta here."

"You don't know where you are? How did you find me?"

"You're welcome, by the way."

"You want me to thank you? I had things under control before you showed up!"

"Under control? Is that what you call a gun in your side? My department's gun at that."

"Tony would never shoot me."

"And why is that? 'Cause he's in love with you?"

"No, asshole. Gerard would kill him."

Hunt slammed on the brakes. They skidded sideways for a few feet. The gravel was loose, but Hunt showed no concern about losing control. "Just who the hell is Gerard, and who the hell were the goons, Mandy?"

She crossed her arms. "I told you not to get involved. You couldn't just let me leave the fucking hospital."

He held her arm. "Who were they?" Before he could even tighten his grip, he winced in pain and leaned his head back and closed his eyes.

"Hunt?" Mandy slid forward in the seat and tried to direct Hunt to lie down. He wasn't putting up a fight. She lifted up his blood soaked shirt. "It's not a graze, Hunt. There's no exit wound."

She reached into his glove box, looking for the stash of fast food napkins that should be there, but there weren't. "That's right," she said with a sigh. "You've probably never had a Big Mac in your entire healthy-Mister-Workout life."

"Shit'll kill you."

Mandy removed her blouse since she still had on a tank top underneath. She wasn't willing to get naked to help him. Okay, she probably was. She tried wiping away the blood to get a better look at it. He winced but didn't smack her hand away.

"The bullet is right at the surface. I can feel it. I have to get you to a hospital and get it out, Hunt."

"I'm not going in and having them knock me out so you get the chance to split again."

"You don't have a choice."

"The hell I don't." He sat upright and tried to grasp the steering wheel with his left arm, but it wasn't cooperating. He smacked the steering wheel with his right hand and bellowed, "Shit!"

"Scoot over."

"No way."

Mandy leaned as far as she could toward the dashboard. "Scoot the hell over. I'm driving."

"We both know how that turns out."

She took his shirt by his collar and then slid him over. He screamed, but she showed no emotion over it. She got behind the wheel and took off.

Hunt woke up in a warm bed in a dimly lit room. There was a fire crackling on the far wall. He tried to sit up but his side hurt. He reached down for it and found a bandage neatly covering his wound. He took in the items on the nightstand next to him. There was half a bottle of tequila sitting there and a bloody rag. He picked up the rag and found the bullet.

He scoffed. "Small caliber. Amateurs."

Events of the night were gradually coming back to him. Mandy had driven them to Bass Lake. She got them a room and some supplies. He recalled screaming into a pillow not so gentlemanly as she dug out the bullet with his buck knife. Damn his stubborn attitude. She probably enjoyed it. A lot of good it did him. He was in pain and she probably still took off.

Light escaped from under what had to be the bathroom door. The light suddenly went out and Mandy came out in a towel.

"I didn't expect you up already."

"You mean you were hoping I was still out cold so you could slip away."

She let out a loud sigh and dropped her arms. "You're an idiot."

"I love you, too."

"Fuck off, Hunt. I didn't exactly enjoy my little surgery you made me perform."

"I don't recall I enjoyed it much, either."

"You should have let me take you to a hospital."

"This is one horse I'm pretty sure we've beaten to death. Did you get any pain killers when you got the bandages?"

"You've already taken four. Not to mention the booze."

"Give me a couple more." He hesitated then added, "Please."

She returned to the bathroom, got a glass of water, and picked up the generic pain relief. After handing the glass and bottle to Hunt, she stepped back. Hunt watched as she adjusted how she had the towel fastened.

"I wouldn't take more than two," she said. "We really should get some food in you, too. Will you eat pizza, or does that fall under the junk-food-don't-touch-my-lips category? I really don't want to go out and risk be seen."

"Pizza is fine."

"One problem."

"I don't care what you put on it."

"No. I need money."

"You took money out of my wallet last night for supplies."

"So? I'm not going in your wallet without asking."

"I give you permission to take money for pizza, Mandy." He gave her a hard stare. "You have me intrigued."

"Why? Because I keep company with hired thugs?"

"Besides that. You are going to get around to explaining this whole mess to me eventually, you know."

"Then what?"

"I don't know 'then what.' I can barely handle you one step at a time, as it is." He stared at her for a long moment again. "Why didn't you take my money and my truck and split again?"

"Because you were wounded, dick. It's your fault not mine, but you still make me feel responsible. You're like that irritating neighbor's dog. I hate you, but if you're squished on the road, I'd still want to get you to a vet."

Hunt laughed. "You're all heart."

She picked up a T-shirt and shorts she'd purchased at the convenience store and went into the bathroom to get changed. When she came back out, Hunt was sound asleep again.

Hunt woke up again after a few hours. The lights were off but the fire was still going, giving the room a soft glow. He immediately searched for Mandy and found her asleep next to him. She was above the covers and shivering. He gave her a tap on the shoulder and she bolted up.

"What is it? You okay?"

"I'm fine. You're cold. Get under the covers. I don't bite."

"It's not so bad. I'll go put more wood on." She got out of bed to add a few logs to the fireplace, and he held his tongue about her "wood on" comment. The cotton shorts she bought were a little on the short side. He wouldn't deny loving the view as she bent over, adding the wood to the fire.

When she got back to the bed, Hunt held the sheet and blanket up. She hesitated but she climbed in with him. There was a good two feet separating them.

"Are you hungry?" she asked. "The pizza wasn't too bad."

"I'm hungry. But I don't want pizza."

"You told me to order pizza, Hunt!" she said, getting upset. "What do you want?"

He slid closer. "You." Hunt kissed her and was a little more than surprised when she kissed him back. His initial hesitant gentle kiss of, *I have to do it, but I'm waiting to be smacked,* was replaced with hard kisses that matched his aching hunger for her that had been building up over the past two days. She returned them with the same force. He was beyond surprised, but wasn't going to dare stop and say a thing.

Within seconds they had greedily removed each other's underwear and he was inside her. She felt so good he couldn't even feel the pain in his side. He did not take her gently, nor was she giving any signs for him to do so. Sexual frustration or pure lust drove them through their near animalistic actions.

Mandy tightened around Hunt. Every part of her drew him closer. The noises she made sent him over the edge. His orgasm was only seconds behind hers. He was both in ecstasy and sad it was already over.

He stayed on top of her, breathing hard for a few minutes. She didn't seem in a hurry for him to leave. She stroked his back then stopped when her hand reached his bandage. "Are you okay?"

He rolled off to her right so he wouldn't land on the bandage. "Didn't feel a thing. I meant, as far as my side went." He gave her a kiss. "Damn, girl. Why didn't you let me do that two days ago? We could have saved a lot of beating each other up."

"You were an asshole two days ago. I'm still not so sure you're not. I guess I have that whole Florence Nightingale effect on you. That or you're still drunk. I'm sure it'll pass."

He kissed her again. "I don't think so."

"Let me get you some pizza," she said as she tried to get out of bed.

He held her arm. "Just stay, Mandy. I like this. Believe it or not, this is the best rest I've had in days."

"Something on your mind, Barney?"

He chuckled. "You wear a guy out. From the inside out, in all honesty. You are one tough broad and when I wake up, I want your story." He scooted closer to her and gently pulled her head to his chest. "And if you even think about not being here when I get up, you're going to be sorry."

He was sound asleep again in seconds.

When Hunt woke up the next morning, he was fit to be tied when Amanda was nowhere to be found. He threw the sheets off of the bed and got to his feet right as she came through the hotel door.

"Where were you?"

"Getting you something to eat." She slammed a bag on the counter. "I didn't think you'd want day old pizza." She was a little more careful in placing the tray of drinks down.

She glanced down his body. "You mind at least putting some pants on?"

Hunt was never a shy one about being naked. Least of all after he had been intimate with someone. This was not how he'd hoped this morning would go. Had he been so delirious he dreamt up last night? Couldn't have. He'd never had that good of a dream before. He pulled up his jeans without putting on any underwear and walked over to her.

"How can you do that?"

"Do what? I know you're not referring to a sex marathon. I'm a little embarrassed at the time on that one.

I was hoping to better my score this morning." Hunt reached for her face but she pulled away. "Jesus. You are one fickle broad."

She gave his hand an added push as he dropped it. "That shouldn't have happened."

"Well it did. Now what?"

"Now nothing. You go your way and I go mine." She took the breakfast items out of the bag. "I found a small diner. I thought you'd be hungry, so I got a little of everything." She sat at the table and unwrapped a plate of hash browns, scrambled eggs and bacon. "You want scrambled or over-easy?"

Hunt sat down across from her. "I don't care. You pick."

She passed him the plate then unwrapped one for herself. A third plate held pancakes. She put it between them and dug for packets of syrup. They both ate a few bites in silence.

Hunt finally spoke up. "You seem to do the morning after thing pretty well, if I do say so myself."

Mandy slammed her fork on her plate. It would have made more of an impact had it not been plastic. "Stop being so damn smug, Blaine. You got shot and you got laid. I figure that's about par for the course for your profession, isn't it?"

"You're half right," he returned with equal attitude.

"Shot much?" She returned to her food.

"You think just because you let me screw you I'd let you go? That kinda makes you a whore, doesn't it?" Hunt thought that would get a plate full of food thrown in his direction but instead, she continued to eat, trying hard to ignore him. Mandy ate half of what was in front of her then took her coffee and stood. She walked over to the window and parted the curtain.

"It's starting to really cool off. They say snow for Friday."

"You really want to talk weather?"

"No. I don't, Hunt. I don't want to talk anything. I didn't want you following me and I certainly didn't want to sleep with you last night. I don't know why I did. Maybe it does make me a whore. I don't care. Just please, please leave me alon—"

A knocking on the door cut her off. Hunt stood, snatched his gun off of the dresser, and rushed to the peephole. The goon Tony had called Bennett was standing there.

"It's for you," Hunt said, quietly.

"How'd they find us?" she whispered.

Before Hunt could think of a smart ass reply, the door was kicked in. Hunt managed to jump close to the wall and avoid being hit. Bennett stood in the entry with his gun aimed at Mandy. "Get out where I can see you, friend. This is none of your business."

Hunt pushed the door hard enough to knock Bennett back. "I told you. I'm not your friend!" Shots flew at him from the parking lot. Bennett wasn't alone. Hunt actually didn't expect him to be, but didn't have a second to think from the time they had heard the knock.

A bullet hit above Hunt's head and he reacted in an instant the only way he was trained. He fired back. Hunt's aim was better than the hired thug. He went down after only one shot.

This had happened in seconds. Hunt remembered Bennett and returned his attention to the room. Amanda had gained control of Bennett's pistol and now had it aimed at her captive on the floor. He rushed over to his duffle bag and pulled out a pair of cuffs. He stood Bennett up and cuffed his hands behind his back. Hunt removed his cell phone from its holster and dialed 9—1—1. He hesitated when the woman answered. "Nine-one-one. What's your emergency?"

"Why did you do that?" Mandy asked, as they sped down the road in Hunt's truck.

"Because I'm not ready to spend the next three days trying to explain what this is when I don't even know myself. You're a great piece of ass, doll face, but I'm not ready to lose my badge over shooting back at someone who shot at me first."

Hunt told the 9—1—1 operator there had been shooting at the hotel, but that was all. He hurried Mandy through packing up what little they had, and they rushed out the door. He wasn't worried about Bennett. Whoever this group was, they weren't going to say anything and probably had a lawyer on speed dial that would have him free in an hour. They were either dealing drugs or some type of Mafia. Hunt would figure it out, but not until they were clear of this town.

"Can't they trace your gun?"

"That wasn't my work gun. That one can't be traced back to me."

"You have a throwaway?" she scoffed. "The great Hunter Blaine, Sheriff extraordinaire, has a throwaway gun?"

"Confiscated it off of a punk city kid. I never expected to use it."

"But it's what you happen to have in your holster?"

"It's called instinct. I knew I'd find you and I knew there'd be trouble. I didn't plan killing a thug was going to be part of it."

"He shot at you first."

"It doesn't matter!"

Amanda was quiet for a few moments. Maybe she sensed Hunt needed a minute to compose himself, but she couldn't keep quiet for long. "Was that your first kill?"

He glared at her hard. "Don't go all shrink on me."

"Was it?"

"How much action do you think I get in podunk Vermont? I'm not the idiot Barney you think I am but no, I've never had to resort to killing anyone."

"He was just a piece of shit. Don't lose any sleep over it."

Hunt took a dirt road that led to a picnic area off a small lake. It was cold enough no one was out. The lake would be frozen soon, and icehouses would be scattered about. He slammed his truck into Park and got out. He walked around to the passenger door and pulled it open, again using too much force. Reaching in, he pulled Mandy out of the truck. After her feet hit the ground, he shoved her hard against the truck. He pulled his gun out and held it to her head.

"You tell me what the fuck this is right now or I swear I'll blow your brains all over my truck. It'll go nice with the bullet holes in there now, thanks to you!"

He never saw it coming. She pulled a gun out from behind her back and held it to his head. "Go ahead, Hunt. See how far you get with half a face yourself."

Hunt stared at her hard with his nostrils flaring before he dropped his gun and spun around. Mandy went after him. Hunt spun around again and relieved her of her gun. He backed her against the truck again and held her there with his hips as he held the gun in her face. "Where in the hell did you get this, Mandy?"

"Let go of me!"

"Where?" he yelled louder.

"I took it off of Bennett. There were shots flying everywhere. You think I wasn't going to be protected?"

"What do you think I've been doing?"

"You think you've been protecting me? Is that what you call this? I keep telling you I was fine on my own!"

"Right. Left for dead in the street, then in a bar with a gun at your side. You're doing a great job so far."

"Well, at least I didn't have to kill anyone."

That comment sent him over the edge. He held the gun to her head again and held her gaze with his nostrils flaring as he pulled the hammer back. After a moment, he dropped the gun back to his side and headed toward the lake.

He was sitting on an old wooden picnic table when Mandy walked up.

"I'm sorry. That was a foul." She took a seat next to him. "Look. I know you think you're going all 'knight in shining armor' on me, but I don't need help."

He mumbled, "The hell you don't," then turned to her again. "Spill it."

"Spill what?"

"Stop it already, dammit! What is this? Who are these people and what are they after? You're not even after a kid, are you? I'm pretty sure you aren't married to that Bennett character and he's not the father of your kid like you claim. What did you do? Run off with their drug money or something?"

"There's no money, Hunt. I told you. That bastard has my daughter."

"That Gerard they mentioned?"

"Yes."

"Why did you say Bennett was the father?"

"I didn't want to throw another name into the mix. You shouldn't even be involved. I just want my daughter back. It doesn't get any easier than that."

"Honey, if this is your idea of easy, I don't want to know what you do for a living."

She hopped off the table. "Will you let me go now?"

Hunt stepped off as well. "Are you insane? You've got thugs with enough weapons to start their own army after you and I'm supposed to just let you walk?"

"You're the one with enough weapons to start an army, Hunt. What were you expecting?"

"What were you doing in my duffle bag?"

"I was curious. It was heavy as hell."

He raised an eyebrow.

"I carried it in, or did you forget that part? You were kind of delirious. You were insistent about it not being left in the truck."

"You need to keep your nosy ass out of my stuff."

She took a step closer to him and poked him in the chest as she spoke. "Then don't get shot again, Barney!"

Hunt took her by the arms. "You know, I don't know what the hell I'm doing chasing you like this. A smart man would have left you lying there."

"Well it's a good thing 'smarts' isn't your strong point then, isn't it?"

He let her go and strode angrily back to his truck. Mandy stayed by the water for a while. Hunt was sure she just wanted time away from him. There was no way she was feeling bad for what she said. He'd done 'cold hearted bitch' before, but she sure took the cake. He almost regretted sleeping with her. Almost. It had been good. Great, in fact. He wished he could have another shot, but with the way she was acting, slamming his dick in the truck door sounded equally good right now.

CHAPTER FIVE

Mandy climbed into the truck. She slammed the door then leaned against it, trying to get as far away from Hunt as humanly possible.

"So, what now? You taking me back to jail?"

"Why? So you can beat the shit out of my men again?" She pelted out a laugh. "That was pretty pathetic."

"Maybe. But where I come from, men care about women. You can't blame Luke for worrying about you."

"No. Just for allowing me to get the upper hand on him so easily."

"Would you...forget it. It's not worth it." Hunt put his hand on his key then pulled it back again. "You ever give that attitude a rest? Shit, Mandy. You get by your whole life on your looks and not have to work on your personality?"

"Screw you, Blaine."

"Well, that's a step up from Barney, anyway. Tell me the story or we don't go anywhere."

"I told you the story."

"Right. You're trying to get your daughter back. Why did he drive from New York to Vermont to hide a kid?"

"Look around you. Is there a better place to hide her than in the middle of nowhere?"

"Upstate New York is pretty vast, too. No reason to come shit in my backyard."

"There's family here. They own a resort."

"Why head here if you'd expect that? Didn't he think you'd follow him here?"

"I'm sure he knew, but he just didn't care. You witnessed for yourself the company he keeps. He didn't expect me to follow and figured they'd stop me if I did. It's easy enough to figure out."

Hunt sat so he was leaning against his door as well. He wanted to face her better. "Are we talking about this Gerard now?"

"Yes."

"And what exactly does he do that he needs armed men around him?"

"The family has money. They're just...eccentric about things."

"My aunt Nellie is loaded. She's what they call eccentric. She has fourteen housecats and eats cheese at every meal. She does not have armed assassins at her beck and call. There's something you're not telling me, Mandy."

"What do you want me to tell you? They think the world is after them and their money."

"Where did it come from?"

"It's old money. The family has had it since before the Civil War. I think they invest now."

"You think? Weren't you married to the guy?"

"Don't remind me."

Hunt ran his hand down his face in frustration. "How did you end up in the bar and why did they have guns on you?"

"I was snooping around to see if they had shown up. I thought maybe I beat him to town."

"He beat you here while you were in the hospital?"

"Look…I don't know. He could have taken Darci to Paris for all I know. I just figured I had to start somewhere."

"Darci is your daughter?"

"Yes."

"And this is finally the truth? That's her real name?"

"Yes. And my last name is really Smith."

His expression said he still didn't believe her. "So you went to the bar looking for him and his goons were there instead?"

"Yes. They were surprised to see me."

"Because they left you for dead in St. Ann's."

"I suppose so."

"You suppose so?"

"Yes. Yes, I guess that's why they were surprised. They threatened me before they beat me. They didn't think I'd have the balls to keep going."

"Well, then apparently I know you better than they do."

She tilted her head. "You think I have balls?"

"Brass ones the size of coconuts, sweetheart." Hunt started the truck.

"Where are we going?"

"Right now? I want to get breakfast. We got interrupted and I'm starving." He took off for the highway.

"Then what?"

"Then we find a motel even more out of the way than the one we were at. My side is killing me and I need some rest."

"I need to get my daughter, Hunt."

"Let me rest. We'll figure it out. I'm not buying what you're selling, but I'm not letting you do this alone."

"You believe me?"

"I never said that. I still don't trust you as far as I could throw you. Right now, that isn't very far. You're still playing the New York card, but your car was registered to a Pennsylvania address."

"It was a vacation cottage. Insurance was cheaper so we registered my car there."

"Right."

"I mean it, Hunt. That isn't bullshit. We were a normal married couple with a kid and vacation days like everyone else."

He sighed, still unsure what to make of it. "I don't like these men in my state. If they're investors, my aunt Nellie is a 3-legged nun. I don't know what the story is with all the guns, but kidnapping is something else altogether. I can't vouch for your motherliness, but I don't think it's in Darci's best interest to be with them either. I need to rest then we'll figure this mess out."

"But—"

"No buts. They shot me. Now I'm pissed off."

They drove for thirty minutes before Hunt pulled over at a gas station with a restaurant attached to the convenience store.

"I feel like shit. Get some food to go, then we'll head to a motel," he said as he tossed her his wallet.

"What do you want?" Mandy's tone finally softened. Either that or Hunt was starting to get delirious.

"A burger and fries."

"Seriously?"

He let himself fall to the seat. He seemed exhausted all of a sudden and didn't want to fight anymore. "Yes, seriously. I could use the protein. Now go get it, would you?"

"Want me to buy some pain killers? I don't think we brought what was at the last place when we bugged out."

He mumbled "sure" into the seat.

Mandy was out in twenty-five minutes. She peered through the truck window. Hunt wasn't moving. She thought about taking off for a split second, then changed her mind just as quickly. Walking around to the driver's door, she opened it up. Hunt sat up, looking like he had been in a dead sleep.

"Ready?" he asked as he rubbed his eyes with his palms.

"Yes. Scoot over. I'll drive."

"I got it."

"Hunt. Now is not the time to be macho. Let me drive, for cryin' out loud. You look like shit."

"Sweet talker," he said before he scooted over. He took the bag from her and pulled out his burger and had a bite taken out of it before she had the truck in gear.

"You are starving."

"Getting shot at, skipping a few meals, killing someone, and fabulous sex will do that to a guy."

Mandy didn't reply as she headed down the highway.

Again Hunt woke up in a warm hotel room. There was no fireplace this time, though. He hadn't expected one, by the looks of the outside, but he hadn't paid any attention when he let Mandy help pour him in bed. He was hurting bad and wanted nothing more than to sleep for a day after he had finished his burger. He'd had better fries but they went down great. Anything tasted great when you were starving. After he ate, he downed four of whatever pain reliever Mandy had gotten and washed them down with the Sprite she'd bought him.

"This is disgusting," he had complained.

"It was that or orange soda. I didn't want to get you something with caffeine. You need to sleep."

"I think I could drink a pot of coffee right now and it wouldn't make a difference."

"Sorry. Guess I should have asked for plain water."

He took her hand. "Sorry. I don't mean to bitch. You put some thought into it. Thanks."

She made no further comments and drove them to the next hotel they came across. He was out as soon as he hit the bed.

Hunt stirred, Mandy walked over to the bed and sat down. "How are you feeling?"

"Better. How long have I been out?"

"Five hours."

"Five hours?" Hunt sat up but got a head rush, so he dropped back down.

Mandy placed her hand on his shoulder. "You needed it. You want more pain killers?"

"It's not so bad right now."

"Probably 'cause it's still in your system. I was taught to stay on top of the pain. Don't wait till it's killing you." She got up and came back with a glass of water and the pills. "Just three this time. It'll eat at your gut if you're not careful."

Hunt sat up and took the pills. He said, "Thanks," after lying back down.

"I know. The water tastes like shit. Want me to run for something?"

"It's fine. I grew up on well water. This isn't so bad."

"Makes me want to yak."

Hunt laughed. "You could light the stuff at my grandpa's place."

"Really?" She scooted closer. "You were a farm kid?"

"Not really. I lived in a town about the size of St. Ann's, but my grandparents farmed out of town. We went there a lot. I worked with him a few summers when I was a teenager."

"Then what?"

"Then I guess I figured out farming wasn't for me."

Mandy laid herself on the bed and propped her head up on her hand. "Did you always want to be a cop, Hunt?"

Hunt was intrigued at the sudden calm that had happened between them. He was enjoying having a regular conversation with her and silently hoped it would last. "I guess I always did."

"Played cops and robbers a lot with your friends when you were a kid?"

He laughed. "I was always the cop. What about you?"

"I was usually Jill."

"Jill?"

"Monroe. Charlie's Angels."

Hunt laughed until his side ached. Mandy laughed along with him then playfully smacked his arm. "Quit it. I think I'd outrank you in a round of cops and robbers."

Hunt slid closer to her and wrapped an arm around her waist. "How about a round of hostage instead?" He leaned into her and gave her a gentle kiss.

She had closed her eyes and accepted the kiss. After swallowing hard she said softly, "I don't think that's such a great idea."

Hunt kissed down her neck and whispered, "Why not?"

Again she swallowed hard, seeming to search for an answer. "I uh...we...we just can't, Hunt."

"Your lips say no, but your body language tells me something else, Mandy." He kissed down her chest then lifted up her shirt as he came back up. She allowed him to take it off.

"When we're not screwing, we're fighting," she said softly.

"So, let's stop fighting." He began to work on her jeans.

"What about your side?"

"Chicks dig scars."

"Aren't you in throbbing pain?"

"There's only one throbbing I'm worried about right now."

He got her naked and brought her under the sheets with him. He thanked above that Mandy insisted he strip to his boxers before crawling in bed last night. They were removed in an instant. Again they made love.

Mandy must have sensed him flinching and made her way to the top. She wasn't much easier on him, but Hunt wasn't about to say a word. Things moved a little slower this time, but the wanting was still too great. It wasn't long before Mandy was lying flat on him whispering obscenities as he sent himself deeper inside her, sending them both over the edge.

Mandy kissed his neck gently a few times before settling her head on his shoulder. "Not bad for a gimp."

He smiled and stroked her back. "Wait until I'm healed up, doll."

She sat up enough so she could meet his gaze. "You think we won't kill each other before the opportunity presents itself again?"

"The opportunity is always there. We need to learn to seize the moment."

She playfully slapped his arm again. "I'm serious, Hunt. You hate me. What's with the sex all of a sudden?"

"I don't hate you. You just have a knack for pissing me off."

"And the difference?"

"One on one, when you're not trying to run away from me or deck me or my men, you're a very fascinating woman, Amanda."

"And when I am?"

"You're an absolute spitfire in bed."

"I'm serious, Hunt."

"So am I."

She glared at him.

"Okay. Honest time? You've intrigued the shit out of me since the moment I found you. Sure, you drive me nuts, but this whole 'mystery lady' thing is kind of a turn-on."

"You're such a straight arrow, Hunt. Besides the whole throwaway gun thing. This isn't going to work."

"Why? Because you're involved in something that will probably lead me to hauling your ass away in jail?"

"Would you?"

"Shit, Amanda." He sat them up but held her in place, wrapping his arms low on her back. "I can't help you when you don't tell me what this is."

"I want my daughter back."

He brushed hair away from her face and tucked it behind her ear. "Then I'll help you. But we do it my way."

Mandy gave Hunt a quick kiss and agreed to let him help, but she wasn't so sure she could follow up on her promise. She was starting to like Hunt's company, and whether she wanted to admit it or not, he had saved her ass back at the bar. Surviving another surprise run in with Gerard's goons probably wasn't in the cards for her. She hadn't expected this much trouble when she set out after Gerard, but she had to finish what she'd started. There would be no peace for her until this was over.

Getting involved with Hunt definitely wasn't on the list, but it was a little hard to go back now. Damn his persistence! She enjoyed having someone there for backup—and of course, the sex was outstanding—but she couldn't let this relationship go past her quest. When he found out what she really was, it would be over anyway.

She settled in next to him and they fell asleep.

Amanda stirred and searched for Hunt. She found him zipping up his jeans.

"Hey," he said as he leaned back down and kissed her. "I think we both needed to catch up on a little sleep."

"What time is it?"

"Seven. I was going to run for something to eat."

"Get back in bed. I'll do it." She tried sitting up but he pushed her back down.

"I'm fine. It's my turn to go for food." He kissed her on the nose. "I'm not so sure we'll have much of a selection. You have any particulars on the 'hate it' list?"

"I'm pretty much okay with anything."

"I'll be back in a flash."

Hunt was back in less than an hour. Amanda had just gotten out of the shower and was drying her hair when he walked in. She jumped when he showed up in the doorway.

"Sorry, Mandy. Guess you didn't hear me over the hair dryer. You all right?" He closed the gap between them and placed his arms on her shoulders.

"I'm fine. Just jumpy I guess. I suppose I'm waiting for more goons to kick the door down again."

"I'm sure we're fine." Hunt took a step closer and wrapped his arms around her. "Mmmm...you smell squeaky clean."

"Not bad shampoos and soap for a dump."

He smiled and gave her a kiss. He found it hard not to kiss her with every sentence. Their kisses grew heavier and he picked her up. Wincing, he released her back down.

"You okay?"

"It really isn't that bad."

"Maybe we should take it a little easier on you."

He grinned and kissed her again. "I'd take another bullet for more sex like that."

"Animal."

"Look who's talking." He dropped her towel and kissed down her chest. He cupped her breasts and kissed one.

"Hunt."

"Hmmm."

"I'm starving."

"Me, too."

"For food."

He straightened up. "Good call. We need our strength." He bent down and picked up her towel and wrapped her in it again. "I'll get things set up. You get dressed." He paused as he walked out of the bathroom and turned back around. "Too much too fast? You don't hate me again already, do you?"

"Not yet," she teased, as she turned the hair dryer back on.

Mandy joined Hunt at the small table. He had two plates in the middle of the table. One was a fried chicken platter and one was a steak. The mashed potatoes and veggies were the same for both. He also had two small salads.

"Quite the spread, Barn...Hunt."

He laughed. "Anything but Barney sounds funny coming from you. As long as you say it with love, I'll let it slip." He pointed at the plates. "Pick your poison."

"I'll take the chicken. You probably can't stand anything fried."

He slid her the steak. "I could eat a rhino's ass right now. Doesn't matter."

She switched their plates. "That's okay. It looks good. I only like steak when I make it anyway."

"What do you want for dressing? I got blue, ranch and French."

"You going to fight me for the blue?"

"I got two of those just in case."

They said together, "The chunkier the better," then laughed.

"My mother kind of made me a cheese-a-holic," Hunt said. "Probably why I started working out."

"Cheese isn't the bad guy anymore. Didn't you read Atkins?"

"Read it. It's crap. Stick to the food pyramid, not these hokey shit diets."

"I didn't say I do it, I'm a cheese freak myself. I liked the vote for more cheese."

He smiled at her. "You're one of these people who make up your own rules, aren't you?"

"And not just where food is concerned."

"I guessed as much there."

"You trying to start a fight?"

"Definitely not. Unless you want to so we can have make up sex."

"Your sex drive always been this insatiable? Never mind. You're a man. Of course it is."

He opened up an iced tea and gave it to her. He took one for himself and went to toast her with it. "Here's to dessert."

"What did you bring me?"

"Me."

She laughed then got suddenly serious. "Don't get me wrong, Hunt. I'm having fun and all, but—"

"I know. We'll get back on track in the morning." He cut a few pieces of his steak. "Don't take any of this wrong on my end either. I'm not looking to get tied down. Girlfriend-wise or literally getting tied down by your goons."

"Of course not. This whole thing was a mistake. I didn't think I needed any help, but there you were. I'm mistaking help and companionship through a stressful time for something else altogether. All of this is a mistake. You shouldn't even be involved."

"Well, I am...in the case, anyway. And I never call great sex a mistake. I need you to know, I can't guarantee you any outcome. I don't like the looks of what I've seen so far and whatever it is, however it goes down, you need to know I may not be able to protect you from the law."

"I'll take my chances. I want my daughter back. I'm not the one breaking laws."

"Except for what you've done to me and my deputies."

She ignored his last statements. "I really wish you'd just let me go. You don't know what you're in for, Hunt."

"How much worse do you think it's going to get? I've already been shot."

"And you could have been killed."

"Your goons have terrible aim."

Amanda stood up. "This isn't a game, Hunt. They mean business."

"Now we're getting somewhere. Sit back down and eat, then I want you to start talking to me."

They ate mostly in silence. Hunt brought up the latest weather forecast he'd heard while he went for the food, and Mandy nodded along. She cleaned up her plates and picked up Hunt's when he said he was done as well. She tried breezing by him, but he took her by the hand and sat her on his lap.

"No more fighting. Just tell me what is going on."

"I told you what's going on, Hunt."

"You said your ex ran away with your daughter. I want to know what that has to do with armed bodyguards or whatever those men are. Why were you beat and left for dead, and why when you show up in a bar they have you pinned in minutes and a gun pointed on you? Who is this Gerard, and why is he sending men after you? And how the hell do you make it through digging out a bullet without puking your guts out, and where did you learn how to field dress a wound like that?"

Mandy motioned to get out of his lap and Hunt let her. "It's...difficult to explain."

"Is he a drug dealer?"

"I wouldn't have gotten involved with a drug dealer, Hunt. Do I look that stupid?"

"What is he then? Some kind of Mafia? Does that sound as lame to me as it does to you? Help me make this make sense, Mandy."

"It may sound lame, but I guess that's as close as you're getting."

"Mafia? You have got to be shitting me. Why the hell would they come out to Vermont? Not cold enough in New York for them?"

"It's not what you think. You probably watched one too many movies. Gerard isn't like the 'Don' or anything."

"Son?"

"Nothing that grand. I swear I didn't know any of this when we got involved. When I found out, it was too late."

"Afraid to leave him?"

"That, and I didn't want to. I really loved him at first. I found out I was pregnant, and there was no way I was going to do it alone. He was a great guy."

"Besides the whole running the city thing."

"I told you, he wasn't like that. I never knew, Hunt. I swear. In the beginning, we lived a normal life. I wasn't showered in diamonds and furs. We didn't host grand balls every weekend and rub elbows with the cliché corrupt mayor and such. I didn't have bodyguards and we didn't have machine guns in the house."

"What changed? When did you realize who he was?"

"I can't pinpoint it to any one thing. I remember men like the ones from yesterday showing up more often. Gerard was always in his den with one or two of them. I was never allowed in. I tried bringing in drinks once, and he was in a hurry to hide a big wad of cash. He rushed me out of there in a flash and I was scared he was going to hit me."

"Did he?"

"That time, no."

"That time? So he did hit you."

"Not a lot. When I found out what he was involved in, we would get in fights. I wanted to move away. He wouldn't go with me and said he'd kill me if I ever left him."

"Sonofabitch."

"I didn't want to tell you these things, Hunt. Getting angry at him personally isn't going to help matters."

"He was scum before, but hitting a woman...there is never an excuse for that."

"Hell, Hunt. I slapped him first once. I'm hardly innocent."

"I don't care." He walked over and held her face in his hands and kissed her gently. "I'm sorry."

Mandy shrugged it off and went over to the window. She pushed the curtain aside. "It's snowing." Her tone had dramatically changed, and she was now smiling wide. Hunt joined her.

"Shouldn't amount to much."

"It's still beautiful."

"That it is. You're in God's country now, sweetheart." Hunt turned to her again and locked his gaze with hers. "Will you tell me more?"

"For all the good it's doing?"

"I need to know what I'm up against. Tell me about this resort you're heading for."

"It's just an old lodge. There's a huge kitchen and twelve rooms. It was probably a bed and breakfast in its day. We stayed there once by ourselves, years ago. Something was going down and I got sick of the bodyguards, or whatever they were, floating around our house. Gerard brought me there to get away. I guess he knew we were safe enough there. No one came with us. It was a great week actually. I was six months pregnant and the mini vacation was great. It did our marriage some good."

"Even knowing what he did for a living?"

"I was pregnant, Hunt. I don't expect you to understand. I always thought I'd get him to change his mind and let us leave. Go to Mexico or something. Australia. Anywhere to get away from this. Yes, I loved the sonofabitch. I knew he'd be a good father, too."

"So much so he kidnapped her."

"I shouldn't have packed a bag. I should have just left. Things could have been replaced..." Her voice trailed off and she sounded like she was fighting tears.

Hunt placed his arms around her and gently rocked. "Shhhh. Take it easy, sweetheart."

"He came home when I wasn't expecting him. He was furious to find the bag." She paused again. "I wasn't left alone after that day."

Mandy moved her head away from him and wiped the corner of her eye. Hunt broke away from her. "Hang on a second." He went to the duffle bag and pulled something out of the side pocket. He stood in front of her and held up her locket. Mandy snatched it from his hand.

"I thought I lost this to the lake."

"It was in my pocket. The pictures didn't fare too bad. That glass covering them must seal pretty well." He took it back. "Turn around." She turned around and he clasped it around her neck. He spun her back around and held it in his hands again.

"How old was Darci then?"

"We had just celebrated her second birthday." She rested heavily against Hunt's chest.

He kissed the top of her head and rocked with her for another moment. "Can you draw the layout of the resort for me?"

She leaned back. "Sure." She dug in the nightstand drawer and found a notepad and pen next to the bible.

Hunt watched as she drew the layout in great detail. Her perspectives were amazing. It wasn't at all the plain lines for walls and open spaces for doors he was expecting her to do. She even added in where the sink was in the kitchen.

"Did you go to school for architecture or something?"

"I had a semester of drafting. Nothing fancy."

He took the paper from her. "This is amazing."

"Well, let's hope there isn't a panic room or any other hiding places. Remember, I wasn't so paranoid when I was there last."

"It was all about the make-up sex, wasn't it?"

"Pretty much," she said as she took the drawing back and continued her sketching.

Hunt lifted her up out of the chair and she squealed. He tossed her on the bed and her squealing turned to more playful giggles. He crawled on top of her and pinned both hands above her head with one of his. He reached under her shirt and unclasped her bra with the other one.

"Floozy," he said, as he gently nibbled at her breast through her shirt.

"What took you so long, Hunt? I've been waiting on dessert."

"One only has to ask."

CHAPTER SIX

gain they lay together, completely satisfied and not letting their worries concern them. No matter how intrigued Hunt was with what she was telling him and how eager he was to arrest this Gerard, he couldn't keep from being more incredibly turned on by Mandy with every glance. He wanted her bad, and to even think of her being with another man made him insane. The desire for animal sex had won over the desire to make gentle love and let her know she would never again have to know what it was like for a man to hurt her. Hunt would never allow it. He was trying to play it cool, but he was falling for her and didn't want it to be over after he made the arrest. He had been planning what he could tell his deputies about her. About why she did what she did and wasn't locked up. Hunt wasn't one to break rules or to let a lawbreaker slide, but he could only imagine what she was going through and what caused her to do what she did. Things would be different when this was all behind them.

She lay with her back facing him and he pulled her in even closer. "Damn, girl. I wish all of my cross-state arrests were this much fun."

She spun around and faced him. "I'm not under arrest."

"Maybe not anymore, true enough. But I sure as hell wanted to haul your ass in for what you've done."

"I hope I convinced you with my story and not just the sex."

"I couldn't be bought and turned corrupt with sex. I would think you knew me by now." He kissed her on the forehead. "How did you get so good at escaping?" He propped himself up on his elbow. "You did try getting away from Gerard before, didn't you?"

She turned away shyly, but he held her chin and brought her back to meet his gaze.

"Yes. It wasn't as easy with Darci, though. I could have left a few times when I didn't have her with me, but Gerard knew I would never leave without her."

Hunt stroked her cheek. "You really make me wish I'd settled down and had kids. I can't imagine loving someone else so much."

"I highly recommend you give it a whirl someday."

"Maybe I will," he said as he claimed her mouth with his once again. They were making love again before Hunt had time to think. She drove him crazy, and his body took over. They moved from the bed to the dresser to the shower before they had finished. Mandy was not shy about her sexuality and had a couple of orgasms before Hunt was rendered 'out for the count.' After lightly toweling off, they collapsed back in bed, finally falling asleep for the night.

When Mandy woke up at six, Hunt was already awake and staring at her sketch. He joined her in bed when she stirred. Sitting up against the headboard, he waited for her to join him. He pointed to a small room on the end. There was a door going in from the outside and a door to what appeared to be the kitchen.

"Is that a walk-in pantry?"

"Good morning."

"Sorry." He leaned down and kissed her. "Good morning. So...pantry?"

"Yes. Gerard said it was set up that way so they didn't have to haul supplies through the house."

"Is this first bedroom a master room?"

"I guess it's designed for the caretaker. It has its own bathroom. It's the only room that does."

"And how far is it to the lake? Any chance we could sneak up that way?"

"There's a hundred and sixty-two stairs to the lake. It's steep. We wouldn't be seen but we also wouldn't see if someone was coming down. We'd probably hear them, but I'm not so sure we'd get away without being seen by them first."

"That's a hell of a lot of stairs."

"I walked them twice a day. I counted. There's an old mechanical lift chair, too. It still works—at least it used to, but it's as loud as hell."

"What about neighbors?"

Mandy spent the next twenty minutes describing the closest neighbors and the layout as best as she could. She sat up and inspected his side. "I want to redress your wound, Hunt."

"I'm sure the air has been fine for it."

"Maybe, but if your shirt rubs, it's bound to start bleeding. Just let me do it."

As she was getting up, he took ahold of her wrist. "We never did get to how you dealt with my wound so well."

"Hunt, when you're a mother, you see everything. Blood, vomit, and gore don't bother me."

"Not buyin' it."

She let out a heavy sigh. "That goon you shot?"

"Yeah?"

"I did the same for him. He showed up one night with a bullet in his thigh. Gerard wasn't home and I was scared to death. I hadn't known then. I thought he was just a business associate of my husband's. We had met at a party once."

"Go on."

"I didn't care for him. Now, I guess I understand why he acted the way he did all the time. He thought he was bigger than his own britches. It was one of Gerard's men who shot him for mouthing off. They were probably aiming for his knee. When they showed up, I thought I was going to be murdered."

"Why did they barge into your place? Don't those guys have doctors on payroll?"

"I guess we were convenient. I can't say for sure. Gerard came home and was furious. It was the first time I had witnessed him getting violent. He pulled a gun out of a holster he was wearing. I never even knew he owned a gun. He pinned the guy who brought the wounded one in against the wall and held the gun to his chin. He thought they were going for me as well. When he realized what I was doing, he lightened up a little."

"How did he explain that away?"

"Not very convincingly. It was at that point I was beginning to wonder, anyway. I went from suspicions to full blown guns and gore. I hated the man. I actually enjoyed hearing the fucker scream as I tended to him."

Hunt laughed. "Did you enjoy hearing me scream?"

"You weren't that bad." He raised an eyebrow. "No, Hunt. I didn't enjoy it. You were different. He had it coming. It was my fault you were shot. I don't know what I would have done..."

Her voice trailed off and Hunt pulled her to his chest. He wanted to make light of it before she became scared and serious. He faked a laugh and touched a finger to his chest by where her head now rested. "Like a bullet could penetrate this."

That caused her to laugh for real. She stroked his chest. "You have a good point there."

"Let's hit the road. I want a good breakfast, and we have about an hour drive to get to this cabin."

"What if they aren't there?"

"Then we keep looking."

Hunt checked in with Roy from the diner. He didn't give him any details; he just said he was still in pursuit.

"Where the hell are you, Hunt? Texas? That GPS should have taken you right to her."

"I'm still in Vermont. Things are just...complicated."

"Complicated. Tell me you ain't fucking her. Goddammit, Hunt. She totaled a cruiser, broke Luke's nose, and stole my truck and you're on a muffin buttering vacation."

"It's not like that, Roy. You know better."

"Oh, I know you all right. I thought you were going all possessive on her because of what she's done. You're in love with the little bitch."

"You watch your mouth when you're talking about her, Deputy!"

"You are fuckin' her!"

"Just shut up and listen. Things are going in a way you can't even imagine. I may have to call in another department once this gets rolling."

"Tell me where you are! I'll leave Luke here and call in Ole."

"You stay where you are. I'll call you if I want backup. I need you there."

"But, Hunt—"

Hunt hung up before Roy could protest any further. The last thing he wanted was the doughnut king of St.

Ann's showing up and getting his fat ass shot off. Hunt was lost in his thoughts about why Roy would go straight to assuming he and Mandy were sleeping together when she came up from behind and startled him. He jumped at the sound of her voice.

"Everything okay?"

"It's fine. Roy had a great idea about showing up here and trying to help me apprehend you."

"He still thinks you're after me?"

"Actually, he thinks I'm sleeping with you."

"He what? Is this some kind of habit with you?"

"You know that's not true. I don't know why he went there. I had fire in my eyes when I left the station to come after you. He knows that's not what this is about."

"Maybe, but your poker face sucks. You gave it away in your voice, Hunt."

"No way. I'm great at poke-her." He grasped her hips and pulled them toward his.

She shoved him back. "This isn't funny."

"Hey," he said, reaching for her hand. "I'm just trying to make light of all this. I swear I don't know why he said that."

"I'm not mad, Hunt. My nerves are really getting worn. I need to get Darci and get the hell out of this godforsaken state. Everywhere I turn there's nothing. I need to see some buildings, for crying out loud." She rubbed her arms trying to warm them up and walked to the truck. Hunt caught up to her and helped her up. Before getting in his side, he reached in back and pulled out a sweatshirt.

"You should have said you were cold. We don't think about coats around here until it's thirty degrees out. I'm sorry."

"Thanks. Sorry for snapping."

He started the truck but waited to put it in gear. Turning sideways, he faced her with a serious look. "I'm beginning to second guess having you along."

"No way, Hunt. You need me there. This is my task, not yours! You're not handcuffing me in some hotel room and going there by yourself!"

"Look, don't get upset. I admit it. My senses were dulled with all the sex. It's just instinct for me to want to take care of you."

"Cop thing or lust thing?"

"I don't know. What I do know is, I don't want you getting hurt. Maybe I need to call the local authorities and let them handle it."

"No! You promised me! They aren't going to do anything! I told you that! You can't call them in over a kidnapping they'll say didn't happen."

"Stop shouting. I'm trying to talk this through and figure it out. I can't have you or your daughter getting hurt. What happens if the bullets start flying? I can handle Gerard and two goons, but what if there's more? I can't go against semi-automatics."

"They will be expecting me to show up—that's all. They won't be waiting on an attack."

"Wrong. They know I'm with you and something else is coming. They're going to be more prepared than you think."

"All the more reason you need me with you. You can't go alone, Hunt. I won't have it."

Hunt slammed his palms onto the steering wheel then gripped it tight. "Dammit. You're the most stubborn broad I know."

"Hate me?"

"Probably."

"Good. Channel that energy where it'll do the most good. You need me as backup, Hunt. We'll get through this. They're morons."

He spun to her again. "That's another thing."

"What?"

"How did you get so good with guns?"

"There wasn't a lot I could do when I was basically Gerard's prisoner. I learned to entertain myself. He thought I was interested so he took me to the firing range with him."

"He thinks you just acquired a sudden interest in guns?"

"I became good at pretending what he did didn't bother me."

"If you can't beat 'em, join 'em?"

"Something like that. He didn't like it at first, but he never would tell me no."

"I suppose not," Hunt said, as he backed out of the parking spot.

"What's that supposed to mean?"

"I'm finding it hard to tell you 'no' myself."

"This is different. You know two is better than one."

"You know the layout and the men and their habits. I guess I do need you after all."

"So, what's your plan?"

"I want to go back and get Roy's truck."

"Good thinking. We should have two escape routes just in case. I was thinking—"

Hunt cut her off by placing his hand over her mouth. "This is my gig. I told you if I helped, it was my way."

She licked his hand and he pulled it away. "I thought we'd pretend to be a team and brainstorm together."

"You have experience planning a stakeout, freeing a hostage, and avoiding getting shot?"

"And you do?"

"At least I'm trained for it."

Mandy threw her head back against the headrest. "Fine. Tell me *your* plan."

Hunt and Mandy drove to retrieve Roy's truck from the bar. Hunt was pleased to find it untouched and with no tow warnings. The owners probably figured someone had too much to drink, found a driver to take them home, and just hadn't retrieved it. Mandy drove it and followed Hunt back into town. Wanting to get to the cabin after dark, they spent some time in the local coffee shop trying to get the lowdown on the surrounding homes by Gerard's lodge. The lady who ran the coffee shop gave them the information they needed, and more.

"Oh, you folks won't have any problems from the neighbors if you plan on your party getting a little loud. Everyone has winterized and locked up their cabins for the season. The Leonards bugged out of here yesterday, don'tcha know. That little Liam of theirs is such a hoot! Going to be a regular comedian someday. He's growing like a weed, too. Have you met Cheryl and Joe? Sweetest people ever. Cheryl is expecting again. Twins! Isn't that the cat's pajamas?" She clapped her hands together when she said twins.

Hunt was used to the small town lingo and the friendly enthusiasm, but Mandy was having a hard time fighting her laughs. Hunt figured she didn't have much by way of friendly neighbors, being so isolated by her husband and his line of work.

"I haven't had the pleasure. Maybe we'll catch them and the baby next year. What about our neighbors to the west?" Hunt asked her.

"Long gone. Earl had to start his radiation. They wanted it over before the holidays, so they cut the season short. They've been gone for about a month now. Yessiree, Bob. You'll be alone out there on your side. Only the Erpstads are left, but they are as far as you can go east on the lake down the skinny point. Can't get there with a regular boat, but you always see them tooling around on that paddle boat of theirs. Harvey has put on a few. Bertha keeps trying to make him lose it. If you ask me, she could stand to lose a few herself. Great baker that one, but you just shouldn't do it if you can't keep your hands out of it. You know what I mean?"

Now Mandy couldn't keep from laughing. She hid it as best as she could through a cough. "I'm so sorry. I got a tickle in my throat."

"That's all right, dear. Maybe some tea with lemon will help."

"Tea sounds great. You want anything, honey?" she said to Hunt, obviously trying to keep the couple status going.

"Just a regular coffee sounds perfect. I'm going to make a call, I'll be right back, sweetheart." He kissed her for added show.

"He's not here, Hunt," Luke said when Hunt asked for Roy.

"Where is he?"

"Out on patrol, I suppose. He told me to hold down the fort. Probably craving some doughnuts."

"More likely Selma over at Dunkin' Doughnuts."

"He banging her?"

"You kidding? You'll never make detective if you don't hone in those senses of yours, Luke."

"He said you're banging your prisoner. Are you?"

"She's not my prisoner."

"So, you are banging her."

"Since when is my personal life so much of a concern for you two?"

"Since I got my nose broke, you took off, and I have to deal with Ole's farts again. I thought this codger was gone for good. Why can't we hire another deputy?"

"No budget. Look, Junior. Shut up and listen. This is going down tonight. Get ahold of Roy and have him head to West Bolton. I have my walkee. It'll work when he hits town. Tell him to not use it under any circumstances. You got that? Do not have him call me. I'll call him when I need him."

"What should he do till he hears from you?"

"Scratch his balls. I don't care. Just have him pick a spot and sit until I call him."

"Bitch has his truck."

"Who does?"

"I'm sorry. The lovely young woman whom you are fucking and broke my goddamn nose."

"Work on that attitude, Junior, unless you want to get put on traffic detail."

"Don't call me—"

Hunt hung up. He joined Mandy and the jolly woman with the nametag that simply read, "Mom." He accepted his cup of coffee with a smile and immediately sent it flying when Mom said, "So, when are y'all expectin'?"

"Excuse me?" Mandy said as she placed her hand on her stomach. Hunt glanced down as well. It was as flat as ever. Maybe his sweatshirt made it appear as if she had a bump there, but he didn't see it.

"I have fourteen grandbabies. I know a glow when I see it."

"I'm not pregnant, Mrs..."

"Call me Mom. I have to tend to my customers. You come see me next season. And lay off the booze this weekend, honey."

"But I'm not pregnant." Mandy's words were wasted. The jolly woman scurried off to her seated customers.

Mandy turned to Hunt. "Is everyone in Vermont this friendly and/or nosey?"

He was grinning. "Some more than others."

"Where I'm from, if you ask someone if they're pregnant, you'd better be damn sure they are or you'll get slapped." She placed her hands on her stomach again. "How can she think I'm fat enough to be pregnant?"

"Don't dwell on it, doll. I'm sure my ratty sweatshirt made it look like you were hiding something."

She strolled over to a rack of sweatshirts with the coffee shop logo. She picked out a small pink one and tossed it to Hunt. "Then add this to the friggen bill...honey."

He laughed as he approached the register.

They waited until dark before heading to the cabin. They'd left Roy's truck at the house of the couple whose husband was getting radiation, then drove Hunt's to the couple with the comedian child and expecting their second. After all Mom told him, it was like he already knew them and didn't think they'd mind if he left his vehicle there.

He pulled out his night vision goggles, but nothing could be seen from the neighbor's cabin. The trees were too thick. If Gerard was expecting company, he didn't think enough to have men on watch, or at least none Hunt could see from here. He opened his door.

"We ready?" Mandy asked.

"I'm ready. You sure I can't get you to stay?"

"We're not having this conversation again." Mandy pulled a gun out from under her sweatshirt and cocked the hammer back.

"Whoa! I didn't tell you it was okay for you to take a gun."

"I'm not going in there unarmed." She opened up the door and climbed out before he could protest any further.

Hunt and Mandy slowly made their way through the trees toward the cabin. It wasn't easy to keep quiet. The little snow that had fallen the other night had already melted. Fall was in full swing and the leaves were plentiful. Add the thousands of twigs already there and you'd have a more successful sneak attack charging with a herd of elephants. They could only do their best and be cautious. Music was playing loudly ahead. That had to count in their favor.

Mandy tapped Hunt on the arm and pointed toward the back porch. He could make out it was Bennett. No one else could be that huge or have a profile that ugly. He was keeping an eye on the lake and not trying too hard. He was attempting something close to a moonwalk to Michael Jackson's "Beat It" as he stood watch. *Definitely a few sandwiches short of a picnic.*

They made it to the side of the cabin without being seen or heard. Hunt crouched down and went to the screen door off the back porch. As he stood and got ready to open the door and surprise Bennett, his walkie-talkie squealed. "Hunt? This is Roy. What's your twenty?"

A few bullets flew past Hunt as he crouched down, cursing. The screen door opened and Bennett dove onto Hunt. Bennett had size on his side, but Hunt was the better fighter by far. He maneuvered himself to having Bennett in a headlock. The victory was short lived though. Hunt was hit on the back of his head by something. All he could hear were Mandy's screams as his world faded to black.

Hunt didn't know how much time had passed before he came to. His head hurt like a sonofabitch. He remained still as he fought the urge to throw up. Trying to move his arms to hold his throbbing skull, he discovered he was tied to a chair. He finally managed to open his eyes. The room came into focus and he was greeted with a hard punch to his chin.

"Good morning, sunshine." The voice wasn't familiar, but Bennett soon came into focus.

"Hello, sweetheart. Have you missed me?" That earned him another punch. This one in the gut. "It's nice you got out of jail so fast. Connections?"

"You might say that. Mandy's old man is still as swift as ever."

"Old man? Where is she?"

"Getting what she has coming."

"I swear to God. If you lay one hand on her!"

"You'll what?" Bennett said as he punched Hunt so hard in the chin again his chair went flying backward. "It's not Gerard's *hands* I'd worry about. I'm sure he's good and horny after being up here with nothing but us men for the past few days."

He leaned down to stand Hunt's chair up, and Hunt spit a mouthful of blood on him. That earned him a hard kick to the gut.

"Stop it!" Mandy's scream brought Hunt's attention to the doorway where she now stood. Her new sweatshirt was torn down the front and her eye had a welt under it.

"You sonofabitch!" he shouted to the man holding her. Hunt assumed this was the ex-prick.

The man shoved Mandy toward Hunt. She ran to his side and threw her arms around his neck. She glared at

Bennett. "Help me stand him up, you oaf!" When he ignored her she turned to the man who had shoved her. "Come on, Gerard. There's no need for this! I'm here. Now let him go!"

Gerard nodded to Bennett, who took it as an order to put Hunt upright.

"Are you okay?" Hunt asked Mandy.

She tried pulling her shirt together as best as she could. "I'm fine." She turned to Gerard again. "Let him go!"

"I know you're not serious. You've created quite a mess for me, Amanda. You just had to try to follow me."

"Did you think you could take her daughter and have her not come after you?" Hunt said. "I hardly know her and I know her stubborn streak. I'm here unofficially. I don't care what you do. Just give her the kid and you guys will have to let the courts decide custody like normal people."

"What the hell are you talking about?" Gerard asked. "What kid?"

He glared at Mandy. "There's no fucking kid? You lied to me?"

Gerard let out a hearty laugh. "You get used to that."

Mandy held Hut's gaze, begging for forgiveness.

He wanted nothing more to do with her. He glared hard at her and said, "Get out of my face, you conniving bitch," before Bennett hit him again.

"You don't talk to a lady like that."

Mandy jumped on Bennett's back and wrapped her arm around his neck, trying to cut off his air supply. "I told you to stop hitting him!" A gun shot caused Mandy to loosen her grip. When she stopped fighting, Bennett slammed her backward into a wall. She cried out. Hunt struggled to get to his feet, but hands pressed on his shoulders from behind, pinning him.

Mandy stood and faced the man holding down Hunt. "Willy?"

Hunt tried to turn around to see the man at his back. His right eye was swelling and he couldn't get a good view of him. "Another lover?" Hunt said angrily.

"Lover?" Willy laughed. "Tell me he has no clue, Mandy."

"I had no clue you would be a part of this, asshole. I stuck up for you. Why would you do this?"

"You had to have a clue. Come on. You weren't that stupid in love with the prick you didn't see what was right in front of your face."

"I'm right here, Willy. I'd watch it," Gerard said.

"Or what? You'll up my payoff? You wanted her. Now you have her, so shut the hell up." He waved his gun toward Hunt and addressed Mandy. "Just who the hell is this guy, anyway?"

"He's nobody," Amanda blurted out. "He's a loser cop from a small town. I escaped his jail and he followed me. Just let him go. He doesn't know anything."

"Damn straight. Call me Barney and cut me loose. Us small town hicks don't know Jack shit about big city mobsters and their whores."

That earned him another punch to the gut. "I told you not to talk to a lady that way. Right, whore?"

That earned Bennett a punch from Gerard. "That's my wife you're talking about."

"Ex-wife!" Mandy screamed.

"All of you shut the hell up!" Willy shouted over everyone. He waved his gun around to show he meant business. "It's like I'm running a preschool here!"

"I don't get it, Willy. How?"

"I'm glad you defended me and all, but you had me pegged. I was a better actor than I thought. I thought you were going to kick my ass back at the restaurant."

"So you were our agent."

"To start, but the Menuscos pay better."

"Why didn't Abbey tell me?"

"I wasn't his. One office had no idea what the other was doing. It was convenient for you to show up and take the heat off of me."

"But Vince knew you were a double agent?"

"Helpful for him to have someone a step ahead. You think you just happened across that cashier job in the building where Menusco was starting up his headquarters? I gave them the tip. We knew what you were, Mandy. You were good, but nobody is that good. Cashier to bodyguard? Come on. Get real. They needed you distracted."

"You even set up Angelo's fight? He knew?"

"You have me there. But the little punk ass mama's boy wasn't in on it. It was funny how that worked out. We were figuring how to set up to keep you giving info and make you think you were doing something bigger. But well...even you screwed up getting killed. Pity to have lost Lonny and screwed up that last drop. You did drop a bomb on us there, Smith. I wonder if you would have pieced things together quicker if you hadn't started banging your own mark."

"Your what?" Hunt asked, staring down Mandy again.

"That's right, pretty boy. So you're the big bad Sheriff of your teeny little town. How's it feel to bang a full-fledged FBI agent? Better lay than one of your everyday bar flies?"

"FBI agent?"

"Could have been something great if we hadn't known all along. Made things even better when she fucked it up though. Had to go fall in love with her mark."

"That's not true and you know it, Willy. I didn't know he was involved when we got married. You know it."

"You still playing that card?"

"It's the truth."

"I didn't mind either way. You are one hell of a lay." Gerard said.

"Stop it! I did fall in love with you, asshole. You know I loved you. It happened so fast…I'm not going to apologize to any of you for my actions then or now."

Hunt finally piped in again. "And after you found out he was involved?"

"It was practically the same instant. I was so deep into both covers…I couldn't do anything about it."

"Both covers? The FBI and his bed? So everything was a lie? The pregnancy, making up at the cabin, the birthday party…Was anything you told me not total bullshit?"

"I'm sorry, Hunt. Once I said I was after my daughter the rest of the story just…flew out."

"And the bullet story?"

"You wanted me to come out and say I had field training with the FBI after all the other lies I had to tell you?"

"Can you two carry on later? I'd really like to get down to business, Gerard," Willy said. He turned to return to the lodge.

"What do you want me to do with her?" Bennett asked.

"Tie her up out here with him. Maybe he'll gnaw through the restraints and kill her and save me the trouble."

Bennett backhanded her and she was out cold.

"When I'm free I'm going to fucking kill you. I hope you realize that." Hunt said the words through bared teeth.

Walking over to Hunt, Bennett took hold of his chin. "Not if I kill you first." He spat in Hunt's face before tying Mandy into a chair not far from him.

CHAPTER SEVEN

Hunt stared out the screens, wishing now the cabin wasn't so secluded and that he'd called for backup. Wait...he had. That dumb sonofabitch was what got them in this situation in the first place. He had told Luke to make sure Roy didn't use the walkie-talkie first, and the dumbshits didn't communicate. He tugged at his restraints, but it was no use. He wasn't getting free. Movement caught the corner of his eye. Mandy was finally coming to.

"Hey. You okay?"

Her head went side to side a few times before she answered. "What do you care?"

"Because if I'm going to be killed, I'd at least like to know the truth for a change. You're FBI?"

"Ex-FBI. They dropped the case out of the blue, saying we had nothing to go on. I spent too much time working on putting Menusco away. There was no way I was just walking away."

"You were so undercover you married someone involved?"

"I thought he was unrelated in the beginning, then...yes. I thought he would be useful and used it to my advantage."

"So, you stayed with him even after you knew?"

"I'd like to say 'what better cover?' but that's not all it was. Call me stupid, but I honestly thought we'd get out together someday."

"How did you sleep at night knowing what he did? What you were allowing to take place?"

"How did I sleep? Usually with his big Italian dick between my legs! That's how I slept. Is that what you want to hear? Ever hear the phrase, 'you can't help who you love?'"

"Don't remind me."

"Oh, bullshit, Hunt. You don't love me. You practically used me the way I used Gerard in the end."

"Wrong, doll face. I was here to help you get your daughter back. I didn't care what he did. I didn't use you to catch him. Until you strolled into my life, I had no idea this shit would ever cross my path. I'm a small town sheriff for a reason. I don't do killings and extortion. I like knowing everyone by name and getting cats down out of trees for little girls. But most of all, I like going out of town for my sex. Until now, I didn't think I'd ever get involved with someone like you!"

"Stop your damn arguing so I can come save your ass."

A voice outside the screen caused Hunt and Mandy to freeze in their seats. "Roy?" Hunt whispered.

"In the flesh."

"Get your ass in here. They're in the house, but I don't know for how long. You have your knife?"

"Of course."

Roy hustled up the small flight of steps, gun drawn. He took each one cautiously and kept one eye on the door to the house at all times. As he cut Hunt loose, Hunt asked how he found them.

"Gotta love that tracker on my truck. I found it down the road. The rest wasn't hard."

"You paid a visit to Mom's coffee shop, didn't you?"

"Yup. She knew I was a new face and asked if I was here for the party. Some party you throw here, Hunt."

When Hunt was free, Roy went over to Mandy. He whispered as he cut her free. "If there is one scratch on my truck, I'm taking it out on your hide."

When he pulled the last of her ropes free, Mandy stood and hurried over to Hunt. "Now what?"

"Now we get my arsenal and some local back up and come back and take care of these guys."

Mandy turned to Roy and slipped the gun from his holster before he knew what was happening. She ran for the door of the house.

As she ran, Hunt ripped the shotgun off of Roy's shoulder and took off after Mandy. There were several shots before he reached her. Hunt walked through the door in time to see Willy on the floor with a shoulder wound and Bennett flat on his face. Her gun was pointed at Gerard. His hands were up and he was begging her not to shoot him.

"We can work this out, Mandy. Don't do this. I'll see to it you have anything you want."

"Anything? How about Darci, asshole." A tear ran from her cheek as she spoke the name.

"Darci? I thought there was no kid," Hunt said with great surprise.

"You still busting my balls about that? It wasn't my fault." Gerard took a step closer and Mandy shot his arm. He screamed and stepped back. "Don't do this!"

"Mandy, stop," Hunt pleaded. "Let the law handle him."

"The law? What are they going to do? I turn Gerard in and there will be another mob lawyer to set him free. All of them."

Roy had joined them at this point and was covering them with a backup gun he had on his calf.

Hunt was grateful he thought to bring a few extras, considering he'd never had to discharge the one he'd had on him for the past four years. Maybe he wasn't as dumb as Hunt gave him credit for.

"You killed her, Gerard," Mandy said. "She was an innocent child, and you killed her."

"I had no control, Mandy. You know that. I had to do as I was told like everyone else. She got in the way. I'm sorry." He tried to step toward her and she fired again. Hunt was surprised she missed. At least he thought she did, until there was a thud behind Gerard. Another man had entered the kitchen. Hunt was so intent on Mandy he hadn't even noticed the man approaching them.

"How many more are here?" Hunt asked.

"None." Hunt cocked the gun. "None. I swear. We wanted to keep this simple. We didn't expect the hassle." He glared at Mandy as he said so. "Do you really think I wanted to kill my own niece?"

"Your niece?" Hunt said as he turned to Mandy again.

"Darci was my niece. His niece. She was the only thing worth staying in this fucked up family for." The tears grew stronger and Mandy struggled for a steady aim with the gun. "He took it upon himself to see that his brother-in-law left the family business. He killed her in the process."

"That's not my fault, Mandy."

"You pulled the trigger!"

"I didn't know she'd be there!"

"Liar! It was their home. You knew I was there visiting her!"

"He had to go and he had to go then. It was unfortunate she got in the way."

"Unfortunate? They wanted out, Gerard. Why couldn't you just let them go?"

"You don't leave the family business, doll. You know better than that. Saying it was his mistake. I thought you loved me, Amanda. Stop this. We'll talk about it. I'll set you up away from all this. We can still have a life together. I'll make it work. I'll figure it out."

"It's too late, Gerard. Way too late for that. I stopped loving you long ago. I knew it was over for good when you couldn't even shed a tear for Darci. No 'I'm sorry' to your sister."

"I never found her. How could I tell her sorry?"

"You didn't even try. You didn't give a shit about anything. How could I be so stupid? Why would I want a life with a heartless man like that?"

"I want to set you up, baby. No money worries. No more dealing with my family if that's what you want. No more FBI. What more do you want?"

"Darci back." Mandy shot him three times in the heart before he hit the floor.

Mandy sat by the fire in sense of shock. She hadn't spoken, only stared into the fire. Five police cars showed up after Hunt called it in. One of the officers was a woman. She put herself in charge of Mandy and tried to see to her comfort. It was obvious she had been raped. They were treating her with kid gloves while they sorted out the details.

Hunt was fast on his feet with explanations. He had sent Roy on his way so things didn't become more complicated with his involvement. He didn't care what Willy said. No one would believe him anyway. It worried him he couldn't get Mandy to talk. He kept glancing her way as he talked to the officers. Revenge isn't as sweet as they say. She set out to kill Gerard and did, but he knew that only added to her burden, not relieved it.

He couldn't believe the lengths she went through to get her revenge. Looking back, he wished he opted for beers at home that night instead of walking to the Ace bar. No, not really. He had fallen in love with her, and it hurt. He knew better, but he became involved anyway. Reality told him it was over before it even started. All he could do was get out of here and never look back. Hunt had said terrible things to her. Things she'd never forgive—and he couldn't blame her. She had done nothing but lie to him from the beginning. He had been a pawn in her revenge. There was no kidding himself about any kind of relationship after this.

The local PD bought his explanation hook, line, and sinker. Tests would show Gerard had raped Mandy. Her rope burns from being tied to the chair and bruised face would help their story. Hunt's face showed enough damage to support his story of just passing by and hearing her screams and having to fight the group of men he didn't expect when he rushed in the house. They could sort out the details of who they were on their own time. Being a sheriff, there was no reason to question him.

He had no reason to be in the area. Oddly, no one dug deeper into his story of staying at a friend's cabin. He threw around some names he got from Mom, and that bought him enough trust. Roy's gun Mandy used was licensed to the department. Things pieced together fine for a self-defense plea.

Hunt declined any medical attention for his cuts and bruises and the offer of being driven home. After he was done with telling and retelling the story, he asked for a minute alone with Mandy. The female officer was hesitant, but agreed.

"I suppose since you're the hero of the hour, it's okay. She probably hasn't had a chance to properly thank you." She patted Hunt's shoulder in thanks as she walked away.

"You holding up okay?" Mandy didn't look at him or reply. "I didn't tell them anything about who anyone is. I suggest you don't try to hide it. They'll find out. I know your thoughts on small town cops, but we're not as stupid as you think." She still offered nothing for a response. "You have a boss of sorts you can call? Someone at the FBI who will stand by you?" Hunt reached for her hand but she pulled it away.

"I can take a hint." He stood. "Goodbye, Mandy. I'd like to say it's been great knowing you."

Hunt made sure the local PD was done with questioning him. He said his goodbyes and left. One ambulance was pulling away with Willy, and another was pulling up for Amanda.

"Shake it, Blaine," Hunt said to himself. "There's hundreds more like her in the cities. Less history, less baggage, less firearm involvement." He went to the neighbor's house to claim his truck, trying everything to get her out of his mind. He'd send Roy and Luke back for Roy's truck later. He'd worry about that tomorrow.

Eleven months later, Hunt watched Amanda from across the courtroom. She wore large sunglasses and a scarf over her head. He wasn't sure who she was trying so hard not to be seen by, him or the mob, but the get-up attracted more attention than it deterred.

Everyone listed as the judge read the verdict. No witnesses were called. No final statements given.

Hunter's Find

Due to the circumstances of the shooting, Amanda was never charged with murder. Hunt's testimony was enough to deem it self-defense. He wasn't quite sure why he had lied for her, but once he lay the story down for the officers, there was no taking it back. He didn't even need to go to her trial, but couldn't help getting into the state computer to look up the final outcome of it. He conveniently took a week of vacation and went to see his parents in Florida when her trial date was set two months after the incident. No one questioned him needing to get away mid-winter.

The only one left to face charges was Willy, who was dealt with in true government speed. Eleven months after being arrested for criminal activity with the mob, he was being sentenced. Hunt listened as the long list of charges were rattled off, then he applauded quietly as they announced multiple life sentences. When the judge hit his gavel, Amanda was nowhere to be found.

Hunt's knocking on the hotel door got louder as he received no response. He grew angry, mostly at himself, as he stood there. Thinking he avoided making a fool of himself, he turned to leave right as the door opened up.

"Hunt? What are you doing here?"

"I'm wondering that myself." He stood there, staring at Amanda, knowing it was a bad idea he was here. She was even more attractive than he remembered. Her breasts more than filled the low-cut blouse she wore. He didn't remember them being that big. Catching himself staring at her cleavage he met her gaze, embarrassed. "Can I come in for a second?"

"I...uh...I'm not sure..."

"I'll only be a second. We need closure on this." He didn't wait for an invitation, he let himself in and brushed

113

past her. He pretended to be interested in the hotel room. "This is nice. I've never been in the suites here."

"I certainly didn't need anything this big. Government picking up the tab and all."

"I see." Hunt said, suddenly feeling very hot. He loosened his tie, hoping it would help. "I saw you at the courthouse."

"I saw you there, too. I just didn't know what else there was to say, Hunt."

He took a few steps closer to her, closing the large gap between them. "I'm sorry, Mandy."

"For what?" She tried a little too hard to laugh off his apology. "You have nothing to apologize for."

"Yes, I do." He took her face in one hand and held it so he could look in her eyes. "I was horrible to you. I said things—"

Mandy trembled as she spun to get out of his grip. "It's okay, Hunt. I got over it a long time ago."

She tried to walk away from him but he took her by the wrist and spun her to face him again. "Well, I didn't. I was a jerk. I always assumed the worst about you. I need to tell you I'm sorry."

"Apology accepted. I'm not angry with you. I know what it looked like. I take responsibility for the things I did. I was never able to thank you for lying for me. So thank you, okay? Now I really have to get packed for my flight back." She tried to pull free again, but he didn't lighten up his grip.

Hunt kept trying to get closer and Mandy kept backing up until she was against the wall.

"Please, Hunt."

"I tried to find you a few months ago. You moved."

"I was under protection. Willy still hasn't spoken. They aren't sure if Gerard put him up to this or if the Menuscos will be after me themselves."

"Why didn't you try to contact me?"

"Why would I, Hunt? You hate me."

"Far from it." He lowered his head close to her. He could feel her shaking even harder. Her breaths were getting shorter, too.

"You certainly called me a whore enough times."

"I said I'm sorry." He brushed his cheek against hers. "I'm sorry for every hateful thing I said. Everything I thought about you. I was wrong." He took her face in both hands. "I missed you. I've been waiting for this day, hoping beyond hope you'd have to come to testify."

She pulled his hands away. "Don't do this to me, Hunt."

"Do what? This?" He placed his lips over hers and plunged his tongue possessively into her mouth. She struggled at first then let out a loud moan and wrapped her arms around his neck.

Hunt moaned in relief when Mandy returned his kisses. He leaned his midsection into hers, grinding at her for only a moment before picking her up and sitting her high on his hips. Reaching under her skirt, he broke her thong then gave a hearty pull at his button-fly jeans and lowered them. He entered her in one thrust, both of them searching for a gasp of air. Hunt covered her mouth with his again and kissed her hard as he made love to her, holding her against the wall.

Mandy's whole body quivered. She threw her head back as Hunt nestled deep within her. It was only minutes before they came together. Hunt dropped his head to her neck. It was a long moment before he could speak. "I've been dreaming about this every day for the last eleven months, Mandy."

She still couldn't or wouldn't talk.

"I haven't even been with anyone else. I could only think of you. You know what a grouch I am to begin with. Imagine the guys putting up with me after almost a year of no sex."

She still wasn't talking. Hunt rested his cheek to hers again. They were wet with tears. He leaned back. "What is it? Did I hurt you?"

She shook her head no.

"Then what?"

"I'm sorry. I'm so, so sorry."

"What are you sorry for? Your lies? I don't care. I want you, Mandy. Stay here with me. Transfer. I know you more than qualify for a ton of local jobs with your background."

"I'm not in the service anymore, Hunt." Her voice was soft.

"Then what's keeping you?"

He smothered kisses down her neck and across the top of her breasts through her blouse. After stopping in surprise at the wet spots at her nipples, a baby crying caught his attention.

His gaze met Mandy's. "You have a baby?"

"Let me down."

He gently placed her on the floor. He pulled up his jeans as she pulled down her skirt. Her gaze fell to her shirt, and she cursed at the two wet spots now on it. "Dammit." She pulled her shirt off and threw it to the floor. "I've leaked through every shirt I brought."

Hunt stood dumfounded at how she could worry about a wet shirt at a time like this. *She had a baby? Who the hell is the father?*

He entered the bedroom where she was sitting on a chair, nursing the baby. The baby was bundled in a pink blanket, he assumed it was a girl. He was a great detective that way.

"You had a baby?"

"Eight weeks ago yesterday."

"I take it you don't love the father, or we wouldn't have done what we did."

"Wrong, Hunt. It's about time I admit to myself I do love her father very much. I've just thought for the past several months he didn't care for me."

"And you made this decision when you were fu—" he glanced down at the baby. Even at two months old, he didn't want to swear in front of her. "Humping me senseless?"

"You always jump to the wrong conclusion first, Hunt. You always did and always will."

"What are you talking about, woman?"

"Look at her. Just look at her, Hunt. See anything remotely familiar?"

He closed the gap and stood close to Mandy and the baby. "No. What's her name?"

"Hannah. Look closer, Hunt."

He reached out and took the baby's hand. She stopped nursing. Gripping his finger tight, she smiled at him. Her big brown eyes opened wide. *His* brown eyes.

"Whoa. What is this, Mandy?"

"She's yours, Hunt."

"Mine?"

"Mom was apparently 'spot on' when she guessed I was pregnant. I haven't been with anyone else, either. Don't think it's because pregnant ladies can't pick up men. I've turned away my share. Let me tell you something. It wasn't easy to do during the horny months."

"There are horny months?"

"You have no idea." She turned the baby to switch breasts. Hunt watched in amazement as she nursed. "Never watched anyone nurse before?"

He could only shake his head no.

"It's amazing. She's really mine?"

"Ours, Hunt. Please tell me you're not going to be a raving lunatic again. I don't think I could take it." Tears formed in her eyes.

"Hey..." Hunt leaned down and gave her a kiss on the cheek then on the mouth. "Shhh...I can't even put into words how I feel right now."

"Well I can. I was just given the okay for sex two weeks ago."

"Are you okay?"

"Hell yeah. In fact, when she goes down, I want some of that again."

Hunt smiled and kissed her gently on the lips. "This is a little late to ask, but should we be worried about this happening again? I stopped traveling with condoms months ago."

"I'm supposed to be okay while I'm nursing. I'm not worried. I never went unprotected before, Hunt. You have to know I didn't mean for this to happen."

"I never did, either. You have always brought out the devil in me."

"And the good apparently," she said as she smiled down at the baby. Hannah had finished eating and was looking between the two of them.

"Can I hold her?"

"Of course. She needs to be burped. I'll warn you, don't aim her at any windows. They say breast fed babies don't have as much gas, but she could probably put you to shame."

Within a few seconds, it was proven Mandy didn't lie.

"That's all the paternity I need. She's mine," Hunt said with a laugh. With the baby in one arm, he took Amanda in the other. "What now, Mommy?"

"I don't know."

"I do. Marry me."

"Marry you? Up until half an hour ago, we thought we hated each other."

"Because we were idiots. I've wanted you every day. Every day we were together I fooled myself I wasn't in love with you. Even through everything that happened, I loved you every step of the way. I'm pissed off you killed that bastard Gerard. I wanted to kill him for what he did to you. Stay with me, Mandy. Be my wife. Be Mrs. Sheriff of podunk. I love you. I've thought of nothing but you for months now. Please say you'll stay here with me."

Another tear ran down her face as she nodded yes. As promised, when the baby went down for her nap, they made love again. Hunt was far gentler this time, but Mandy made it obvious she didn't want him to be. She took over and tried to make up for the months of sex lost. Hunt took her breast in his mouth and was led into a choking fit by the blast of milk he didn't expect.

"Sorry, lover. Job hazard."

He laughed. "Makes me want cookies."

As they lay tangled together, Hunt reached for the heart pendant she still wore. He opened it up. There was still a picture of Darci, but baby Hannah had joined her on the right side.

"You could have told me the truth."

"That I was out to kill the son of a bitch? I don't think so."

"I wouldn't have opened with that, but I think we could have worked through it."

"Hunt, please don't. You would never have let me go anywhere near them. They'd be back in New York and back to the same old tricks. Part of you will always view what I did as wrong. I actually can't believe you lied for me."

"I love you, remember? Besides, I only partially lied. The bastard did horrible things to you. He had it coming one way or another." He kissed her forehead and pulled her close. He wished more than anything he could take away her being hurt by Gerard while he was unconscious. "I wanted to beat the crap out of Roy for giving us up. It was hard to do after he actually came through and rescued us."

"I don't want to talk about it, Hunt. It's history."

"It's our history. What do we tell our grandkids when they ask how we met?"

"We have a few years before we have to come up with something." She yawned. "I'm exhausted. Will you stay?"

"I'd like to see you try to throw me out."

"I could take you, and you know it," she said through another yawn.

She cuddled into his chest and Hunt held her tight.

"Yeah, I do know it," he whispered to deaf ears. Mandy was sound asleep. Hunt wished he could fall asleep as easily as she did. His mind was too busy racing. Part of him was worried there was someone out there still looking to cause Mandy harm. Even though Gerard's father was long dead, there was always a never-ending trail of cousins in families like that, just looking for a reason to claim revenge. Hunt knew he could protect her. He finally drifted off to sleep dreaming of doing that. Him—only cooler and better accessorized, with weapons fitting of Roger Moore.

Mandy woke up to an empty bed and sat up with a start. Hunt walked through with Hannah within seconds. "Hey," she said as she scooted back, preparing to nurse.

"I'm glad you're up. I tried to occupy her, but I think she's hungry."

"That's a guarantee. She has her mother's appetite." She lowered the sheet and revealed her naked breasts and Hunt let out a whistle.

"Hello, titty fairy. I noticed they were bigger last night but holy hell, Mandy. They fill up overnight?"

"You could say that. It downright hurts some mornings." Hannah fussed at hearing her mother's voice and began to cry. Mandy reached her arms out. "Can't keep the princess waiting."

"What's her middle name?"

Mandy smiled. "Blaine."

"Really?"

"Really, Hunt. I loved you, you asshole. Of course I wanted you to be a part of her life somehow."

He crawled up the bed and sat next to them. "As much as I love it, we'll have to change it."

"Why?"

"Because after we're married, I don't want her to be Hannah Blaine Blaine. They'll call her bling bling or something."

Mandy laughed. "Okay. You get to give her a middle name."

"Can I think about it? You had nine months to pick out a name. I haven't even had nine hours."

"Of course." She leaned over and kissed him. "This is not at all how I expected this trip to go."

"You would have really left and not told me?"

"I didn't think I had a choice, Hunt. I wouldn't have done it, trying to be mean."

"I know." There was something on Hunt's mind, but he was afraid to say it.

Mandy must have sensed it because she spoke first. "I know what you're thinking, Hunt. I promise you, she's yours."

"I wasn't thinking anything like that."

"Yes, you were. You're worried because Gerard raped me, he could be the father."

"Okay. It crossed my mind for a second. Would it matter if I said I didn't care if I was the father or not?" He sat up so he could look at her. "I was finding it hard to understand the lengths you were going through when I thought we were after your daughter. I couldn't imagine loving someone so much you'd do anything to get them back and safe in your arms. The second I held Hannah, I felt that. I mean, how could I love something so much I only known for twenty seconds?" He stroked Hannah's cheek and she stopped eating. Again she smiled at Hunt.

"They tell me she's too young to really be smiling, but I don't buy it for a second. She loves you, too, Hunt. She knows you're her daddy."

Hunt stood and took the baby from Mandy. "You know I have no doubt. She has my eyes."

"He used a condom, Hunt."

"He what?"

"He called me a filthy whore and used a condom. He didn't want to get anything you might have given me. That's what he said, anyway."

"Who would have thought the..." he paused and glanced Hannah's way. This watching his mouth was going to be tough stuff. "Who would have thought the D—I—C—K—H—E—A—D would have had the smarts. I really am sorry, you know. No one should be treated like that. Ever."

"He wasn't that rough."

"He hit you."

"I hit first."

"Doesn't make it okay."

"No, but it sure made me feel better."

"I'll never hit you, Mandy."

"I know, Hunt."

Hannah belched and added comedy relief to their serious conversation.

"She nap soon?"

"Almost right after she eats."

"Hot damn. Cookie and milk for breakfast."

CHAPTER EIGHT

"This road looks familiar," Mandy said as she drove with Hunt toward his house.

He didn't want her to fly back and get her things. He arranged for a mover to do it all. Mandy protested only slightly. She admitted she wasn't looking forward to a flight with Hannah again so soon. She really hadn't traveled well.

Hunt took her explanation as the green light to take care of things. He was looking forward to spending the next eighty or ninety years taking care of things with the two of them.

"It should look familiar. This is where you drove after you kidnapped me."

"It is!" She squealed as she took in the scenery. "Looks different in white."

"The snow isn't here to stay yet." He reached for her hand and gave it a squeeze. "You still going to love me when it's ten degrees?"

"I think you'll find ways of keeping me warm."

He gave her hand a kiss. "Aaaaaand to the left..."

"Oh, honey. It's the pond where I almost killed you."
She pretended to wipe away a tear. "It's so touching."

"Smartass. This isn't just a tour down memory lane."

"You actually lived on this road? You never said anything."

"If I did, I certainly wouldn't have said anything, but I didn't. I do now, though. Correction. *We* do now." He pulled into a driveway and Mandy brought her hand over her mouth.

"You bought the farm?"

"That I did," he said with a big smile as he put his truck in park.

"Not that I had the chance to see much of it, but I loved this house!"

"I found the owner. He was anxious to unload it, actually. It needs work, so I bought it for a steal. He even threw in the old truck."

Mandy began to remove Hannah's car seat, but Hunt stopped her. "I have her. You go on in." She didn't wait to be told twice. Mandy rushed in. When Hunt walked in, she was coming down the stairs.

"It's huge!"

"What every man wants to hear."

"You nut. There are rooms everywhere. It's gorgeous. Did you do much to it? I didn't exactly get a tour of the upstairs when we were here last."

"I haven't done anything to it. I've only been here for two months. It was cheap, but still a bitch to close. Inheritance issues and stuff."

Mandy stood in front of him. "What made you do it, Hunt?"

He put Hannah down and wrapped his arms around her. "Isn't it obvious? I missed you, babe. If I couldn't have you, I was going to make myself miserable and surround myself with everything that reminded me of you."

"You really are hopeless, Hunter Blaine."

"And I'm all yours."

Mandy glanced down at Hannah. "And the baby is still asleep."

"You're making up for those horny months, aren't you?"

"You bet I am. Now shut up and do me, Mr. Blaine."

"I love a woman who..." Hunt caught himself and grinned.

"Yes. I do recall you liking a lot about women." Mandy pulled him closer by the hips.

"Only you from here on out. That's a promise. I finally have you back. There's no way in hell I'm messing this one up."

Hunt couldn't get enough of looking at Mandy. He had almost forgotten how stunning she was. As they lay together naked in bed, he ran his hand gently down the side of her face and angled her chin up slightly to kiss her again.

"You're really making me sorry I stayed hidden."

"That's my intention. I don't want you away from me again for any length of time."

"I really should be in touch with the office. There has been no indication of anyone looking for me, but I'm not sure if it's the smartest thing to move here."

"I don't think anyone would attach you to me after all this time, but do what you need to. I mean what I said. You're not leaving me again. If I need to relocate and change my name, we'll do it."

Mandy propped herself up on her arm. "Really? You love this town, Hunt."

"What do I have here? Roy? My life is you and Hannah now. I can be a cop anywhere."

She snuggled into his chest. "This is so not what I expected at all."

"You think you would adjust to a mellow life after all you've been through?"

"I welcome it with open arms."

Hunt held her tight and kissed the top of her head. "Will you tell me something?"

"Is it something you think I don't want to tell you?"

"Maybe. I want to know about the night I found you."

"I figured you would have pieced that together long ago." She tried to scoot back but he held her tight.

"Don't go anywhere. I've waited a long time for this." He paused to kiss the top of her head again. "I figured it was Bennett and the other goons. I guess I'm wondering how you ended up in the bushes."

Mandy rested her cheek on his chest, but remained silent.

"Are you searching for the right words, or are you trying to make up a convincing lie?"

She sat upright. "I know you don't have much to go on with me, Hunt, but I only lied when I had to. I don't make it a habit, and I promise you—you don't have to ever worry about me lying to you."

"Do you want to tell me? It's okay if you don't."

"There's really not much more than what you've figured out. They were on to me tailing them and seized me first chance they could. I let my stupid guard down for a second. They were taking me to the cabin, but I put up a fight."

"I'm well acquainted with that. You have your fiancé shaking in his boots. I don't ever want to cross you." He said it in jest, but the look on her face implied she took it differently. "Hey. I'm teasing."

"I know. It's just...it's a past I want behind me. All of it, Hunt. I know I wouldn't have met you without every detail that happened, but I want it to be left in our past. Please?"

"Of course."

Hannah stirred. Mandy got out of bed and began to get dressed. "I took quite a beating in the car, but I was lucky and punched Bennett good in the nose then nuts. I bailed out of the car, and I guess hit my head on the sidewalk. I swear that's the truth. They were doing probably sixty down the street. When I bailed out, I must have rolled into the bushes. You have to take my word on that. No more lies, Hunt. I promise you that much."

He walked over to her after pulling on his own jeans. He wrapped his hands around her waist and she snuggled into his chest again. "I trust you, Mandy. I only wish I could kill Bennett again for what he did to you."

Hannah's stirring was now accompanied by a wailing that brought a halt to the hug. Hunt was satisfied...for now. The rest of the night they wandered through the house as Mandy explored every nook and cranny, discussing the possibilities of what to do with the space.

"Screw the Menuscos. I love this house. We're staying."

Hannah woke them both up at three a.m. She had a dry diaper, didn't want to eat, and was completely inconsolable.

"I don't know what's wrong," Mandy said, almost breaking out into tears herself. "Maybe we should take her to the hospital."

"I don't think we need to jump to that right away. Give her to me." Hunt paced around the room, bouncing with her, but her crying didn't lighten up at all.

"I'm worried, Hunt. We need to do something."

"Give me a few minutes. I'll go take her temp. If it's up, we'll go in. Otherwise it's probably gas or something simple."

"Since when are you an expert on babies? I'm her mother. You think I would know when something is wrong."

"I know, babe. I'm not taking this lightly either. I have been down this road with two sisters plenty. You have the world's greatest babysitting uncle right here."

"Then do something, Great Uncle. That screaming is piercing my skull."

Hunt walked into the room he had claimed as an office and opened up his desk drawer. He returned with Hannah to the room they were going to turn into the nursery and put her in her car seat. He rocked it with his foot as he began to play Lee Oscar's "Before the Rain" on the harmonica he'd removed from the desk. Hannah immediately stopped crying. She stared at her father as he played.

Mandy entered the room, wide-eyed at both the baby's sudden silence and at Hunt's playing. "For the love of all that is holy, you stop and I'll kill you."

Hunt's smile caused him to goof a note or two, but it hadn't affected Hannah at all. She was enthralled by the music. The song itself was over nine minutes long, but three minutes into it Hannah pulled her legs close to her chest and let go of enough gas to blow a hole in the floor. They both laughed hard then Mandy picked her up.

"What did I tell you? Gas," Hunt said.

"I can't believe you know that song."

"I've always loved that song. It's what made me pick up my first harmonica."

"When you mentioned it that night we stayed here, it blew me away. No one I know knows that song."

"You've never known anyone as cool as me before."

Mandy playfully smacked him and Hannah cried again.
"She doesn't like it when you abuse her daddy."

"I think she wants you to play again."

"I think Mommy wants me to play again."

"This is true."

Hunt played the song from the beginning, and once again Hannah was quiet in an instant. Mandy rocked with her as he played. She was asleep before he reached the end. Mandy placed her in the spare bed and double checked the pillows surrounding her. Hunt lingered for a second longer than Mandy. After reaching the door and discovering Hunt wasn't behind her, Mandy turned back around.

"Something wrong, Hunt?"

"No." He reached down and stroked Hannah's back. "I'm afraid I'm going to wake up tomorrow and we'll be listening to her valedictorian speech as she graduates college."

"It does seem to happen that fast, doesn't it?"

"I've already missed her first eleven months. Yes, I would have loved to know her in your belly, too. I don't want to miss anymore."

It was Mandy's turn to wrap her arms around Hunt's waist. "We're not going anywhere. I promise."

"You're what?" Hunt's men said in unison.

"You heard me. I'm getting married."

"To who?"

"Some hot FBI chick who kicked the shit outta Junior here and stole your truck."

"Now I know you're pulling our legs. Her? You ain't even seen her in a year."

"Eleven months, give or take a few days."

"You made this decision at the hearing?" Roy asked.

"Just after."

"You hate her! Are you insane?" Luke shouted.

"I don't hate her. I love her. Always did. I was just too stubborn to admit it."

"Well if that don't end all," Luke said. "Maybe now that you'll be getting it on a regular basis, you won't be such a dick."

Hunt pointed his finger at him. "Watch it. I still sign your checks."

"No, you don't. Becky at the courthouse does."

"I meant theoretically. I don't want any flak from you guys. When she comes in, I want her treated with respect. You know why she did what she did."

"Yes, Hunt. You've drilled us on her evil ways enough. 'She had to do it...blah blah blah...It's okay—she was FBI...blah blah blah...' Hey, is she still a fed? She going to be your boss now?"

"She's retired. Her job is staying home with my kid for now."

"Your what?" they said together again.

"My kid. Most beautiful little girl you've ever seen."

"Who are you and what have you done with my boss?" Roy asked.

"How do you know it's your kid? How many times could y'all have screwed in a couple of days anyway?"

"You're crossing the line, Luke. It's my kid. Soon as you hear her fart you'll be convinced."

Roy laughed, Luke didn't. "You're getting hosed, man."

"Right. She's after me for my riches. My family fortune is what drew her to me in the first place. Get over it, Junior."

"Knock it off, Hunt. I ain't no kid. I deserve better than this."

"Then start acting like it, Luke," Roy said. "I have a pimple on my ass older than you and it's better behaved."

"I don't need this shit. I have streets to patrol."

"Take it easy out there," Hunt said. "If I get one more pissed off parent calling me to yell about you scolding their kid for riding their bike the wrong way down the street, I'm making you go over there to apologize."

"I'm just teaching street safety."

"Then create a class. Stop wasting the warning slips."

"Yes, sir." Luke over exaggerated a salute and walked out.

"What the hell is eating him?" Hunt asked.

"Can't say. He probably needs to find a woman and quit whacking off 24/7. Must be wearing at his nerves."

Hunt walked in the house at five-thirty that night with a spring in his step. He could get used to having someone to come home to every night.

"Hi, home. I'm honey," he said as he took off his coat then his utility belt. Mandy exited the kitchen with Hannah sleeping in her arms. Hunt came over and kissed them both. "I picked up the marriage certificate this afternoon. There's a three day wait, then we can go to the courthouse. Roy and Joy agreed to be witnesses."

"Joy?"

"She works at the courthouse. You sure there isn't someone you want to call?"

"I'm sure, Hunt. Living with a gangster for a couple of years doesn't do much for lasting friendships. I pretty much severed all my ties when I signed up."

"No brothers or sisters?"

"Nope."

"Parents?"

"Both long gone."

He stroked her cheek. "We have so much to learn about each other."

She tip-toed up and kissed him. "I'm looking forward to it."

"Did the movers call? Any idea when your things will get here?"

"Another couple of days. I'm really thinking I should go get her a crib. Even though she's not rolling yet, it scares me leaving her on the bed surrounded by pillows. She's not going to last in the bassinet I have coming for long anyway."

"Let me get dressed and we'll go get one."

"You want to now?"

"Sure. Give me a chance to take you out to dinner, too. We've never had a real date before."

"We ate out plenty."

"I'd hardly call the choke-n-puke places we picked up food and ran as 'date meals.'"

"I found steaks in the freezer. I have them thawing."

"So, throw 'em in the fridge." He gave her a quick kiss and headed for the stairs. "I'll be down in a flash."

Mandy was fastening the baby in her car seat when Hunt came back down. "While we're out, we could stand to do some grocery shopping, too. Your cabinets are pretty bare."

"I don't eat at home much."

She took hold of his shirt and pulled him close. "You'll be home now though, right?"

"Wild thugs couldn't keep me away." He kissed her then picked Hannah up and headed for the door.

Mandy stopped him. "I'm not living under an illusion being a cop's wife is easy, Hunt. I know the drill."

"I know. I'll never try to keep things rosy where they're not, either. But you do need to understand, St. Ann's isn't New York. You won't be getting calls telling you I'll be late for dinner. I almost guarantee that won't happen. At least not often. Your case was the most interesting thing that came through here in...well, ever." He glimpsed at her chest as he said that and grinned when his gaze met hers again.

"What?"

"You need to go change your shirt."

Her attention went to where his had been and she cursed. "I need to get nursing pads while we're out, too. This is crazy. I swear I have enough milk for twins!"

"How about one growing baby and her milk-loving daddy?"

She giggled. "I'll be right back down."

"I'll go get her loaded in the truck."

Hannah slept through the whole meal, giving them a chance to talk without disruption. Mandy had gotten a nice pension from the FBI when she left. She was too young to officially be retired; it was more of a "suggested honorable discharge with pay." Although what she had done wasn't set up by the organization, they had taken full responsibility at its outcome and reaped the reward. Her name was added in the arrests only when absolutely necessary in-house, but kept out of official records and the news media.

Trying to explain it to Hunt didn't come easy. It even looked to her as if she was paid for doing a hit and asked to move on because of it. Hunt squeezed her hand when she reached the tougher to explain areas and gave her looks of sincere understanding.

"I like that you've put the FBI behind you. I wouldn't want to be married to a cop." He took a big bite of salad. "Too easy to cheat."

"Oh really?" she said as she crossed her arms.

"Hell yeah. 'Honey, I'll be late. I'm up to my ass in paperwork. Don't hold dinner for me.' What you're really saying is, 'Honey. My partner has been giving me the look all day. We're going to go bang our brains out before I come home to your sorry ass and have to have sex with you again.'"

She leaned in close. "You are the smart one. I don't know, Hunt. You'd better watch yourself. Roy is a pretty sexy man. I see how he'd tempt you."

"Ew. Now that's just sick and wrong."

She picked up her steak knife and flipped it in her hands like a pro knife juggler. "I'd hate to have to cut off one of my favorite parts on you."

"Vicious. Yet incredibly sexy the way you handle that thing."

She removed her shoe and ran her foot up his thigh.

He jumped when her foot made contact. "You play dirty pool."

"I play to win."

"You won me, babe. Although somehow, I think I got the better part of this bargain."

"That has yet to be determined. I'm not so sure I'll be a picnic to live with."

He reached for her hand again. "I'm sure we'll both have to make adjustments. You're not getting cold feet are you?"

She shook her head.

"Are you?"

"I'm not, Hunt. I thought about you every day. I'm ready to do this. Really. I'm worried..."

"What, Mandy?"

"That if I showed up without Hannah, I'd be back in Connecticut."

"Bullshit. Did I not have my way with you before I knew about her?"

"Yes, but—"

Hunt cut her off. "But nothing." He stood, walked over, and knelt down by her chair. "I don't know what it'll take to convince you how much I've missed you and how badly I wanted to see you again. I want you, Mandy. Hannah is an extremely wonderful bonus I couldn't even have dreamed of. I never knew I wanted kids until I laid eyes on her. Please don't second guess me or my intentions ever again." He reached in his pocket and pulled out a box. He opened it up revealing a stunning carat diamond solitaire. "Marry me, babe."

As she nodded yes, a lone tear ran down her cheek. Hannah squealed and they both laughed. "I think she agrees, too," Hunt said.

Just then, there was a familiar voice from behind. "Hunter Andrew. Just what is this?"

"Mom? Dad? Uh...you're back? Why didn't you call me?"

"I was about to ask the same thing, young man," his mother said as she motioned to his hand still holding Mandy's after he slipped the ring on it. "You're engaged?"

He stood. "Um. Yes. I wanted to be sure she agreed before I called you. Why are you home?"

"My friend Hildy is in the hospital. Denny was afraid she wasn't going to be with us much longer. We came to say our goodbyes." Her gaze found Hannah. "Who's the peanut?"

"Just your granddaughter."

"Lord have mercy!" She sat in Hunt's chair and fanned herself.

"Knock it off, JoAnne." Hunt's father approached Mandy. "Don Blaine, but you can call me Dad. Pleasure to meet you, Miss..."

"Amanda. Amanda Smith."

"You're not from around here, are you? I don't recall seeing you around these parts."

"You're right. I'm not," was all she managed to say before he chimed in again with another question.

"How'd a good looking thing like you end up with my boy?"

"She kidnapped me—" Mandy whipped her head up, afraid Hunt was going to actually tell the truth. He followed with "—with her natural glow and charm."

"You had a baby and you didn't tell us?" his mother said, obviously still upset over being left in the dark.

"It's been a long distance thing, Mom. I wasn't going to have you get attached to someone who wasn't going to put up with my crap."

"You should have thought of that before you decided to make a baby."

Hunt knew it was easier to ignore her than to fight. Instead, he used the best weapon he could. He picked up Hannah and put her in his mother's lap. "She still needs a middle name. I was thinking Marie."

"You'll do no such thing. Hannah Gayle, after your grandmother. It flows better."

Hunt's gaze met Mandy's, searching for a response. She smiled. "It's perfect. I love it."

His mother finally turned her way. "Very pleased to meet you. When is her baptism?"

Hunt muttered, "Oh dear."

Hunt was busy putting the crib together while Mandy paced the room. "I'd rather take on a busload of Mafia Dons than go through that shit again, Hunt. Thanks for the heads up."

"I said I'm sorry. Once they go to Florida they don't ever come back until after April. I didn't expect it. I thought we'd have a chance to get used to each other before I had to subject you to my mother."

"Your dad is sweet enough."

"He cowers under the 'Yes, Dear' policy and opts for peace."

"We're going to have to explain to your mother I'm not Catholic."

"Protestant."

"Whatever. I don't know about this whole baptism thing, Hunt. I don't do church."

"I don't either anymore, but I want her baptized. We can have it done at St. Anthony's. Technically I'm still a member there."

"Is it really necessary?"

"To my family it is, so it is to me."

"I'll do it for you, Hunt, but I don't buy into the whole unbaptized babies don't go to Heaven crap. What could their innocent little souls do wrong before they're even moving around?"

He put down the tools and stood up. "I don't want a battle of beliefs here. If you were Catholic or Jewish and had different beliefs, I'd bend over backward for you so this would work. You don't have any, so let my family have this. Okay?"

"I said I'd do it. I don't have to like it, but I'll do it. Are we going to be expected to go to church now, too?"

"Probably Easter. We can skip Christmas if you want, since Mom and Dad are away, but I'd really like Hannah to grow up knowing Christmas service."

"I don't have a problem teaching her bible stories and wanting her to know right from wrong, but when she's old enough to question things, we'll let her make up her own mind, Hunt."

"Fair enough. You will let her believe in Santa and the Easter bunny for a while though. Won't you?"

"Duh."

They both laughed at the conversation finally taking a comedic turn. Mandy reached her arms around Hunt's neck. "Was this officially our first fight as a couple?"

"Hell. Nothing was even broken. I think we got off easy."

"Can we have make-up sex anyway?"

"You bet your sweet ass."

As they lay in bed cuddling, their conversation from dinner continued. There were serious issues to deal with before they were interrupted by Hunt's parents.

"I'll come get you tomorrow and we'll go car shopping."

"I suppose I need to get one. It wasn't such a big deal in the city when I could catch a cab. I guess out here they'll be a little hard to come by."

"My truck is paid up, so there won't be an issue for me getting a loan."

"I'll manage my own car payments, Hunt. I may have my mind made up to be a stay-at-home mom for now, but I certainly don't need to mooch off of my husband."

Hunt slumped back, frustrated. "Do you have to play so tough nut independent with me? Can't you let me be the man of the family and do shit for my wife?"

"Of course. You are allowed to take out the trash and shower me in *bling* for any occasion you see fit."

"Are you going to insist on paying half the mortgage?"

"I think we should share bills, don't you?"

"No, I don't. I'm the man. I provide for my family."

"But I have money coming in, too."

"Then start a college fund for Hannah."

Mandy propped herself up. "You want separate checking accounts?"

"I was thinking joint."

"Really?"

"Why keep things separate?" He pulled their hips together. "I love you. We'll be married. What's mine is yours. I don't want to live separate lives under the same roof."

"You sure move fast, Blaine."

"All or nothing. It's all I know how to be. If you want a separate account then fine. But I'm making mine joint. We'll both have a checkbook."

She gave him a lingering kiss. "I don't need a separate account."

"I won again? I'm thinking I'll like this arrangement."

"Don't count on it. I specialized in negotiations."

"Really? So what's next?"

"I get the top."

"You drive a hard bargain."

CHAPTER NINE

Things were moving fast with Hunt and Mandy. For knowing very little about each other, they seemed to be very compatible. Conversations came easy for them, they shared a lot of the same favorite foods, and they couldn't keep their hands off of each other. The days were relatively uneventful, but they never had an awkward silence or uncomfortable moment. Other than both being a little tired from Hannah's early morning feedings, they were truly happy together.

Over breakfast on that third morning, Hunt, not being able to take his curiosity any longer, asked her about the Menusco case. He hoped it wasn't a mistake.

"I thought we agreed this was a dead subject, Hunt. I really don't see the point in talking about this."

"I'm just curious. I'm still...intrigued. I can handle any details about Gerard, I promise."

"I'd rather you not utter that name in this house again."

"I'm sorry. I just...I'd like to know. I did put my badge on the line for you."

"Are you going to use that our whole life?"

"No. I swear. I need it to make sense."

"Before you marry me you mean?" She leaned against the counter and crossed her arms.

"No, dammit. No." Hunt closed the gap between them and wrapped his arms around her. "Don't, Mandy. I'm marrying you whether you like it or not. If I need to chain you in my attic, I will. I want you. Don't ever doubt me or think there is anything you can tell me that could possibly make me feel otherwise."

"Then why, Hunt?"

"If you're not comfortable with it, then forget it. I was just curious." He gave her a kiss on her forehead then went back and picked up his orange juice and downed it in one gulp. "I really need to get going, anyway. I need to catch up on a few things if I'm going to take half a day off and get married tomorrow afternoon."

She hurried over and wrapped her arms around his waist. "I'm really sorry. I don't want to think about those days again."

Hannah cried from upstairs, interrupting them.

"Saved by the bell, anyway," Hunt said with a kiss. "Don't give it a moment's thought. I won't bring it up again."

They lay in bed that night. Hunt was ready to doze off, but Mandy wasn't near to anything resembling sleepy. She turned to face Hunt and placed her hand on his chest.

"I ran a small convenience store on a busy corner."

"Hmmm?" he said, sleepily. Hunt struggled to wake himself up.

"When I went undercover."

He wrapped an arm around her. "We don't need to do this."

142

"I want to. I want you to know everything. I don't want you to think you're sleeping with a cold-blooded killer. I never want to give you reason to doubt me or the reasons I did what I did."

"I get it, okay? If anything happened to Hannah, you think I wouldn't do exactly what you did?"

"But you think it wasn't his fault. That he was just a victim. That Darci was in the way and it was sad, but he didn't deserve it."

"I said no such thing, and do not presume to tell me what I think about any of this, babe."

She gave his chest a kiss. "I love when you call me babe."

The room was dark, except for what light trickled in from the service light between the house and the shed. Total darkness was taking some time to get used to. Mandy had only known city life. She still waited to hear sirens speeding by and car alarms going off nightly. She doubted if she'd ever adjust to the peace and quiet.

"I don't want to fight. I want to tell you. I need to tell you. Are you awake enough for it?"

"I am now."

Mandy was recruited out of college for the FBI. The combination of her IQ tests, her straight-A scores, the diversity of her classes, and load of credits had caught someone's eye. She was the president of her debate team, majored in psychology, took fencing and karate outside of school as well as frequented a shooting range. She wasn't allowed a gun on campus, but what the dorm mother didn't know wouldn't hurt her.

Mandy's parents had left her well set up financially when they passed. She was in college at the time and didn't even make it back for their funeral. It was finals week. Mandy hated that she couldn't go, but there was no one she'd see again to give her any grief. She was never close to any of her parents' friends. Oddly, they were both only children as well, which meant no aunts or uncles to answer to, either.

The ceremony was small and they had been cremated. She received their ashes in the mail a few days later. She got drunk that night with her roommate and scattered their ashes along the memorial walk in DC. It was something her parents did every year. She thought they'd like that.

Just before graduation, she was approached by a man fitting of a *Men in Black* audition. Mandy thought the things he told her about a job were a joke.

"Who put you up to this? Harvey? That dick. He's always messing with me." She called around the courtyard. "You can come out now, douchebag. The gig is up."

"Miss Smith, I assure you. This is no joke."

She laughed hard. "Right. The FBI scouts college students for recruits? Why don't you haunt Duke? He's a mean son of a bitch. He'd be ready to blast some bad guys for you."

"He has a 2.7 GPA and breathes through his mouth."

Mandy's jaw dropped.

"And blasting bad guys isn't what we do." He handed her his card. "Be at my office Monday morning at noon. Graduation will be over by then."

"What makes you think I don't have plans?"

"The movers don't show up until Tuesday. You're moving into a studio apartment across town and you have no job applications out."

"Why are you snooping on me?"

"It's what we do. Don't you watch movies? Have a nice day, Ms. Smith."

Mandy showed up at noon on the dot. She was pissed, but she was still punctual. She was escorted to Mr. Abbey's office and offered beverages and snacks. All of which she declined. Mandy was a sight in her jeans with holes in the knees and a bright pink, low-cut tank top, high enough on her stomach the reveal the handcuff belly ring. Her pink heeled sneakers were fitting of something Posh Spice would wear.

Hunt interrupted her story. "You did *not* dress like that."

"I swear, I did."

"You don't have a belly ring now."

"I let it close."

"I think they're sexy. You should pierce it again."

"With my baby belly? Are you insane?"

"Oh bull. You don't even look like you had a baby."

She ignored him. "You going to interrupt through my whole story?"

"Only over incredibly sexy wardrobe."

"May I continue?"

"Please do."

"Interesting choice of body jewelry, Ms. Smith."

"I'm going through a kinky sex phase."

"Will that come around again?"

"Stop it, Hunt!"

"Sorry. Continue."

"You can play hardball all you want, but I know you're perfect for our team," Mr. Abbey said.

"Why is that? Because I have no family so there's no one to miss me when I turn up dead?" Mandy said.

"You have skills you don't even know you possess."

"But you do?"

"Walk with me." He led her to the elevator and they rode down several floors. When they reached to the bottom level, they got on another elevator and went down a few more floors.

"What is this place?"

"Just what it says on the outside. You don't think we keep the bad guys in check with office space do you?"

"Are you leading me to a room where some dude with one initial is going to give me all kinds of cool spy toys and an awesome car that flies and dives under water?" Mandy clapped her hands together, faking excitement.

He let out a heavy sigh. "No." The elevator door opened and he led her down a long hall. Solid steel doors gave nothing away as to what went on behind them. He finally walked them through one of them. A man and a woman were sitting at a desk, staring through a two way mirror at a very handsome young man sitting in a room alone with his hands cuffed together in front of him. He was smoking. The couple turned around, greeted Craig Abbey, and gave Mandy a once over. She curtseyed when he introduced her.

"What did he do?" Mandy asked Mr. Abbey.

"He's a lowlife drug dealer. Street level. Nobody really."

"And you have nothing better to do right now?"

"He killed one of our men. We know he didn't know what he was doing. Dumb accident. We want his supplier."

"Don't you have people that beat people like him up to get answers?"

"I'd like to try another route first."

"What's that?"

"You."

"Me? What the hell am I supposed to do?"

"Whatever comes to you." He brought her to the door. "His name is Melvin."

"No wonder he turned to a life of drugs. Kids probably beat him up all the time with that name." He shoved her through the door and locked it behind her.

Mandy turned around and smacked at the door. "Asshole!" She was pissed. She ran her hands down the back of her head, showing her frustration to Melvin. "Hey," she said as she went over and sat on the table. She picked up his pack of smokes. "You mind?"

"Knock yourself out, gorgeous. What's the deal? They run out of interrogation rooms or what?"

She lit the cigarette and blew the smoke up. "Something like that I suppose." Mandy went to her stomach and lay flat on the table so he had a great view of her cleavage. "What do they have you in for?"

"My gun accidently went off."

"And that's arrest worthy?"

"It went off in a DEA agent's face."

"I see. DEA. That's drugs, right?"

He laughed. "Yeah, that's drugs. Stupid sonofabitch. Don't mess with M. You'll get a cap popped in your ass every time."

"M?"

"That's me."

"You have lots of family and your mama ran out of names?"

"What do you want, sweet thing?"

She sat up and kicked her shoes off. Swinging one leg high and over to the other side of the table, she was now sitting in front of him with her legs spread open. She scooted her way closer to him and watched as beads of sweat formed on his forehead. She flicked her cigarette toward the wall after taking another long drag. She scooted even closer, then lowered one foot to his crotch. He was hard.

"Ohh... sucks to be stuck in here like that with no one to take care of it."

"I see you right here."

"This is true. The least I could do is relieve some of the pressure." She reached down and unsnapped his jeans then leisurely worked the zipper. "Better?"

"It will be when you bend over that table."

"I have a better idea." She scooted onto his lap and leaned in like she was going to kiss him. In a flash she launched him backward and pressed her left forearm over his neck. He tried squirming, but she had him pinned hard. With her right hand she reached down and squeezed his crotch. He screamed.

"What the fuck, lady?"

"Who's your supplier?"

"Fuck you!"

She squeezed him harder. "Like this?"

He screamed again. "Stop it!"

She pressed at his throat. "Do I suffocate you, castrate you with my bare hands, or do you want to talk?"

In another squeeze of his prized "tool" he had given up a name and address of his supplier.

She stood as he lay there curled up as best as he could and gasping for air.

"Thanks, Melvin. I knew you wouldn't let me down."

"Bitch," he screamed through his coughs.

Craig walked in. "Nice work. Although I kind of thought you'd use that psychology degree of yours to convince a confession out of him."

"Fuck you, Abbey. You had no right locking me in this room. You didn't need me for some dime bag junkie's confession." She hurried up through putting her shoes back on. "I'd bet my inheritance you know who that is and are capable of tracing it all the way back to Colombia."

"You're right. But I like the way you work."

She punched him in the gut hard enough to send him back a few steps. "Get me out of here. Now."

"She's pretty when she's pissed...for a cop." Melvin was being helped upright by another agent when Mandy strode back over to him.

She planted a solid kick to his chest, sending him flying back again. "I'm not a cop. Fuck you."

Hunt was sitting up by this point. Mandy had his full attention now. "You're serious, aren't you?"

"Dead serious. I didn't want anything to do with Abbey or his flipping organization."

Hannah cried. "I'll get her," Hunt said. "She can't be hungry." He stopped at the door. "I'm not tired anymore. You want to put some tea or cider on?"

"How about hot chocolate?"

He laughed. "You make what you want. I'll take tea. Something without caffeine though."

"Okay." She stood and put her long robe and house slippers on. They turned the heat down slightly at night. It made for great snuggling in bed, but getting out was chilly. She considered asking Hunt to reprogram it until Hannah was done with the middle of the night feedings.

Hannah was back in bed. Mandy and Hunt sat on the couch sideways so they could face each other. They shared a crocheted afghan over their laps as Mandy continued her story.

"So, you care to guess what I did the next morning?" Mandy asked Hunt.

"Showed up at Abbey's office?"

"Yup."

Mandy was once again escorted to Mr. Abbey's office. The secretary reacted as if she was expecting her, and it pissed Mandy off. When he spotted her, the *Men in Black* reject leaned far back in his chair and twiddled a pen in his hand. "Fancy meeting you here," he said. He eyed Mandy, who was now wearing a stylish blouse, black pants, and pumps. Her hair was pulled back in a sloppy bun. "You done with the rogue tough girl look?"

"Cut the shit. What do you want from me?"

"I want good agents and you have the potential to be one of the best. Your grades are off the charts and apparently you are stronger than you look."

"I didn't think FBI agents got their hands dirty."

"You have to be prepared for everything."

She flopped into one of his overstuffed office chairs. "What do I do now?"

"I personally will oversee your training. You'll need to learn the rules and follow them like everyone else. I expect your hand-to-hand and gun training will go fast enough, but a lot of that college psychology crap just doesn't float in real life applications."

"So what are we talking?"

"Six months or so."

"Six months?"

"Or so. If we rush it. I have something in mind for you, and I'd really like to throw you into it A—
S—A—F—P."

"Was the job he wanted you for with the Menuscos?" Hunt asked.

"Yes. They'd been watching them for a while and wanted someone to try to get inside. He thought someone new wouldn't be such a giveaway. He thought I had enough attitude to pull off some one-on-one contact and not give myself away. I did the training and they dumped me in a shithole of an apartment in Brooklyn."

"And the convenience store?"

"I had to interview for it. They didn't want to chance the owner knowing at all if they could help it. A low-cut shirt pretty much sealed the deal I'd get the job."

"You play dirty pool."

"I always play to win. By the time training was over, I was ready to run."

A man sat at the counter of the convenience store every day for an hour during Mandy's shift. The shop was set up more like an old '50s soda fountain and ice cream shop with a few groceries for sale as well. Her counter sold cigarettes and small bottles of liquor, but there were spinning barstools past the register for customers to sit and have an old fashioned root beer float or coffee. The only food available was bagged snacks and miscellaneous sweets. She drew the line at cooking. She would have told Abbey to take a flying...you know what...if she had to flip burgers.

The man at the counter was a little older than she was, and very handsome. She was sure he was Italian or maybe Greek. His dark hair and eyes made her go weak every time she waited on him. Day after day he sat there sipping his coffee. He said his pleasant hellos and minded his own business. His nose was usually in the newspaper.

Mandy kept trying to figure out what he was doing. He wasn't paranoid in the way he checked the doors and watched his surroundings. No one approached him as he sat there. She couldn't help but wonder at first if he was a part of what she was doing here. Abbey didn't give her any information to start. He said, "We want you fresh. I don't want you knowing what you're looking for. They'll be onto you like a fly on shit. Get comfortable with the neighborhood, go to church, make some friends, join a book club. Then we'll talk about your mark."

"I don't do church, Abbey."

"Whatever. Do something. Just play it cool. You're not in any danger unless you give them reason to be suspicious about you. Don't contact us, we'll contact you."

Almost a month had gone by. Mandy and the man had finally evolved into friendly banter, but she was careful not to cross the line into flirting. She was on business and he could be part of it. Even if he wasn't, she wasn't about to get involved with someone while she was working on a job of this magnitude. They had finally gotten to a first name basis, and Mandy let herself relax around him. His name was Gerard, and he did nothing that made her think he was anything more than an average Joe-Schmo killing time.

That Friday, she had served his coffee and wandered back to someone standing at the register. Something about the man was wrong. She sensed his nervousness, but couldn't act on it prematurely and risk giving anything away. He pulled out a gun before she could blink.

"Gimme all your cash!" he shouted. His gun went from her to Gerard. He acted nervous as hell. An amateur at best and probably his first robbery, Mandy thought.

There was a bat under the counter for times such as these. She tried to distract him for a moment before she reached for it.

"Just hold on there, Skippy. You don't want to hurt anyone. I make minimum wage. I'm not going to get crazy. Take what you want." She reached for the bat as she hit buttons to open the register, but Gerard was on him before she even got it out of the hook. He sent the man to the floor hard enough he was knocked out cold when his head hit the floor.

"Get some duct tape. That'll hold him till the cops get here."

"You're leaving?"

"I don't need to be here when the cops show up. Tell them you clobbered the schmuck."

"Any particular reason?"

"I'll tell you at our date tonight."

"We have a date?"

"Seven o'clock. It's the least you can do. I just saved that pretty little ass of yours."

She wasn't about to correct him about saving her...or about her ass. He'd been nothing but a great customer all this time. She didn't think he could be connected in any way with whatever she was doing here. The office would have warned her if that was the case. She was beginning to think they had her on the wrong corner. After living like a nun for the past few months, a night out sounded good.

She finally answered. "Seven o'clock would be great."

Dinner turned into drinks, drinks turned into animal sex. It had been too long for her, and she enjoyed it thoroughly. What Abbey didn't know couldn't hurt her.

She had waited for Hunt's heavy eyelids to close completely before uttering the last part. It was after one o'clock. She woke him up.

He apologized for falling asleep. "Babe, I'm sorry."

"It's fine. It's late. Let's go to bed. I'll finish the rest later."

"Did I miss anything good?"

"No, my love. I stopped when I knew you were dozing off."

"You will finish for me. Won't you?"

"I promise."

Hunt woke up before Mandy the next morning and checked on Hannah. She was just waking up and not crying yet. She gave her daddy a big smile. He carried her downstairs and removed a bottle of breast milk out of the fridge. He was pacing the kitchen trying to burp her before Mandy joined them.

"She took the bottle okay?"

"Took a little bit, but she did. Is that okay? We were up so late, I wanted you to sleep in."

"Of course it's okay. I'll pump if I get too full before she wants to eat again." She kissed him. "That was nice of you. Thanks. I'll nap when she does later and catch up. Sorry you won't be able to."

"I'm fine. Did I tell you? I'm getting married today. A speeding train couldn't stop me from doing anything."

She smiled. "Okay, Superman. Give me her, you'd better go get your cape on."

After he gave her the baby, Hunt said, "We need to pick up where we left off on your story, too."

"You really need to know everything?"

"I already know you banged him on the first date. How much worse can it get?"

"I thought you were asleep."

"I know." He grinned then took off running up the stairs.

Hunt came flying through the door at two-thirty. Mandy was standing there ready to go. Hunt was late. They were supposed to be at the courthouse already.

"What happened?"

"Sorry. There was a shoplifter at the hardware store. Luke was nowhere to be found. Roy was on patrol, I had to go. His ass is grass when I find him."

"Can we still get married?"

"Yes. I called the courthouse. They'll be ready for us whenever we show up. Judge Finkle is free for the rest of the afternoon. I'm sorry to worry you. Guess I should have called."

"I'm okay. I was worried about you." She stepped in closer to him. "I'm not so sure about this cop's wife thing. Maybe I'm changing my mind."

Hunt held her and growled. "If you don't marry me woman...I'll kill you so hard, you're gonna die to death."

Mandy laughed so hard, Hannah jumped. She wasn't startled enough to be woken up completely, and soon fell back to sleep. "Go get dressed."

"Have I said you look ravishing?"

"No."

"Well, you do. You wanna have sex?" He wagged his eyebrows up and down.

"Sorry, sir. I'm saving myself for my husband."

"Lucky bastard."

Twenty minutes later, Hunt was told he could now "kiss the bride."

Roy turned to Mandy. "Can I kiss the bride, or are you going to threaten my life?"

"You're safe." She leaned forward and kissed his cheek. "No hard feelings?"

"No hard feelings. I need to thank you for taking this bum off the streets for me."

"Is that a fact?" She gave Hunt a playful glare.

"Sure. Now that he's taken, the cop-loving broads will be after me now."

"Dream on," Hunt said with a laugh. "Junior show up?"

"Yeah. I chewed his ass. I don't know what's with him lately."

"Get him in the file room for a few hours as punishment. That would be a good start till I get my hands on him." He turned to Mandy. "Come on, wife. We have a honeymoon to start."

Hunt carried the baby into the house. They had decided to put off a real honeymoon until Hannah was a little older and they were comfortable leaving her with Hunt's parents. A couple of days off would have to suffice for now.

"Speaking of your parents, are you sure they aren't going to have your hide not having them at the ceremony?"

"Don't kill me."

"What?"

"I just...sort of...forgot to mention something to you."

"Hunter Andrew Blaine! What did you do?"

"Nice. We've been married ten minutes and I got the full name already."

"I'm waiting."

"The only way to appease my mother was to tell her she could throw a reception. Please don't be pissed."

"I'm not pissed, Hunt. Why would you think I'd get pissed?"

"I don't know. Maybe because you and my mom butted horns from the second you met."

"She was upset because we dropped a few bombshells on them that night. She'll come around."

"That's what I was hoping."

"Hunt, of course I want to get to know your family and friends. It's not like there's anything on my side. You have any friends with wives, or is everyone you know as devoted to bachelorhood as you?"

"There's a few of both. You'll meet everyone at the party, then maybe we'll have them over in shifts and get to know some better on a one-on-one basis."

"I think we need some one-on-one, too, before we get too into having others over."

"You do have a point there. We sort of have a lot of territory to cover getting to know each other."

"You want me to continue with the story, don't you?"

"You have that wives' intuition already, babe." He pretended to wipe a tear. "I'm so proud."

"Put a sock in it, Blaine. I'm going to get out of this dress before I leak in it. You go ahead and pop the champagne."

"You going to have some with me?"

"Not while I'm nursing."

"Then it will have to wait until we are both ready to enjoy it."

"You don't have to, you know."

"I know. I want to. I'm not this unselfish often. Take it where you get it."

Hunt played with Hannah until it was time for her to go down for the night. He wished she'd stay up later so Mandy could sleep longer, but babies made their own schedules. Mandy said she used to try to wake her up for another feeding before she went to bed, but Hannah would have nothing to do with it. When she wanted to sleep, she stayed asleep.

They walked into the kitchen with the intent of making dinner together. What they got instead was dessert on the table first. Hunt discovered she'd neglected to put any underwear on under her housedress, and it was all over from there.

"Nice sturdy table there, Blaine," Mandy said as she kissed the neck of her exhausted lover.

"Couldn't have planned it better." After a few moments, he stood and helped Mandy to her feet as well. "My aunt always said to have dessert first. That way you always have room."

"Smart aunt," she said with a kiss. "I'll get the wild rice going. You start on the fish."

"Yes, dear."

"Good answer."

Mandy was grateful they had avoided the conversation of her past throughout the meal. However, when they sat on the couch, she knew the gig was up.

"Soooo," Hunt said.

"You sure I can't get you a beer or something?"

"I'm fine. You left off after having sex for the first time."

"I know." She took a deep breath. "Things were fine for a while. We got along great. I hadn't dated anyone so mature before. No offense, Hunt, but you know how most college boys are. It was a nice change for me."

"So you loved him for his mind, not his—"

"If you're not going to play fair, I'm not telling you any more of the story."

He took her hand and gave it a kiss. "I'm just teasing. Please continue."

Mandy spent many days and nights wondering why the FBI wasted the time and training on her if she was only going to be a convenience store clerk. Nothing out of the ordinary happened other than the robbery for another few weeks. She all but moved in with Gerard. They spent most of their nights at his place, but she wouldn't sleep over. She supposed the agency was watching her, but if they wanted to complain, she had her argument ready. After he dropped her off one night, she got her chance to use it. Craig Abbey and her unofficial partner, Dan, were waiting in her apartment.

"This isn't the safest place to do this. What if he came in with me?"

"We already know you...have been serviced. We know your routine, Mandy," Dan joined in. "We need to talk to you about this little affair of yours. We feel it's a distraction."

"Bullshit. You told me to fit in, so I fit in. You wanted me to get local color, so I got it."

"I'd say you're getting it, Mandy. Right between the—"

"Knock it off, Dan," Abbey shouted.

Mandy had met Dan during her training. He was the same level as she was, but always acted like he was her superior. More than once, he was a little too close for her comfort. He never came out and asked her on a date, but

Mandy had always suspected he wanted to. He made several uncomfortable advances, and if she had responded at all, they would have been lovers. She was certain of it. He was behaving like a jealous lover here, not an upset teammate.

"Look, Mandy," Abbey continued. "I'm not happy, but I'll trust your judgment on this. I don't want you getting gaga over this guy and drawing your name with his in little hearts and miss what's going on around you."

"You know me better than that!"

"All right. Chill out. I've given you free reign here. But you screw up and it's my ass!"

"I'm not going to screw anything up. He wants me to move in with him, and I said no. I figure you have me set up in this shithole for a reason. I know what I'm doing."

"Move in together? Already? Don't you think he's moving along a little fast here?"

"That's none of your business, Dan." Mandy sent a stare at him that silenced any further outbursts. She returned her attention to Abbey. "Just what the hell am I doing anyway? You guys have me selling cigarettes and ignoring fake IDs 'cause I'm not supposed to know any better. What the hell is supposed to go down? What am I wasting my time there for?"

"Just keep your eyes open. You'll know soon enough. We're not wrong about this location. We have it on a good source it's about to become the new hotspot. You're going to be in the middle of it, and we need you on the top of your game."

"I will be. Don't worry about Gerard. I'm sure he thinks I'm the brainless bimbo you have me playing. Just let it be. I'll probably end up meeting more people and maybe set up for more leads. Don't underestimate my thoughts on this."

"Yet you don't think he's involved in any of this?"

"I don't. But so far we haven't done much other than..."

"Fuck."

"Screw you, Dan."

"Can't have us all, babe."

"Abbey? Would you get a leash on that thing or don't bring him around anymore."

"Both of you knock it off."

"Come on, Craig. You don't think I've observed him for the past few weeks? He doesn't pack a gun. He doesn't have contact with anyone I've seen. He isn't making drop-offs or pick-ups. He could just like the place's coffee. Let me run with this."

Abbey was still silent.

"It would help if you gave me any indication of what the hell I was supposed to be looking for."

"Just keep your eyes open. We'll be in touch again soon."

They left, leaving her still confused as to her mission, but at least she wasn't in trouble for falling in love on the job. She hoped whatever was going to happen would happen fast. Mandy hated to lie to Gerard, but couldn't bring herself to tell him anything about the agency. She was certain he had nothing to do with what she was here for, but she couldn't risk her cover to anyone.

CHAPTER TEN

The following day, Mandy's convenience store boss approached her with a strange request. She could tell by the way he sauntered over something was finally rolling. Her heart raced with excitement, not fear.

"'Sup, boss man."

"'Sup? How about I give you a dollar an hour raise not to talk like that anymore?"

"Sold. I'll let you touch my boob on my lunch break for two."

He laughed. "You are a feisty one. I need you to do something for me."

"Who do I need to kill?"

"Much easier than that. Program a new key on that contraption for me." He pointed to the cash register.

She took the key out of her pocket and turned the register to program. "Fire away."

"Make it PLU number ninety-nine."

"How much?"

"You figure it out so it comes to $58.25 after tax."

"Why that amount?"

"You just received an extra buck an hour not to ask why."

She knew she had to act curious, but couldn't push it too far and risk her job. "I'll do as you ask, but this don't smell right, Joey. You're not doing anything that could get me in trouble, are you?"

"Of course not. It'll look like a carton of cigarettes. I'll get you the stock. People show up, ask for PLU number ninety-nine and you hand it to them, no questions asked."

"What if a cop asks?"

"No cop will ask."

"But what if one does?"

"Then you hand him a box of Camel Lights."

"Is it illegal?"

"Two bucks an hour raise."

"Fine. No boob touching though."

Again he laughed. "Deal."

"So," Hunt said. "He had you selling drugs?"

"As much as it pains me to admit it, yes. It was very small scale. My guess was weed. I could never get in the boxes without it being obvious. It didn't matter; I had to do what I had to do for both jobs' sake. The small-time buyers weren't who we were after. They were mostly your average businessman. Never anyone underage. That was a slight consolation."

"If it wasn't you, they'd get it somewhere else?"

"Something like that. Anyway, the store's sales went up dramatically. They never only bought PLU number ninety-nine. They always spent more. Made it look legit."

"So, they made him a deal. He'd traffic and they'd boost his legitimate business."

"I'm sure Joey didn't do it willingly. I found out he had been paying for protection. I have no doubt they took more as he made more."

"This sounds so Al Capone."

"That's exactly what it was like. I didn't know how the agency knew to set me up there. You'd think they would have watched this happening and then tried to get in. It's like they had a jump on it."

"Or someone on the inside already."

She tilted her head and stared at him for a moment. "Funny you should say that, because I thought the same thing, but nothing I ever came up with panned out. We were a small team. I always thought there was no way there was any double dealing going on."

"Never say never, babe. Money talks. I don't care who you are."

"You telling me you could be bought, Mr. Blaine?"

"Me? Hell no. You know better. I don't know these pencil dicks you're talking about and wouldn't put anything past them, from what little I've heard. Please go on. Maybe this will help make something fall into place for you."

"Well, of course, I found out about Willy at the cabin. But I never saw it coming." She paused.

"What?" Hunt asked.

"I never thought about it. There were a lot of times Gerard was there and I had someone ask for PLU ninety-nine. He never once said a word."

"Because he knew."

"Of course he knew, Hunt. But back then, I didn't know he knew. I should have been more in-tune with that."

"You were in love."

"Don't mock me!"

"I'm not mocking you. You loved him. You didn't think he had anything to do with things, and you wanted to keep believing it." He held her chin. "Look what you did to me. You were a murderer on the run for all I knew and I couldn't keep my hands off of you. The last thing I want to happen here is to get in a fight over this. I'm okay with your past. He's hardly a threat anymore."

Her eyes squinted and her lips tightened at his comment.

"I'm sorry."

"I want to go check on Hannah."

"I haven't heard a peep out of her."

"I still need to go check on her. I'll be back in a minute."

Mandy spent some time adjusting a blanket that didn't need adjusting, staring at her baby. When she'd found out she was pregnant, she hadn't hesitated for a second about keeping her. She'd wanted the baby whether or not Hunt wanted to see her ever again. Keeping the pregnancy a secret was something she'd always regret. Hunt not being a part of it left a small emptiness in her over the months, but when his arms wrapped around her from behind, it was a void immediately filled again.

"Hey," he said. "Everything okay, Mommy?"

"She's fine. I just can't ever get enough of watching her sleep."

"I know the feeling," he said as he held her gaze. "You keep me up at night."

"I snore?"

He chuckled. "No. I can't stop watching you sleep, either."

They shared a lingering kiss before she led him out of the bedroom. "How about we share a shower before I continue?"

"You know it's not just going to be a shower."

"I'm counting on it."

Squeaky clean, they sat on the couch again with cups of tea. Mandy found a raspberry one she thought she'd like. She hadn't acquired a taste for Hunt's green tea.

"This is hardly a way to spend a honeymoon. I promise I'll make it up to you, babe."

"This is fine. I've had enough of hotels and traveling for a while. This is nicer than you think."

"This is your home now. You feel free to 'woman' it up anyway you see fit."

Again she gazed at him for a moment, struggling for the right words. "You know, I never would have taken you for such an agreeable man for a husband. I thought you'd be a bachelor until the day you died."

"I was on my way to that before you came along, thank you very much."

"I'm serious, Hunt. We fought like cats and dogs until we—"

"Had sex? Humped our brains out? I took the skin boat to—"

"Stop it!" she said through a laugh. "Yes, that."

"I wanted you and thought I shouldn't have you. Of course, I put a wall up and was a dick to try to push you away. You took psychology. Tell me you didn't figure that one out."

"I know that. It just seemed like it went further than that for you. I really thought you weren't a woman kind of guy."

"You thought I was gay?"

She laughed harder than before. "No, Hunt." She had to lean in his chest to muffle the laughing that continued. His reactions to surprises were priceless. She'd have to remember to zing him more often. When she composed herself, she continued. "I thought you hated women or something. One night stand, Hunt. 'Don't get close to me— I'm not going to get close to you.'"

"I won't say I hated women, but you were right. I was a two-date kind of guy."

"Always?"

"There was one girl during and after college, but it ended badly and I never wanted to go through that again."

"If I didn't show up for court?"

"I'd still be looking for your ass."

"If I didn't have Hannah?"

"I'd knock you up on sight. You just married me. You still going to play the 'what if' game?"

"If I'm spilling my guts here, I want a little dirt in return. That's all. What was her name?"

"Whose name?"

"The one who broke your heart."

"We don't use the name of 'she who should not be mentioned' around here."

"Come on, Hunt. You owe me that much."

He dropped his head back. "Annabelle."

"And what happened?"

"She got pregnant."

Mandy sat up straighter. "Why'd that break you up? Were you not ready to settle down back then?"

"Just the opposite. I proposed. She said she wanted to think about it. I didn't hear from her for a few days. She showed up and told me she'd had an abortion."

Mandy gasped.

"I couldn't look at her after that. She killed my baby, and I couldn't forgive her. We parted ways. End of story. I don't even know where she is now."

Mandy was silent for a while. She wished she hadn't made Hunt tell her. All she could say was, "I'm sorry."

Hunt shrugged. "I have my girls now. That's all that matters." He pulled her hand to his lips for a lingering kiss. "What was next, oh mob queen of mine?"

"Things became strange, fast."

Renovations in the office space that spanned the two floors above the store had been completed the following week. It was then when things really start to hop. Mandy had all her senses on overload, trying to keep up with what was going on.

Cars came and went all day. The men weren't the typical accountant-looking types either. Most were built as if they'd done their share of jail time and used that time pumping weights. Color was not a factor. There were men of every race, and so were their women. They varied from ladies of the night to the overdressed and over-jeweled wives with undersized dogs.

Mandy remained friendly to them as if her job depended on it. It did. Both of them. She continued her affair with Gerard, neither of them mentioning anything past the counter and bedroom.

After closing up one night, she ran the bag of garbage to the dumpster like she always did. She found two men beating up a young man and couldn't bring herself to turn away. Dropping the bag of trash, she headed for the larger of the two. She had the element of surprise on him, but wouldn't have needed it. She was easily the better fighter. A few well-placed kicks and a good right to the chin had the man on his back. When she knew he was out of the fight, Mandy turned to help with the other attacker, but discovered she didn't need to. Once it was a fair fight, the boy didn't do too badly. Anxious to bring it to an end, she picked up a discarded block of 2x4 from the remodel and hit the second assailant on the head. He went down hard and the other man ran off.

"Thanks," the boy said as he wiped his bloody nose.

Boy? He looked around twenty to Mandy. Still, she couldn't bring herself to say man.

"Kind of embarrassing to be saved from a brawl by a chick."

"A chick with a great right hook. And two on one never is fair."

"I've seen you before. You're the cashier, right?"

"That's me."

"Obviously your talents would be better served elsewhere."

"Oh, no you don't. Don't you dare tell anyone. I'll get fired or something."

"Not likely. Come with me." He took her by the arm and led her to the back fire escape. It was down at the moment. It had been rigged to stay that way.

"Did you do this? We could get a fine for that."

"Again, not likely." He motioned for her to go forward. "After you."

She did as she was told. As they climbed, she asked him, "Who were those two, anyway?"

"Someone not friends of my father's."

"Your father? You're not Joey's son. Are you?"

"Nope."

Once they were up to the second landing, Mandy waited for him. He breezed past her and crawled in the window. She followed. Immediately they were greeted by screams.

"Angelo! What on earth—" The shouting quit when the man's gaze fell on Mandy. "Why is she here?"

"Can it, Pops. She just saved my ass."

"Saved your ass? What happened?"

He stepped away from the window and motioned for his father to look out it. "Gino's boys?" his father asked.

"Yup. Jumped me the second I hit the ground."

"Well, what the hell were you doing going out? You know better than to go without Bennett! What were you thinking?" His father pulled a gun out of a holster and pointed it out the window. The man on the ground was coming to. "You'd better tell your uncle to watch his ass, boy! You want a war, you'll get one!"

Mandy pretended to be frightened by the appearance of the gun. Angelo cackled. "First gun, sweetheart?"

"Hardly," she replied, trying to now act insulted.

The man on the ground stood and ran away. Angelo's father came back in, holstered his gun, and straightened his coat. "So, why is it you bring this cashier into my home?"

"I told you, Pop. She saved my ass. Two of those goons jumped me."

"And what did she do?"

"Kicked their asses. Give her a job."

"She has a job."

"Give her a better one."

"Wait a second," Mandy interrupted. "Do I get a vote here?" She had to at least pretend to protest. Her ploy worked. Angelo's father liked the fact she pretended to be uninterested. He was obviously a man who was used to making people do what they didn't want. He wanted the challenge. The forcefulness. She had read him well.

"No. My name is Vince. I'm the boss of your boss. That makes me your boss, too."

"I just got a raise. I'm not leaving my job. I don't care who you say you are."

"I'm doubling it."

"My raise?"

"Your salary."

"Why? What do you want me to do? I'm not doing anything illegal."

"You already are. Might as well make money at it."

"That PLU ninety-nine, right? I'm not an idiot, but at least I could play stupid if we were busted."

"Playing dumb wouldn't help you, not that you have any worries, anyway. You'll be well protected. I guarantee it."

"I suppose you're going to tell me you have cops on payroll?"

He only grinned and turned to his son. "Next time a woman has to save your ass, Angelo, find one with bigger tits and less brains." He returned his attention to Mandy. "Come to my office tomorrow morning."

"What about my job?"

He waved as if it wasn't such a big deal. "I'll have someone cover your job. You'll learn to do as I say, Amanda. We'll get along much better that way."

"I prefer Mandy."

"Of course you do, Amanda." He stepped forward and held her chin. He gave her an obvious once over. "I suspect you have nicer clothes."

She jerked her head out of his grasp. "Yes."

"Then wear them tomorrow. See her out, Angelo."

That night Mandy was afraid to say anything to Gerard. Not that she even really knew what to say. Tell him she thought she was just hired by the mob or tell him she was an FBI agent. Both sounded too stupid to be true. She hated that she had fallen in love with him in the middle of all of this. It was a distraction she shouldn't have allowed. Wearing a negligée, waiting for him to come over, she planned on breaking it off tonight. Having sex one last time sounded great, though. It was easy enough to find something small to fight about and give her an excuse for a break. She'd miss him but she couldn't risk ruining this job over him. Maybe after it was all said and done she could find him again.

Things were moving too fast, and she had to put some space between them. She was beginning to doubt her ability to do either job effectively and keep him in the dark. That's what her head told her, but when Gerard showed up with a two-carat weight diamond, a wedding dress, and flowers, she had a hard time doing anything but smothering him with excited kisses. She unbuckled his pants, wanting to make love, but he stopped her.

"Later. We're getting married tonight."

"Tonight? Why the rush?"

"Because I want you now. I want you living with me. No more of your excuses."

She wanted to marry him, but she couldn't live a lie. "I need to tell you something first." Mandy was still deciding whether to tell him about her job with the mob or being an FBI agent. She hadn't made up her mind which. He stopped her by placing a hand over her mouth.

"All I want to hear out of those lips is, 'I do.'"

"But, Gerard—"

"Shhh. Get dressed. There's a limo downstairs."

Before Mandy could blink, she was Mrs. Gerard Teluso. They drank champagne in the back of the limo and then made love in it.

Hunt interrupted again. "In the limo? Lucky son of a bitch."

"So, get me a limo on our honeymoon."

"Porsche."

"A little harder to make love in, don't you think, Hunt?"

"It's always been a dream of mine. Read it in a book once."

"Any. Way. You. Want." She kissed him between each word.

"Shameless hussy."

"And all yours."

"Yowza."

The limo came to a stop and Mandy assumed they were back at his place. She straightened herself as best she could and stared out the window. They were in the richest neighborhood for fifty miles.

"Why are we here?"

"I want to show off my wife."

She frowned. "What if I said no?"

"You wouldn't," he said, with a devilish grin.

Mandy took a little more care in making herself presentable. "Who lives here?"

"My boss."

"So, I finally get to know what you do for a living?"

"I told you I was a consultant."

"That's a little vague."

"You'll see in a minute." He opened the door and pulled on her gently. "Come on, wife. Been married for an hour and I'm waiting on you already."

She climbed out and gave him a lingering kiss. There would be hell to pay with Abbey, but she didn't care. There had to be FBI agents with families. As long as her cover wasn't blown, there was no harm in it. Wives of FBI men knew what their husbands did. This would be no different. As soon as they were out of here, she would explain it to Gerard and life would go on. Abbey would have to accept the fact the agency was her job—not her life. Abbey wore a wedding ring, but never mentioned a wife. If he could do it, why couldn't she?

After being greeted by a butler and entering the ballroom, she suddenly felt differently about her decision to spill the beans to Gerard and was glad she'd held her tongue. How could she be so stupid?

The room was filled with too many familiar faces. Just about everyone in eyesight came and went from the floors above the convenience store. The man who dropped off the phony cigarette cartons of drugs toasted toward her as she caught his eye. Mandy played it cool and held on to Gerard tight. "These people work upstairs."

He grinned. "Yes they do."

"You don't work upstairs, Gerard."

"No." He hesitated and pointed to Vince. "But my boss does."

Mandy froze. "Vince is your boss?"

He turned to her and put his hand on her face. "*Our* boss, I hear."

"I...I tried to tell you." Her words stammered out. She became weak in the knees and needed fresh air. Abbey and Dan would really have her hide now. Not only did she up and get married mid-job, she married into what she was supposed to be watching over.

"You okay?"

"I think the champagne went straight to my head." She fanned at her face as if she were hot.

He pulled her close. "Does this scare you?"

"Scare me? No. I have an idea of what I'm in for. Even better if we are in it together." She made a mental note to tell Abbey to put drama class on any new recruit training from now on.

Vince made his way over to them. "I see one of my best men has just claimed one of my newest, soon to be best men. So to speak." He gave Mandy a kiss on the cheek. "Welcome to the family in more ways than one, Amanda."

"Family?"

"Vince is my uncle."

"I see," she said with a forced smile. "Then it is a family business after all. I'm proud to be a part of both. I hope I don't let you down."

"I'm sure you won't." Vince wandered away.

"Come on," Gerard said. "I want you to meet everyone. I need to stake my claim, too. You've been the talk of the family ever since you started. I knew it would only be a matter of time before you were recruited for better things."

"Why didn't you tell me what you did? Why the secrecy?"

"What if I came out and told you I worked for…"

"The mob?"

"There has to be a better word for it."

"It is what it is, lover."

"What would you have done?"

"I can't say. I'll be honest and admit it scares me a little. I really didn't sign up for this when I took that clerk job."

"But you joined willingly enough when Vince spoke to you today."

"He didn't really give me much of a choice. Besides, I'm intrigued. I don't know what to think, really. This whole day has been a whirlwind."

"But you love me. That much is true. Am I right?"

She kissed him. "That much is true."

"Good, because I'm not really a consultant. I'm more like their lawyer."

"I want a divorce."

Gerard laughed. "No deal. I'm more of the behind the scenes guy. We have some pencil dick to be the public face. My skills are better spent…elsewhere. Come on. Let's make our rounds and get home and back in the sack. I want you again, wife."

Of course she left that last part out when telling Hunt. Her job with the FBI was the first thing she really took seriously in her life. She couldn't believe she'd let her love for a man interfere with it. All she'd been able to do to keep her sanity was to convince herself she could do her job more effectively with the insight Gerard's position now offered her. Mandy had planned to bide her time, collect the information she needed to for Abbey, and convince Gerard to leave with her.

"You did what?" screamed Abbey.

Mandy wanted to fess up and tell them right away, rather than wait for them to find out. She made an excuse to be late for work the next day and drove to headquarters. Mob employee or not, she was a woman first. Vince made a comment about her wardrobe and she pretended to need to expand it to suit him. He expressed he was, in fact, pleased at her effort and would not be upset at her tardiness this one time.

"I didn't know he was a part of it, I swear. You know that. This is your fault!" She screamed at Abbey.

"How is it my fault?"

"You should have given me some clue as to what I was doing. You knew everything and everyone involved. You could have laid out some kind of plan of attack. If I hadn't helped Vince's son in a street fight, I'd still be pushing coffee and smokes at that damn counter."

"You know why we couldn't tell you."

"You should have given me some credit and filled me in, dammit. But it doesn't matter. It's that much better now that I'm married."

"How do you figure that?" Dan said, joining in with the screaming.

"Now I'm in. I'm really in. They are never going to suspect anything."

"Bullshit. This isn't going to fly, Mandy. You love the guy, don't you?"

She chewed at her bottom lip in lieu of an answer.

"Answer me!" Dan roared even louder.

"Yes! I do. So what?"

"So what? You're not going to turn him in. You aren't going to do anything that will get him arrested."

"He's not even a big part of it. Don't you think I would have sensed it? All he did was sit there for coffee each day. I had no idea he was a part of this. My guess is his role is to stay clean. There has to be some reason he doesn't get involved at a higher level. He's a good guy, Abbey. He said he's like a lawyer. Jokes aside, what he does *is* probably legal from every angle." She was ignoring Dan as best as she could.

"A good mobster. Listen to her."

"Go to hell, Dan. He's not a mobster, but he's my 'in'. You keep trying to slice this up any way you want, but you know I'm right. I'll get closer, faster, with him on my side. I don't know why you're even in on this case. All you do is bust my balls. I'm the one out there putting myself at risk."

He got right in her face. "This case is mine! It's you who was the afterthought! Don't you forget it, doll!" He pulled her to her feet by her arms then brought her closer to him by her hips, holding her to his midsection. "You just couldn't keep your legs shut. Could you? You like the feel of that?" He said as he backed her into the desk. "You want to—"

"That's enough!" Abbey shouted. "What the hell are you doing?"

As if he were in a trance, Dan let go and stepped back. Mandy slapped him hard. "You fucking pig!"

He held up a finger and pointed it in her face. "And you're off the case, you cheap slut!"

"He did not call you that!" Hunt said.

Mandy shrugged. "He did."

"Has he been killed?"

"No. He's still there."

"I'm on it," Hunt said, acting like he was standing up. Mandy pulled him back down.

"His day will come. I'm not worried about him anymore."

"Anymore?"

"He really flipped after that."

"Oh no you don't! I've worked hard to be where I am. Abbey? Come on! This is a good thing. You had me jerking off a coffee machine for months and now I'm the boss's son's right hand man and married to the lawyer. It doesn't get any better than this. I've gained access to everything in one day."

"Pillow talk included," Dan griped.

"Yes, dickhead. Pillow talk included." She turned her attention back to Abbey. "I'm able to keep my identity a secret as long as you guys don't blow it for me. I'm telling you, Gerard isn't a major player here, but he'll keep me close, and that means I'll be the first one with the knowledge of anything you want."

"Why didn't we have an ID on Gerard if he's the lawyer? It doesn't make sense."

"He said he's the behind-the-scenes guy. I guess he's family and they try to keep the name off the books as much as possible. I don't know how he's turning out so high profile, but you have nothing on him. We do now, though. That's what matters. Everything I learn will help us."

"I still don't like it," Abbey said.

"Why? Why is sleeping with him any worse? I'm safer than I was before. He loves me. You think he'd let something happen to me if suspicion suddenly fell on me? He'd be the first to defend me."

Abbey turned to Dan. "She has a point."

"You're off your nut, boss." Dan stormed out of the office.

"Ignore him," he said to Mandy. "You really think your cover won't be compromised?"

"I know it won't. Even more so now. You have to let me do the contacting from now on, though. If you show up at the wrong time...I don't even want to think about it."

"We'll leave you be for now. But I have to have a way to contact you. I want regular updates. You figure it out. We're too close on this, Mandy. We don't have enough to run them in. I can't afford to stop this now."

"You don't have to stop it now. We're only just getting rolling."

"I hope you're right about this. You've put me in a hell of a position here."

"You were right about me. I'm the girl for this job. I know I am. Let me do this."

"All right. I want you to stay away from Dan. You report only to me."

"No problem there. Thanks, Abbey."

"Would you call me Craig already? Damn it all, Mandy. I swear I'm going to take my wife's last name."

She laughed softly. "I never thought of it like that. I swear."

"Just watch your back. I don't want to lose my best man. You get pregnant and I'll kill you myself."

"No worries there. I'm not ready to bring a kid into this mess."

"Wise woman."

"You going to fill me in now on some names and specifics or are you going to let me shoot in the dark here?"

He pulled a large file out of his desk. "I think you should know the main players. I don't want you wasting time on dipshits like Melvin. I'm not sure what Vince will have you doing with Angelo, but he's about as second in command as you get." He flipped open the file. "Do keep your eyes open around that Bennett guard dog of his. He could be trouble."

"We've met."

He took Mandy's hand. "I mean it, Mandy. I hate what you've done. Your judgment is clouded. You need to look out for yourself."

"I can handle it."

He sighed and focused his attention back to the folder. After about an hour, Mandy said she had to get back.

"Take care of yourself, kid."

She saluted him playfully. "Yes, boss. And thanks."

"For?"

"Everything. Keeping Dan at bay and not killing me for marrying Gerard. I swear I wasn't going to let it happen. It just...did."

"Oh, don't get me wrong. I want to kill you plenty. I have to go with your gut here. I don't see as I have much of a choice in the matter."

"I'll check in after a bit."

"Soon, goddammit. I don't like the rogue agent bullshit."

"I promise," Mandy said before she walked out the door.

"Did you mean it?" Hunt asked.

"Of course I did. I wanted to do the job, Hunt. I was upset about the possibility of being sidetracked. A man can do the job and be married. Why shouldn't I have been given the chance?"

"It wasn't a man/woman statement. I would have been worried if I were Abbey, too."

"I don't want to fight with you about this."

"I don't either, and not just because I don't want you to get mad and hold off on sex. I'm saying he was right about you being too close to the situation. If it came down to it, I would have worried that you—or anyone in that position—may have chosen love over what was right."

"Give me one example," she said, angrily.

"Me."

"You?"

"You were essentially my mark. I fell in love with you. Look what I chose?"

"But this was different."

"Not really. My first duty was to bring you in, but I banged you instead."

"Banged?"

He scooted closer. "Made love. Love makes us do crazy things. That's all I'm saying."

"Can I be done with storytelling tonight?"

"Absolutely."

CHAPTER ELEVEN

Mandy was grateful the recap was put on hold. Telling the story was bringing back unpleasant memories. She hated that, even to her, she sounded like a lovesick teenager who was risking a career over love.

Her belongings showed up early the following morning, and they were busy getting things organized. Secretly she hoped they never went back to their conversation, but she didn't think Hunt would let it go.

As they carried in boxes, she apologized numerous times to Hunt.

"I didn't imagine I had acquired so much stuff again. I really got rid of a lot before I moved into protective custody."

"Don't apologize, babe. The house is more than big enough for this and more."

"We're doubling up on a lot of appliances. Is there a Goodwill in town?"

"Not far from my office, actually."

"I'll start a box then. This is ridiculous. I should have gone to pack up and saved them from sending it."

Hunt pulled her close. "Then we would have been apart. No way," he said with a kiss. "I'd have spent four times what they cost to keep you here."

Mandy cuddled into him. "You sure know how to spoil a gal."

"You two are all I care about. Stop sweating the petty stuff, babe."

The phone rang, interrupting them. Hunt walked over and answered it. After a few murmurs of "sounds good," "we don't care," and "all right," he hung up.

"Who was that?"

"My mom. Last minute decorating."

"Crap. I forgot that was tonight."

He returned to her and held her tight. "You'll be fine."

"I'm sorry. I don't mean to be a party pooper. I want to meet your family and friends. I just hope no one knows how we met."

"Only Roy and Luke know that, and I made sure they'll be quiet. I also put Luke on duty tonight."

"Afraid he'll spill the beans?"

"He has a loose tongue when he drinks."

"We need to come up with a good story."

"Let's stick to the truth."

That surprised Mandy. "Are you crazy?"

"I meant mostly the truth. We met on a case. That's all they need to know. You don't care if people know you are retired FBI, do you?"

"I suppose not. I just don't want to give out details."

"Then don't."

"They'll ask why I'm retired at my age."

"Your reason is upstairs. That's the best one in the book. You'll be fine."

"Promise not to abandon me?"

"I'll stay by your side all night."

"Promise?"

"I promise." He grinned.

"What?"

"Big bad FBI agent can take on a mob boss, but not sixty-five-year-old in-laws."

"Your mom is scarier than one-eye Devon."

"One-eye Devon?"

"He was always picking his teeth with a buck knife. Threw it by my head once to make a point."

"What happened to him?"

"I threw it back. My aim is pretty damn good, too."

Hunt placed his hand at his crotch. "I'll remember that."

Mandy smirked. "I didn't hit them, but I bet I gave him a little trim."

"You scare me."

She pulled him by his shirt, down for a kiss. "Good."

Trying to find an outfit for Hannah was tough for Mandy. Even though it had only been a week, she had outgrown almost everything.

"No problem, babe. We'll stop at the mall before we hit the American Legion."

"Would you mind? I'd really like her looking nice since this is her coming out party, too."

"Of course not. We're the guests of honor. Who can complain if we're a little late?"

"That'll score points with your mother."

He had to laugh at her. "She's not that bad. Just wait and see. The news was thrown at her all at once. I know she's really thrilled I'm settled down, and even more so about Hannah. Trust me and relax. Would you, please?"

"I'll be fine. I wish I could drink."

"How long are you planning on nursing?"

"As long as she'll let me. A year. Maybe more."

"That long?"

"It's the best thing for her, Hunt. So I behave for another year. No big deal. You don't have to, though. I mean it. You drink with your friends—I'll drive us home."

"You sure you don't mind?"

"Of course not. You ready to go?"

"Don't I look ready?" Hunt was in a black pullover and jeans.

"You look casual."

"That's all it is."

"Am I overdressed?"

"You're gorgeous. Don't change."

"It's the only dressy thing I have that fits these boobs." Mandy wore a white sundress. She tugged at the ties at the chest as she spoke. "And have access to be able to nurse."

"You look great. I like that dress. It's what we were married in. It's fitting."

"You sure?"

"Positive. Stop being so nervous. I promise my friends are harmless. You'll have a blast." Her emotionless gaze met his. "Do you love me?"

"Very much."

"And I love you. That's all this is about." He gave her a strong kiss. "Let's go."

They wandered together through the kids' aisles at the department store with Hannah asleep in Hunt's arms. Mandy wasn't thrilled with the selection of dresses in Hannah's size.

"There's another rack of dresses over there." Hunt pointed across a rolling shelf unit he could see over but Mandy couldn't. "I'm going to go pick up some socks since we're here. Meet you over there in five minutes."

"Okay." She continued to flip through the rack she was at, harshly pushing the hangers away one at a time as she grunted in frustration. "There isn't much to choose from."

"We'll go to the city this weekend if you want. It's only an hour away. You'll have more luck there. Just get what you need to get by for tonight." Hunt kissed Hannah's sleeping cheek. "She'll be adorable in anything."

Mandy smiled at him then wandered to the other rack.

Hunt was digging through a large wire display bin of socks, looking for his size, when someone came up behind him. "Hunt?"

He spun around at the familiar voice. "Annabelle?"

"How are you?" She leaned up for a kiss on the cheek and as good of a hug as she could give him with the baby on his shoulder. She went around to Hunt's back so she could see Hannah's face. "Hunt, she's beautiful. She yours or did your sister have another?"

"She's mine."

"I hadn't heard you were dating anyone. You know my mom," she said as she rolled her eyes. "Always hated that I let you slip outta my grasp. She still brings you up on occasion." Her gaze went to the baby again. "You know, it took a long time getting over my decision. But it was what I had to do. Getting over you was harder than I thought. I had no idea—"

"We don't need to rehash this, Annabelle. I'm sure you've moved on and have a great life."

Just then a young boy came running up to her. He appeared to be around three years old. "Mommy!" he said as wrapped one arm around her leg and another held a dump truck tight. "Can I have it?"

"Sweetheart, you already have six dump trucks. What are you going to do with a seventh? Go pick something else."

"Okay." He took off as fast as he showed up.

"You have a son?"

She smiled and nodded her head. "I guess I never did watch carefully enough. I wasn't ready for him either, but I wasn't going through...you know...again. I haven't regretted having him for a minute. Makes me wish..." She turned away and bit her bottom lip, like she was fighting tears. Hunt pulled her into his chest for a hug and she wrapped her arms around him.

"Don't, Annabelle." Hunt looked up as Mandy approached them. He didn't know her well enough to gauge the look on her face. He straightened up. "Hey, babe."

Annabelle turned around. "You must be the lucky Mrs. Blaine."

"That would be me."

Annabelle stretched her hand out. "Hi, I'm Annabelle. An old friend of Hunt's."

Mandy accepted her hand. "Nice to meet you." Hunt cringed at her expression. *Crap.* She remembered the name. "Do I need to give you two a minute?"

"No. I'm sorry. Don't mind silly old me, lonely and weepy for an old friend. My husband is overseas and I'm home visiting my mom."

"He's in the war?"

"Marine. I thought being married to a cop would be bad." The look on her face revealed she immediately regretted her words. "I'm sorry."

"That's okay," Mandy said. "I'm ex-FBI. I know what you mean."

"FBI?" She eyed Hunt. "Hunter Blaine. You're outranked." Annabelle laughed and Mandy joined in. Her laugh stopped abruptly when the little boy came running up again.

"This one, Mommy?"

"Another fire truck?"

"My ladder is broked."

"Broken, sweetie."

"Can I? Please?"

"All right. Let's get going."

Mandy stopped her. "Do you have plans tonight?"

"No. Just hanging out with my mom."

"Why don't you two join us at our reception at the Legion? It's going on now, actually. We're being fashionably late."

Annabelle faced Hunt, whose expression was that of pure shock. "Hunt? That okay?"

"Uh...sure. Of course. Bring your mom, too. I'm sure my mom would love to see her."

"I will. Thanks. See you there in a bit."

After she walked away, Mandy turned to Hunt.

He tried to stall what he figured was coming. "I see you found something."

She gave the dress a once-over. "This will do. So..."

"I didn't know she was in town. I swear."

"And the hug?"

"Like she said. She was getting weepy."

"Over her husband or you?"

"Don't do this, Mandy. I didn't ask to see her. I didn't want to see her. Why did you invite her tonight?"

"Just trying to be polite. She sounded lonely."

"Of all times to try to prove you're tough." He turned to leave but she stopped him. "I'm not fighting with you about this. Least of all here, Amanda."

"Amanda? No babe?"

"Stop it."

"We need to check out and get going." Mandy hurried to the register. Annabelle was walking out and waved at them as she left.

"Hey, Hunt," the elderly woman at the register said. "This your pretty new bride your mom was bragging about this afternoon?"

"This is her. Don't know how I was able to get her to say yes, Karen. Mandy, this is Karen. You might as well say she's my aunt." The women exchanged pleasantries. "You coming tonight?"

"I'll be done with my shift in an hour, then I'll be there."

"See you then."

Amanda was quiet until they climbed in Hunt's truck and settled Hannah in her car seat.

"Please don't let this ruin our night."

"Was that your son?"

"What? No. I told you she didn't have it. That's what you're pissed about?"

"I'm not pissed, just in a little shock I guess. Your tender hug with someone you supposedly hate caught me off guard. Then when the child ran up...I didn't know what to think."

"Shit, Mandy." Hunt scooted over the bench seat and held her tight. "We've been broken up for over five years. The kid had to be three. I'm sorry. That thought didn't even occur to me."

"I'm being an idiot."

"No, you're not. I'm sure you felt like I did, only I had it a little worse. I knew what Gerard had done to you."

"Shhhh." Mandy put her fingers over Hunt's lips. "Let's not do this. This is our night. Let's start from scratch. I'll try not to get jealous over every ex-girlfriend of yours who shows up."

"Not a long list, babe. I told you, I didn't keep it local for a reason. I really wish you hadn't invited Annabelle."

"It's history, Hunt. Maybe I was being selfish and wanted her to know what she gave up."

"You're the devil, woman." He laughed and gave her a kiss.

"And you married it."

As soon as they reached the American Legion, Hannah woke up. She wasn't pleasant about it, either. She started wailing immediately.

"I'll get her fed and dressed, Hunt. You go in. I'll find you."

"I can wait."

"I'm fine. Really. You go have a beer. I'll be no more than fifteen minutes. Just leave the heat on please."

"You sure?"

"I'm sure." She kissed him, crawled over the seat and picked Hannah out of the car seat. Mandy unzipped her coat, lowered the neck of the dress, and Hannah greedily attached to her breast.

"I'll come out if I don't see you in fifteen minutes."

"You think I'm going to make a run for it?"

"Absolutely."

She laughed. "Nut job. I promise I'll be in."

He leaned over and kissed her again. "Fifteen."

"Maybe twenty. I want to change her tights, too."

"Do whatever you need to do, babe. See you inside." Hunt finally closed the door and entered the building. Mandy sunk low in the seat trying to stay out of sight. Hunt's windows were pretty heavily tinted, but she wanted to be sure not to be giving a free peep show to any passersby.

After switching breasts, Mandy was startled by a face at the driver's window. His hand was cupped to it and the man was peeking in, but if he could see her and Hannah, his face never gave it away. She gasped when he tried the handle and sighed in relief when she discovered Hunt had locked her in. The last thing she wanted to do was panic for no reason, but after the person circled the truck twice, she called Hunt. He answered on the first ring.

"What the matter? You need help?"

She watched as the man finally walked away. Now she felt silly. "Um...no. I'm fine. Sorry, I guess I butt dialed you."

Hunt laughed. "You almost ready?"

"Just getting her dress on. I'll only be a minute. Sorry."

"You miss me. See you in a few."

As Mandy dressed Hannah, she kept looking up for the man, but he never reappeared. It was just her imagination getting away with her. Hunt's truck was a white Toyota 4-door. She could see three others from where she sat. No doubt someone had too much to drink and was trying to get in the wrong vehicle. "Shake it, Smith," she said, scolding herself. "I mean, Blaine." She opened up the door and backed out of it.

When her feet hit the ground, hands gripped her waist and she screamed.

Hunt laughed and spun her around. "You scared the shit out of me, Hunt!"

Hannah cried at the screaming and yelling.

Hunt took her. "I'm sorry. I didn't mean to. Just helping you down. You okay?"

Running her hand over her face she said, "Fine. Sorry." She crawled in front and turned off the truck then removed the keys and climbed back out. "Let's do this."

The night went over better than Mandy imagined. Hunt's friends were very friendly, and happy someone had finally managed to get him to settle down. They didn't pry for details about how they became a couple and how they managed to carry on the relationship with no one knowing about her or Hannah. Everyone who laid eyes on the baby, said there was no denying she was Hunt's and raved about her beauty. Mandy was glad her daughter adjusted well to being handled so much. She really hadn't been exposed to too many other faces up to this point in her life.

Hunt's mother was cheerful the entire night and eagerly introduced Mandy to everyone, showing her off as her daughter-in-law. That was unexpected and warmed Mandy more than she knew. Maybe she had judged her unfairly. She also took Hannah for most of the night and insisted she and Hunt dance a few songs.

"This is something we never covered, babe. You're not too bad on the floor."

"I was about to say the same about you."

Hunt shrugged. "It's foreplay."

She giggled and waited for a kiss. "I'm ready to go when you are."

He pulled a garter out of his pocket. "Roy gave me this, and Mom has a bouquet for you. We have to do the rituals. You game?"

"Of course."

After making a presentation out of removing Mandy's garter belt, Hunt sent it into the crowd like a sling-shot. One of his single firemen friends caught it and hurried out to the dance floor.

"This means I get to kiss the bride right, Hunt?"

"That's up to the bride, Jon."

Jon had a few inches on Hunt. Mandy took ahold of Hunt's hand and stepped up onto the chair she was just sitting on, to bring her closer to his level. She now stood taller than him, but the action got the desired laughs from the crowd. He took that as a yes. Jon placed his hands on her hips and planted his lips on her. He dipped her backward, again causing roars of laughter from the group of friends. When he finally stood Mandy up again and stepped back, Hunt placed him playfully into a head lock. After a few pictures, the two shook hands and Jon left the floor.

Hunt was about to help her down when his mother came out onto the floor with a bouquet of white and red roses for Mandy. She announced the available ladies should gather where the men were previously. When they were ready, Mandy turned around and tossed it over her shoulder. When she turned back around, a woman around Hunt's mother's age was holding it up like the torch on the Statue of Liberty.

"Who's that?" she whispered to Hunt.

"Annabelle's mom."

The woman approached the two of them and stood in front of Hunt. "Try to dip an old woman like that and you'll have me in traction, boy."

He gave her a gentle kiss on the cheek then introduced her to Mandy, who greeted her with a warm hug. "Very nice to meet you."

"You too, dear. Now if you'll excuse me, I'm off to beat my daughter for letting this one get away." She tenderly took Mandy's hands. "You have a keeper here."

Mandy smiled back. "I know."

Again they posed for a few pictures and the woman wandered away. The music played right away again and Hunt pulled Mandy in close to him. "You almost ready to go?"

"I'm ready when you are. I don't want to rush out, though. Everyone is having such a good time. I really like your friends, Hunt."

"Well, hopefully we'll get to that one-on-one time soon. I'm sure this is a blur for you now."

"I've actually always been pretty good with names. I think I'm doing okay."

"You think so, huh?" Hunt pointed to a heavyset man talking with two women. "Who's that?"

"Jimmy. He runs the bank."

"And her over there?"

"Peggy. She runs the hair salon on First Street."

"And those two?"

"Jerry and Jerri. How could I forget a couple with the same name? Must be hell when someone calls for them."

"You are good at names."

"It's important for me." She leaned into him and he wrapped his arms around her.

"Is something bothering you? You seem a little...distracted. You sure you're okay?"

"The night is wonderful, Hunt. It's just...never mind. It's not even worth mentioning."

He leaned her back. "Anything on your mind is worth mentioning."

Mandy glanced over to Hannah.

Hunt thought she was looking for an escape to a serious conversation. "What gives, babe?"

"I'm sure it's nothing. When I was out in the truck, I thought someone might have been trying to break in."

"What?" He said it a little too loud and a few people glanced his way. He smiled and waved and pulled her back in and swayed with the music again, as if everything was fine. "What do you mean someone tried to break in? Did they see you?"

"I'm sure he didn't. He cupped his hand, looking in the window, then tried the handle. When it didn't budge he walked away. I figured it was just someone drunk and at the wrong vehicle."

"Why didn't you say something?"

"Because I didn't want to make a fuss. It was probably nothing."

"Probably, but you still should have told me. Even if it was someone with too much to drink, that's not someone I want on the road. I'm going to call Luke and get him patrolling out here just to be sure." He took her by the hand and went over to his parents.

"It's about time you gave up that pretty little thing, Hunt," his father said. "I've been waiting for my chance at a dance all night."

Mandy outstretched her hand to him. "I'm all yours, Dad."

Hunt went outside and called Luke. After he hung up, he wandered around his truck. Tracks were easy to see in the light snow, but there were too many. He removed his gun from his glove box and tucked it into the waist of his pants. While he waited for Luke to show up, he wandered around the perimeter of the parking lot and checked the service entrance side of the bar. There were a few sets of tracks going into the employee entrance, but nothing that could make him suspicious. A flash of red on the wall caught his eye and he turned around. Luke showed up and flashed his lights to let Hunt know he was there.

"Find anything?" he asked Hunt.

"I'm not seeing anything but tracks from about a hundred guests."

"How's the party?"

"Fine. Sorry you're on duty. Someone had to be."

"No sweat. I'm still afraid of your wife, man."

Hunt laughed softly. Maybe he was too hard on the kid. He'd make it a point to lighten up on him. "I'll bring her and the baby by someday and give her a chance to apologize face to face."

"No worries. If you're happy, the station is a much happier place to work."

"Will you do a few extra passes over the next hour?"

"You think it's something to worry about?"

"Probably not. But I especially don't like the fact they singled out my truck."

"Could be one of the Cadence boys. Ralph is still pissed about his car in impound."

"It was impound it or let him get behind the wheel and kill himself or someone else."

"I know that. I'm just saying he has a grudge right now. Could be him."

"Call his mom up and see if you can get a twenty on him. Otherwise we'll have to assume it was random until we have reason to think otherwise. Hang out and make your presence known for a while. Maybe that'll deter whoever it was from trying anything else."

"You got it, boss."

"Thanks, Jun—er, Deputy."

CHAPTER TWELVE

Hunt and Mandy got in after midnight. They were both amazed how Hannah had slept over the music and crowd noises. She had more than her share of attention and being passed around. Mandy was sure she'd sleep like a rock through the night. After hearing from Luke nothing else suspicious had happened, she was a little more at ease, but something about it nagged at her. She hoped she wasn't making a mistake not staying hidden. The past couple of years were something she was anxious to put behind her. A normal life with Hunt and Hannah was all that she wanted now.

Both of them too exhausted to make love for the first time since they reconnected, Mandy simply cuddled into Hunt's chest and drifted off to sleep.

It had been months since Mandy dreamed of the night of Darci's death. The nightmare haunted her again this night. This time though, after laying Darci's lifeless body on the bed, she turned around and picked up Hannah from her crib. She ran to the doorway in time to see Hunt shot in the chest and sent flying back. The 'No!' she shouted in her sleep carried into her sleeping body. She bolted awake and Hunt woke up, joining her.

"What is it?" he asked as he gripped her shoulders. She leaned into him, quaking in fear. Hunt held her tight with one arm and stroked her head with the other. His hand brushed the sweat at her scalp. "Nightmare?"

She could only nod.

"Want to talk about it?"

She now shook her head. "It was nothing."

He leaned back and held her chin. "You sure?"

She nodded again and held her cheek to his bare chest. Hunt leaned back to the bed again, bringing her with him and still holding her tight to his chest.

"Maybe I shouldn't be pushing you to talk about things. I don't want to be bringing up any bad memories and causing nightmares."

"That wasn't it, Hunt. I promise."

"Just the same. I give you permission to lay off storytelling this weekend. Let's explore the house and decide on paint colors and such."

"We really shouldn't paint until spring."

"Can't stop us from planning ahead. This dump is in dire need of a nice paint job. If you leave it to me, it'll all be white."

"No way." She cuddled tighter into him. "I'll go pick up some books from the hardware store and show you some fun color combinations."

"Anything you want, babe. I'll help paint, but you pick colors."

"Free labor?"

"Don't be ridiculous. I only paint for sexual favors."

"Deal." Mandy let out a content moan.

"You sure you're okay?"

"I'm always okay in your arms."

He stroked her back as they lay there, and they both drifted off again. Hannah woke them up at six sharp. Mandy zombie-walked to her room while Hunt went down to get coffee going. After entering the kitchen, Mandy handed Hannah to Hunt and went to the coffeepot.

"You're going to have coffee?"

"Just half a cup. It'll be all right. I can't believe I feel like I have a hangover without the fun of drinking. How are you feeling?"

"I'm fine."

"I saw you down a few shots with your friends. I thought you would have been tipsier last night."

"Tipsy? I don't get tipsy. I get good and hammered." He stood and rocked with Hannah. "And I didn't get hammered. I had to go along with the guys, but I have a pretty high tolerance."

Mandy sipped at the coffee. Hunt laughed as she pretended her knees buckled at the taste.

"Taste good?"

"You have no idea."

"How about when we're out getting paint chips, we swing by the dealership and pick you up a car. I don't like that you're out here without one."

"We're fine."

"What if something happened with Hannah while I was at work and you need to rush her in to the doctor or something?"

"I'm pretty sure you'd be here in a heartbeat if that were the case, Daddy."

"You bet your ass I would be." He pulled Mandy's hips close to his, mindful of the precious package he held. "Have I said 'I love you' today?"

"Yes. But I'll take another."

"I love you, Mrs. Blaine."

She gave him a kiss. "I love you, too. Will you hold onto her while I go shower? I really need to wake up."

"Of course, babe." An unmistakable rumpling came from Hannah's diaper.

Mandy took off running. "My timing is excellent. It's yours!"

Their weekend was uneventful by excitement standards, but Mandy was proud of what they had accomplished.

They had gone to a small used car dealership where a friend of Hunt's was the manager. Mandy picked out a small SUV. She wanted front wheel drive with the dirt roads and snow. When they were in the office with the finance manager, Hunt insisted on making the loan joint. "Your responsibilities are mine, too."

Mandy asked Hunt to step outside with her for a minute. "I thought we had this conversation already. I'm capable of taking care of some bills, Hunt."

"I know you are, but I want to do everything together from here on out."

She stared at him then took his hands. "I'm not going anywhere."

"I'm not worried you are. I just get a kick out of being Mr. and Mrs. That's all."

"You sure that's all?"

"Cross my heart," he said as he made the motions.

"All right. You win again. Come Monday, we're opening a joint account and I'm transferring everything into it."

"You do what you want. I want it all out on the line. I'll have no secrets. No 'rat money' that I'll hide from you. Everything is together from now on."

Mandy smiled and pulled him back into the office. "Joint loan application please."

After they arrived home, Mandy taped up color swatches in every room. Along with the samples, she had picked up a few books on decorating and feng shui, a small decorative fountain, and tall twisted Ficus for the living room. She added a fern to the kitchen and a Wandering Jew to the bedroom.

Hunt helped by installing ceiling hooks for her. "This place needs a little life, Hunt," Mandy said as she sprayed the fern after setting it in its long macramé hanger. "I never understood people who don't like houseplants."

"I do like them, that's why I don't have them."

"Explain that logic."

"I could kill a silk plant."

She laughed hard. "I'm here for you, lover."

Again he closed the gap and held her close to him. "And I'm thankful for that every day."

As much as Hunt hated to leave for work the following Monday, life had to get back to routine. "Now that we're back on track, you going to continue your story for me? I feel like I'm reading a crime novel and had to put it aside for a few days. I'm hating this Dan character and have to know more, babe."

Mandy laughed and placed her free hand on his cheek. "My jealous husband. Dan was harmless. I hardly had to see him after that blow up in the office. Abbey made sure of it."

"Call him Craig, babe. Abbey pisses him off."

She laughed again. "At least I see you pay attention to me when I talk."

"I'm sorry. Did you say something?"

She playfully smacked his rear end. "You rotten man. Get to work already. This house doesn't clean itself while you're gone, you know."

"It always worked before."

"Well now you have a baby to consider. I don't want her having a dust bunny for a favorite pet. Now scoot. I promise I'll pick up where I left off when you get home. Any supper requests?"

"Surprise me."

After a final kiss goodbye to both of his girls, Hunt was out the door.

Amanda started her day. Things were becoming routine to her. A routine she never, in a thousand years, would have expected to accept. Cleaning house, doing laundry, feeding a baby. Her life until this point had not been the life for just anyone.

Evening gowns and fancy dinners were replaced with ones she carefully assembled due to Hunt's desire to eat healthy. Gun holsters were replaced with diaper bags. Alcoholic drinks were replaced with "nursing friendly" beverages. She should have felt strange about this, but she didn't. Searching for honesty within herself, she knew she was truly the happiest she had ever been.

She put Hannah down for her morning nap and covered her up. Staring at her sleeping baby, her thoughts went to her parents. She wished they were alive to see her. Again she regretted not making it to the funeral, but she knew dwelling on it was going to get her nowhere.

Her mind wandered to the life she led as an agent. The life she never asked for. She had been placed there by Abbey. She struggled often with wondering why she had taken the job. Did she have something to prove? And to whom? Her parents wouldn't have approved—that was a certainty. She didn't think she had a death wish, and most certainly had no one to try to impress. Mandy knew it would take a long time for Hunt to accept the fact she liked staying home and being a mom. She'd have to work hard at it to keep him convinced.

Mandy walked down to the living room and took in the room. The words Hunt said to her came to mind. *Feel free to girl the place up.* After staring at his curtains, it became clear to her where she was going to start. She dug in a few kitchen drawers, found a tape measure, and went to work. Mandy was on the last window when a car pulled into the driveway. Instinctively she reached for the small of her back, feeling for a gun. It had been almost a year since she'd worn it. Funny how old habits die hard. She knew it was silly and refused to go to her dresser drawer for it. Peering from the small window in the door, she smiled as a familiar acquaintance emerged from the car.

Anxiously she opened the front door and waited on the porch for her old boss to join her. Mandy surprised even herself when she threw her arms around his neck.

"I never thought I'd be so happy to see someone," she said as she held herself there.

Abbey laughed and returned the hug. "I have to admit, I didn't expect such a reception myself." He let go of his hug, but continued to hold her by the hands and gazed at her. "I think domestic life agrees with you. Maybe I had you all wrong."

"Don't be an ass. When I had it, I had it."

"You still have it, sweetheart. Now you just do it without the firepower."

"I almost ran for my throwaway, idiot. What are you doing showing up without calling first?" She was glad to know their banter was still there after all this time. She always could insult with the best of them.

"You going to blow away your UPS man if he doesn't make a call first?"

"If he shows up without his brown truck, you bet I am. I'm freezing my ass off. Come inside, Abbey."

He stepped in and hung his coat up.

"Can I get you anything?"

"Got coffee on?"

"I'm nursing, so no. But it's easy enough to get some going."

"Whatever is handy is fine."

"Coffee is easy. We have that cup-at-a-time thing."

"Sounds great."

"Still take it black?"

"Yes, ma'am."

After they were settled at the table, Mandy dove straight into business. "I know this isn't a social call. What's up?"

"Can't I just want to say hello?"

"No. You always have an agenda."

"I'm sorry I didn't get to the hearing."

"I didn't need you there. It was fine."

"I stood behind you. You know that. I put every effort into doing what I could to keep you clean."

"Were you suspended for long?"

"Not at all. They wanted to make sure our stories jibed. I'm sorry things turned out the way they did. That wasn't the plan. I hate how things went down with you and Gerard. I knew you hoped things would end differently."

"But it didn't, and it's long over. I don't look back anymore. My life is with Hunt now." She paused. "I have to admit, it was strange being kept from you."

"I know. That decision came from higher up. I couldn't fight them. Things already looked bad enough."

"What gives then? You here to tell me to go back into hiding, Abbey?"

"Abbey? Now you make me feel like you've switched back to work."

"You're making this about work. If it was anything else, you'd have asked about the baby."

"How is she? Daddy take a liking to her?"

"Of course." Mandy wiggled her ring. "I know I don't have to tell you anything you don't already know. You probably knew when Hunt bought the ring and house. I'm done with the service, *Craig*. Why are you here?"

"Dan's gone rogue on us."

"He what?"

"He hasn't checked in—in more than a week."

"How do you know someone didn't pop a cap in that dick's head?"

"He's out there. He's on his way here, Mandy. I can feel it."

Hannah's crying gave Mandy the escape she wanted. She didn't have a reaction to what Abbey was telling her. There was no way she'd heard that right. What would Dan want with her? After stalling with changing Hannah into a dry diaper, she made her way downstairs. Hannah would need to nurse, but hopefully she'd give Mandy a few minutes first.

Abbey stood when she came back into the kitchen. He smiled at Hannah. "She's a beauty."

"What does he want?" Mandy was no longer up to pleasantries.

"I can't say for sure. You knew him almost as well as I did. There was something not right about him though. I should have had someone on him long ago."

"Dammit." Mandy paced. "I've been out too long. I should have known…"

"Known what?"

"Someone was snooping around the other night at our reception. There was something not right about it, but I couldn't put a finger on it. It had to be him." She took a step closer toward Craig. "You think he was working with the Menuscos?"

Abbey met her gaze. "I'm not sure what to think. Something just never smelled right for a long time with this. I never told you I suspected anything wrong about him, but I was glad your whereabouts were kept secret from him."

"But it was a secret from you, too."

"It was, but they still gave me courtesy updates when I asked about you. I was worried about you, kid."

"Dammit, Abbey. Why didn't you tell me your concerns about Dan when you had the chance?"

"What chance? All this fell to shit in nothing flat and they hauled your ass off. I thought I was being overly cautious. You only just popped back up on the grid, Mandy. I didn't see you rushing to be in contact with me."

"I didn't think I had reason to. Besides, things have been moving too fast. Getting married, getting settled here." She paused and pointed at paint samples taped up. She glanced back over to him and lowered her voice. "I didn't think you cared to hear from me, anyway."

"Why would you think that?"

"We've had nothing but a professional relationship. I'm out of the agency and never going back. There was nothing to say. I guess I felt bad for letting you down, and didn't know how to approach it."

"You didn't let me down, Mandy. Things played out the only way they were going to. There's a reason these people have the positions they do and never go to jail. I was a fool for sticking you in there the way I did and thinking I could make a difference."

"We could have had them. You just wouldn't listen to me. I knew I was close."

"It was too dangerous and despite what you thought, I know the system. It wasn't enough. You should have come in."

"Darci would still be dead."

Craig sighed. "Probably. Look, I don't want to fight. I'm frustrated, and now I'm worried about you. As soon as I found you, I got on a plane. I was sure you'd just get pissed off and tell me you were a big girl and could handle yourself, but I had to come."

"I *can* handle myself, but now I have a baby to consider, dammit!" At the sound of her mother's raised voice, Hannah cried. "Shhhh, Peanut. It's okay." She turned to Abbey. "I need to nurse her."

"You want me to leave the room?"

"I've never been shy. After having a kid and the world with their hands up my koochie, I hardly give a rip. I'm warning you. Look away if you're uncomfortable."

He could only grin. "I never would have pictured you, of all people, this way."

"Well...get used to it. This is my life now."

Mandy sat down and unbuttoned her shirt only as much as she needed to. Abbey was a tough guy and all talk, but it was obvious he was embarrassed at her bare breast. He picked up his coffee and wandered to the kitchen window.

"Your husband the jealous type?"

"If he is, we haven't been together enough for it to manifest. Why?"

"Because there is a police cruiser pulling in the driveway, going a little faster than it should be."

Mandy stood, keeping the baby attached. She learned she could do more than she thought she could with a baby at her bare breast. Heading for the door, she told Abbey to sit down. "It'll be fine. He's a bear, but he's not going to rip your arms off without a good reason."

Hunt flew in the door. The look on his face was concern, not anger. He instantly relaxed when he found Mandy standing there, calmly nursing Hannah.

"Who's here?"

"Abbey."

"Craig? What's he doing here?"

"Come meet him and sit down, Hunt. I was just sort of finding that out for myself. Why are you home?"

"I was driving by on my way to a call when I saw the car in the driveway."

"Do you need to go?"

"Not right away. I need to fill out a report on some property damage probably from some young punks. It can wait."

Mandy knew how intimidating Hunt could look in uniform, but the look on Abbey's face when he stood and reached out his hand made her grin. Craig wasn't a short man, but Hunt was a good five inches taller than he was. Where Hunt was built for uniform and bullet proof vests, Craig was built for business suits. The two men shook hands firmly.

"I'd like to say I'm pleased to meet you," Hunt said, "But why do I feel like this isn't a social call you're making to my wife?"

Mandy wasn't sure whether she wanted to be flattered or upset at Hunt's use of the word 'wife.' It made Craig pause as well.

"I wish it was a social visit. I wanted to inform Amanda of the situation, then believe me I was going to bring you in on it."

"Bring me in on it? Bring me in on what? What the hell is going on?"

The sound of his voice raised disturbed Hannah again. She stopped nursing and began to cry. Hunt took her from Mandy and brought her to his chest.

"It's okay, baby girl. Shhh..." He bounced her for a moment. "She done?"

"She needs the other side."

"Go feed her, I'll talk to Craig." He gave the baby back to Mandy.

"No way, Hunt. This is about me. I'm staying." Defiantly and holding nothing back, she exposed her other breast and sat down once again with the baby. Hunt could only sigh and return his attention back to Abbey, who had to quickly look away from Mandy's breasts. Not quick enough that Hunt didn't see him. Mandy was grateful Hunt let it slide.

"Have a seat," Hunt said as he pointed to a chair. Craig hustled into it as Hunt asked, "What gives?"

"One of our agents has gone rogue. We think—rather, we know, he's on his way to Vermont."

Hunt interrupted. "Is this that Dan asshole?"

Abbey's gaze went from Mandy then back to Hunt. "How do you know that?"

Hunt sat and dropped his elbows to the table then rested his head in his palms. Still looking down, he said, "Care to tell him, babe?"

She regarded Abbey again. "Hunt and I have a lot of catching up to do. I've been filling him in on...well...me. It wasn't top secret stuff. He could have read any of it in the reports. I did fill him in on a few of my clashes with Dan during the case. Don't bust my balls over it. It never occurred to me it was off limits. You know me better than that."

"I don't care what you're telling him. What bothers me is he's already pieced it together. How could it have slipped me in all this time?"

"'Cause you're not in love with her," Hunt said, looking back up at Craig. He stood and turned to Mandy. "We're not staying here. I think your instincts were right the other night. It could have been him. Go pack a bag."

"He's not chasing me out of our home."

"Wrong!" Hunt lowered himself to his knee beside her. "I'm sorry for raising my voice, but it's not just you I'm worried about." He glanced to Hannah. He didn't need to say anything else.

"I'll go pack for all of us."

Hunt turned to Abbey. "Give me what you have. Description on him, his car, everything. I'll call it in."

Mandy knew better than to fight with him about anything. Only seconds before Hunt showed up, her concern was not for herself, but for Hannah. If it were up to her, she'd stay and deal with whatever this was going to be. She didn't dare dream of risking either Hannah's life or leaving her to grow up without a mother. As she climbed the stairs, she strained to wonder what Dan could want with her other than just a grudge at how they butted heads. Even Hannah's loud belch couldn't bring the usual smile to her face.

"Why Mandy? What does this asshole want after all this time?" Hunt asked Craig Abbey. "It has to be more than the fact he used to want to date her."

"I really can't say. Something happened to the guy after a blowout of theirs. He wasn't the same at the job, and was a little too preoccupied with the case she'd been on."

"He should have been pulled from it."

"He was. I made sure he no longer had access to certain files, but something tells me he found his way in them anyway."

"No offense, but don't you think your security should have been better than that? You're the FBI, for cryin' out loud."

"It was good. That's how we knew someone was in there. If it wasn't him, whoever it was—was pretty damn good. There was never a trail."

"Why wasn't Mandy notified before now?"

"I didn't think it was an issue before now. Keep in mind she only popped back up on the grid when she booked the movers. I wasn't worried about her when she was in relocation. A memo showed up on my desk this morning. My concern was about Dan immediately. When I couldn't get ahold of him, I panicked, so here I am. I'm hoping like hell I'm wrong, but my gut says otherwise. Maybe something is going down in Vermont again and he took off without telling me. I'm not willing to take the chance with her. I trusted the higher-ups and let them keep her location a secret from even me but dammit, they shouldn't have dropped their guard just because the trial was over."

"Look, I don't mean to tell you how to run things—"

"Then don't. This isn't a pissing contest. I'm not turning this into a 'who loves her more' fight, either. I feel responsible for her safety and I'm entrusting that to you. Get her the hell away from here. I don't care where you go. I'll get a man at your office if they'll be hurting with you gone."

"I can get it covered," Hunt said, curtly.

"Look. I'm not trying to tread on your toes here, Jack."

"Jack? I suppose that's better than Barney."

"Barney?"

"Never mind. I don't care about anything but Mandy and Hannah right now. I'll cooperate with you, but there are no guarantees what I'll do if someone threatens them in any way."

"Not that you need it, but you'll have our full support. I have clean phones in my car. Don't tell me where you're heading, just call me when you get there. Go where no one can connect the place to you or her."

"I'm not new here."

Abbey ran his hand down his face in obvious frustration. "I know. Go see if you can help her pack. I'll breathe easier the sooner you two are on your way. I'll go get those phones."

Mandy went downstairs and couldn't find Craig anywhere. Hunt told her he was going to the car to get them their phones. She stepped out on the porch to look for him, but was instead greeted with a pinch at her neck. A familiar face held her focus right before her world went black.

As Craig's car drove away, Hunt hated to admit he was glad. He knew he was being rude, but he hated the "higher up" agencies. Everyone with initials on their badge, instead of a county name, thought they were better than a small town police department. Hunt had yet to have a decent experience with any of them. After he finished packing, he picked up Hannah then his and Mandy's bags with his free hand, and went downstairs. He'd have to go back up for the diaper bag and Hannah's clothes, but he didn't feel safe even leaving her alone for a minute.

Hunt called for Amanda as he dropped the bags by the front door. When she didn't answer he called out again. "Babe? You ready?" His heart raced when she didn't respond again. He searched the house in high gear. "Sonofa—" Glancing down at Hannah, he stopped mid cuss.

Hurrying down the porch stairs, he found Abbey in the hedge by the house. He dropped to a knee and shook him. "What the hell happened?"

"I don't know," he said groggily. "Someone hammered my skull."

"Where's Mandy, dammit?"

"I don't know." He collapsed back again. "Aw hell. I was too late." Craig Abbey passed out.

Hunt stood in an ambulance in his driveway waiting for Craig Abbey to come to. Craig finally mumbled, "What the fu—" and tried to sit up, but Hunt not so gently pushed him back down, cutting him off.

"What aren't you telling me?"

"Where's your daughter?"

"She left with my parents. I need to get her where she's safe. They're going to visit family and I'm not sure I want to tell you who."

"I don't want to know. They can't beat out of me what I don't know."

"Who?"

"I don't know, goddammit! It was just a hunch Dan would be coming here. I knew he was in love with her, but I didn't expect anything to amount to much."

"Bullshit!"

"I mean it!" Craig howled back. He placed his palms on his forehead in obvious pain.

"I'm going to ask you to leave, Hunt, if you two can't be civil," the EMT said.

"Suck it, Dave," Hunt snapped, then returned his attention back to Craig. "What's going down? I have the right to know."

Craig sighed and struggled to sit up. The EMT fussed, but Craig shooed him away. "Get me out of this thing and back in the house."

Hunt's radio squealed. "You there, Sheriff?" Roy asked. Hunt pushed the button on the mic on his shoulder. "What do you have, Roy?"

"A whole lot of nothing. I covered what I could as fast as I could, but no cars even remotely close to matching the description you gave me have gone by anyone I've talked to."

"What about Luke?"

There was a brief silence. "He ain't checkin' in again, boss." Hunt's attention returned to Craig. His nostrils flared. "What the hell is going on? Luke's in on this, too?"

"That's our suspicion."

Hunt landed a punch square on Craig's chin. Craig flew back on the gurney, but Hunt immediately pulled him to his feet. He pulled him by one arm and dragged him off of the ambulance.

"Careful, Sheriff. He may have a concussion," the EMT said.

"If he starts puking, I'll know. And guess what? I don't particularly give a shit. Now get the hell outta here."

The radio squealed again. "Hunt? You want me to call it into the state boys?"

"Call everyone, goddammit. Deputize everyone who has a hard-on for your job and get them out there looking."

"Ten-four."

CHAPTER THIRTEEN

Hunt placed some ice in a Ziploc bag and tossed it on the table. It slid toward Craig and he picked it up. "For my head or my chin?"

"I don't give a shit. Why the hell did we not have this discussion sooner? How could you wait till the bastard was on my front porch before you showed up?"

"We just put it together. We finally had him in the ops room on a laptop looking her up. Someone was helping the guy with the codes. He's not that good on a computer."

"I don't care what his computer skills are. Where'd he take my wife?"

"I don't know where he'll go from here. He can't be stupid enough to go back to the cabin. Maybe there's another we weren't aware of."

"Don't you have a tracking system in your car?"

"Of course."

Hunt tossed him the portable phone. "Call it in."

"Shit," Craig said as he dialed his office. "I should have thought of this an hour ago. I'm not even going to use the excuse of my head injury." He pounded on the table as he waited to be patched through. "Dan will know. I'm sure he's already ditched it."

"At least it'll give us a direction to head in. Put a trace on his phone while you're at it."

"I'll try, but he's sure to have a clean one as well."

Hunt went upstairs to change out of his uniform while Craig made the calls. "Well?" Hunt asked when he came back down.

"My car was ditched on highway twelve a few miles out. Nothing has been reported stolen, and his car was found not too far out of St. Ann's."

Hunt picked up a duffle bag he had by the door. He had packed it while Craig was loaded into the ambulance and being checked out.

"What's that?"

"A little survival kit. I know which direction they are headed, anyway."

"I'm going with you."

"No, you're not."

Craig stood. "Look. This is my fault she's in this situation. I'm going."

"Because you recruited her?"

"Because I was too much of a jackass to not see the signs. I'm going with you. I'll tell you what I know on the way."

Hunt hesitated for a moment before he said, "I'll let you. But if you get in my way, I'll kill you."

"Fair enough."

Mandy woke up in the trunk of a car. She was pissed off. She'd seen Dan a second after the needle went in her neck. "Asshole," she grumbled. Her speech was garbled as if she were drunk. She felt that way, too. Whatever he used was going to take a while to wear off. Not having a clue where he could be taking her, she tried to pay attention to the only thing she could. The roads. The one they currently traveled on was smooth enough; they weren't on any dirt county roads, that much she could tell for sure. Not that it was any help to her.

Her hands were bound together behind her back, but her legs were free. The trunk was almost pitch black. She scooted back and felt around for the corner. When she found it, she peeled away the backing for the taillight. When it was free, she adjusted herself and immediately kicked at it.

"Knock it off back there," was shouted from the front of the car, but she refused to stop. She broke through the light and cried out at cutting her leg on the plastic shards. The car immediately pulled over. Within seconds the trunk was opened and she was blinded by the bright light. She was immediately punched hard in the chin and knocked out cold again.

Mandy came to as she was being carried into a cabin, flung over a shoulder she could only assume was Dan's.

She finally was able to form words as he carried her down a long hallway. "What the hell do you want, Dan?"

"A piece of your ass would be nice."

"You went through all this trouble just to rape me?"

He dropped her down on a bed then straddled her. She struggled as he ground himself against her. He slapped her hard.

"Don't have such an ego, Amanda. Even if I wanted to, I couldn't."

"Impotent? I thought as much." He slapped her again.

"Menusco has bigger plans for you than that."

"Menusco? You're the fucking stoolie Willy reported to?"

"Not as dumb as you thought, huh, hotshot?"

"You're right. Dumber."

He raised his hand to slap her again, but didn't. He held her chin in his hand and gazed at her. After a minute, he moved his hand down to her breast. "That's right. Maybe I should suckle on these babies and see what the fuss is all about."

She spit in his face. He followed through with his last slap after all. Removing duct tape from a drawer, he bound her legs together. He took out a pocket knife and cut the tie he had on her hands then taped them one at a time to the bed post. She gave him a good struggle, but he won in the end.

"Bastard. You fucking rotten, double agent bastard."

He gave her breast another squeeze and blew her a kiss. "Rest well, love. You're going to need it."

An hour passed and no one entered the room. Mandy stopped struggling with her bindings and put her mind to work.

Events were falling into place as she lay there, trying to piece together all the things that had gone wrong, and why, during her days with Vince and his gang. Vince Menusco had Dan on the inside—that's how he'd always stayed just a step ahead of her. Every time she thought she'd gotten close to a bust big enough to lock him up for good, something always happened to blotch it up. She'd gotten really close once. The night Darci was killed. Now it made even more sense. She wished she could kill Gerard all over again.

"So," Hunt said when they were on their way. "Any chance you can fill in some blanks for me?"

"About what?"

"Anything and everything. Mandy was filling me in on things, but she just got to the part where they hired her on for bigger and better things and she found out dickhead was a part of it."

"Gerard was smooth. He certainly wasn't on any watch list of ours."

"You had to know he was Vince Menusco's lawyer. That didn't arouse suspicion?"

"Oh, don't get me wrong. There was plenty of suspicion, but nothing to go on. We knew once she started dating him, it would come out. We couldn't tell her we even knew that much about the guy. He would have known she was only pretending to not know who he was. That's why we used her. We couldn't have someone who knew everything about the case. Those guys can smell a fed from a mile away."

"So, you set her up."

"Not how you think. We hoped she'd get in on her own, and she did. We had no idea she'd up and marry one of them."

"But you allowed it."

"What choice did I have? She's the one who insisted it was such a great deal. It sort of was. We kept as close of an eye on her as we could."

"You had your own man, so to speak, followed?"

"She was under surveillance and she knew it. We looked out for her. It's not like we bugged her bedroom to hear them goin' at it. Sorry."

"Her past that concerns him doesn't bother me. It's the past that's biting her in the ass right now that does. How long did you know Luke was involved?"

"He only just got involved. Your boy became greedy."

"How so?"

"He contacted Menusco. Said he knew where to find her. Wanted to know if they were looking for her and if there was a reward. We intercepted a call. Dumbass used your office phone."

"That sonofabitch pipsqueak! I'll kill him!"

"I'm sure he's already taken care of. Menusco doesn't pay for information. He's accustomed to taking what he wants."

"How did you know to tap my lines? You should have let me know."

"Just a hunch. We had to cover everything we could. As soon as she came back out in the open, I wanted to watch her, Hunt. We were supposed to have backed off, but I couldn't let her go."

"That's when you caught Dan looking her up?"

"Exactly."

"You should have contacted her. Made her go back into protective custody."

"That's exactly what I was trying to do. I just wasn't fast enough."

Hunt picked up his radio. "Roy? You out there?"

After a second Roy responded. "You found something?"

"No word since the car. You at the site?"

"Just arrived. She was in the trunk. Kicked out the taillight. There's some blood, but it doesn't look bad. I almost feel sorry for the guy, Hunt." Roy had to chuckle.

Hunt couldn't bring himself to laugh with him. "She's a fighter. We do know that much."

"You want me to head north or stay with the car till you get here?"

"I won't see anything you didn't. Go ahead and head up. I want to start looking in the neighborhood of the last cabin. It's as good a place as any. Leave the car with the county boys and let the crime scene guys do their thing. I'm going to take back roads up there. Let's touch base after a bit."

"You want me to get the county boys on it ahead of us?"

"No. I don't want anybody screwing this up. We have no vehicle to go on. They have an APB on Mandy and Dan Wright. That's all they can help with for now. I want to get to this cabin and look around first before they tromp over anything that could be a clue."

"Ten-four."

"You trust that Roy?" Abbey asked once they signed off.

"With my life."

"With Mandy's?"

Hunt glared at Craig Abbey hard. "Yes."

"Then let's go."

Even without Hunt to tell the story to, the events still played out in Mandy's mind. As far as her marriage went, life was great. She never knew love could be like this. He couldn't have treated her any better if she were a princess. Loving him with everything came easy to her. Sex was fabulous. The one thing she couldn't get past was what he did for a living. Although she had yet to live any of it or really learn the extent of his involvement, she couldn't help feeling like a hypocrite.

In her mind, she tried to picture him as just the typical family lawyer. He didn't do any of the actual dirty work, or so she justified anyway. If she thought about it too much, it ate her up. The money that paid for the roof over her head came from someone else's suffering, or illegal activity. She repeatedly talked herself into the fact she was undercover. Only her love of the job and her need to get Vince Menusco behind bars got her through the times when she was hardest on herself. The things she did in a day were probably worse than anything Gerard was doing. Knowing it was for her job was still hard to justify. Witnessing the things she did and not being able to do anything about it was eating at her. Trying to hold out to seek justice when this was over with was the only thing that kept her going.

She really loved Gerard and spent more than her share of time worrying if it came down to her or him, would she really be able to put him behind bars or worse...pull the trigger. Mandy spent many days hoping it would never come to that.

When their workday ended, they truly were like any other married couple. Mandy quickly became close to Gerard's sister, Sue, and her daughter, Darci. When Gerard didn't have a fancy night out planned, they often went over so Mandy could play with the two-year-old fireball.

She grew more attached to the child than she ever planned and again second-guessed this whole situation. After things went down, she would be exposed as an agent and never again let into Darci's life. Mandy couldn't bear the thought of that. These people were becoming family and any way she sliced it, it was a mess. As the days passed, Mandy grew increasingly confused as to exactly who she was. Amanda Smith, FBI agent extraordinaire or Mandy Teluso, mob lawyer wife and hired thug for the son of the infamous Vince Menusco. She became so good at it, sometimes she even forgot which part was the act.

Not too unlike her occasional nights with the toddler, Mandy spent her days playing glorified babysitter for Angelo. Babysitting was her closest comparison to the job she held. He was in his early twenties but still behaved like a teenager.

Mandy reported to Vince's office the day after she had her talk with Abbey. The day she claimed to need to go shopping. She walked in and Vince gave her a good once over. She wore a tight black skirt and heels. Her white blouse gave little away to the imagination as far as what her bra held. She had a black blazer on as well. Vince's smile showed he approved.

"I like how you clean up," Vince said.

"Make no mistake. I can still kick in this skirt well enough to break someone's nose."

"You do have me intrigued, Amanda. You a black belt or something?"

"Maybe. Street fighting is more my forte though."

"Street fighting? You don't look the school bully type."

"Maybe I grew up in a rough neighborhood." Her tone was flat. She made sure she gave nothing away.

He opened up his desk drawer and pulled out a small handgun. Holding it up, he waved it motioning for her to come over.

Mandy strode over and took it from him. She was afraid to appear too knowledgeable, but wanted to let him know she did know how to use a gun. She released the magazine and examined it, then placed it back and set the safety.

"I'm more of a revolver kind of gal."

"I can arrange that. So…you do know your way around guns."

"I can shoot the balls off an oaf at two blocks."

Vince snickered. "So, you weren't as afraid as you appeared the other night."

"Shocked, not afraid. I was only an innocent store clerk, remember?"

"Not so innocent as you appear."

"Most people's lives aren't as simple as they appear."

"Jail time?"

"Juvie."

Vince grinned. "I'm really not sure why it is my son wants you." He eyed her up and down again. "Then again, maybe I am."

Mandy caught what his look insinuated. "I'm not here to be his toy."

"Nor do I want you to be. The boy needs guidance."

"I'm not a fucking school teacher or babysitter, Vince." She turned and headed toward his office door.

"Wait," he shouted.

She stopped and turned around.

"Come back and sit down."

Mandy did as she was asked. "Look...I have to admit. This is creeping me out. I was just a clerk and you know I'm capable of more, but maybe that's all I want to be right now. Sure, I put on a tough act, but I don't know what you want from me."

"My son doesn't believe he needs a bodyguard, but I say otherwise."

"Bodyguard? You want me to be his bodyguard?"

"You're not the only one but yes, a bodyguard in every sense of the word. I can't send him alone on his...meetings. And as you witnessed two nights ago, there are men out there he...shall we say, doesn't play nicely with."

"Excuse my ignorance, but you don't know me from Adam. What makes you think I'll take a bullet for your son?"

"I have two grand a week that says you will."

"Two grand a week? Who the hell do I need to kill for that?"

"Hopefully no one. Unless provoked."

"And when I am?"

"That's when your husband comes in handy."

Feeling the conversation now called for some pacing, Mandy stood and walked to the window. When she reached it, Angelo entered the room. She spun around as his jaw dropped at the sight of her.

"Pick up your chin, kid," she said as she crossed her arms. "Your father and I are negotiating."

"Negotiating?" Angelo said as he turned to his father. "I want her."

"Just because she knows a little judo bullshit and takes out a couple of young punks doesn't mean she's good enough to take care of you, Angelo."

"I don't need taking care of, dammit. I've been trying to tell you this for years. If you're going to insist I have a fucking babysitter, at least give me the one with a personality."

"She's a woman, for crying out loud. You think when push comes to shove she can take it?"

Mandy marched over and interrupted. "A woman? Bring in your best goon, Vince, and let's see who gets the job done."

As if on cue, one barged through the door. He was almost too stereotypical of the word 'goon.' He was tall, over-muscled, and a least five cans short of a six pack in the brains department. It was obvious his nose had been broken more than once. Amanda had seen him around. His name was Bennett.

"You wanted to see me, boss?" he said with a cheek full of chewing tobacco. He had a mouthful every time Mandy ran into him, but she wasn't sure whether to blame his slurred speech on that or his lack of education. She imagined it peaked somewhere around eighth grade.

"Right on time, Bennett. We were just discussing you." He turned to Angelo. "If your mother were here, she'd have my hide for hiring her."

"Well Mom's not here. Is she?"

Vince let out a long sigh. "I could never tell either one of you no."

"Give her a chance. No offense, Bennett, but you're fired."

"Fired?" He raised his eyebrows at Vince, confused.

"Reassigned," Vince said to him. He turned back to his son. "Get out of here. You have business to conduct. Take your new toy with you."

Mandy gave him a glare, but figured she shouldn't push it too much. Vince liked a little bit of a fight, but she was sure having someone "off her" if she pushed it too far wasn't beyond him, either.

True to his young-adult manhood, Angelo made an advance on Mandy in the limo on that very first day.

"Your father hired me to keep an eye on you, Angelo. Don't complicate things."

"What's to complicate? You're to do as I say."

"I go where you want to go and get you out alive. I'm not paid to be your whore."

"You're paid better than a whore. I should get the full service treatment here." He ran his hand up her thigh and she promptly grasped it and had it twisted behind his back before he could blink.

"That will be the last time you touch me. *Capiche*?"

He mumbled out a yes. She let go and he rubbed his shoulder. "I got you this job."

"I got me this job kicking the shit out of men you couldn't. Now stop acting like a spoiled brat and let's stick to business."

"You going to tell Gerard?"

"Why? So he can kill you? That would put me out of a job and a husband after your dad has him killed for killing you. Let's keep this between us. But if you try anything like that again, it's not my husband you'll be worrying about."

Mandy wrote it off as more of a test than anything else. She knew enough to know to watch her back and her mouth. You didn't do or say anything you didn't want to get back to the boss.

The limo came to a stop in twenty minutes. Angelo went to get out and Mandy stopped him. "I'll get out first."

"I don't think so."

"Look. Get rid of the attitude, will you? You made a pass, it's out of your system, now let's move on."

"Just hang back and let me work."

She held him by the arm again. "What is your problem? I thought you wanted me with you?"

"I didn't want that dick Bennett on my ass anymore."

"So you pulled me out of the thin air, begging daddy for a broad instead, hoping to bang her in between jobs?"

Angelo slumped back in the seat. "No. I'm sorry. That wasn't my intention."

"Then get over yourself." Mandy was worried she had been a little harsh. She placed her hand on his. "Look. I don't imagine there are too many women in this line of work."

"You have that right."

"But there will be a benefit to that."

"If this were high school, I'd be picked on for having a nanny."

"But this isn't high school, and I refuse to play the part of your whore. I'm not going to wait in the car while you do what you need to do. I intend to do my job."

"I don't know what you're going to expect for any kind of respect. I'm not taking you for mall outings. These guys mean business."

"And I fully expect to get my hands dirty."

"Do you have an idea what you're getting into?"

"I have an idea."

"We'll see about that." Angelo opened up the door and they climbed out.

Mandy held herself tall and proud as she kept beside him. She refused to let him get a pace ahead of her. She had to establish herself and she had to do it immediately.

They walked through the empty warehouse and into a back office. It was smoke filled and smelled of both cigars and cigarettes. Everyone was silent as she and Angelo came through the door. One man reached for his gun. She knew him from photos. He was William Dougherty. "Willy the Face" was his street name. He had either acquired the name because he was strikingly handsome or because of the scar on the length of his left cheek.

"Knock it off, Face. She's cool."

Willy eyed her up and down. "Cool? I'd say she's downright hot. Daddy buy you a new toy?"

"Strictly professional."

"New nanny?"

"Screw you. You and her in a ring? You don't want to guess who my money would be on."

"Bullshit." A cough followed the outburst from a man who stood closest to Mandy. He took a step toward her and reached up with his hand like he was going to brush her breast with the back of it. Before he even blinked, Mandy had his hand behind his back then had him flat on the floor with her knee pressed in it.

All the other men laughed. Mandy held her hand out to shut them up. "This will be the last time I need to tell you boys how serious I am." She shoved off of the man and stood back up, taking her place by Angelo's side.

Willy stood and approached Mandy. "You handle a gun like you do an arm?"

She removed the revolver from the back of her skirt band and shot an old dusty bowling trophy sitting on an even older file cabinet in the corner.

Two of the men pulled their guns and held them at her. It was Willy's turn to hold up his hands in protest. "Cool it.

She's all right." He reached out and took her hand, then greeted her with a kiss to each cheek. "Welcome to the family. You have a name?"

"Mandy."

He addressed the men. "Beat it. All of you." The four men left, not without giving Mandy a good once over. This was a little more than the low-cut blouse glance she received when she walked in. This was with a respectful nod. Except for the last man. The one she had pinned on the floor. His face was slightly crimson and he wouldn't look her way.

"I want no grief on her, Gunner. You understand me?"

He nodded as he pulled the door shut behind him.

Once the door closed, Willy leaned back on the desk. "I got no problem with the broad. You here to deal or what?"

Mandy was worried at first that her position with Angelo wouldn't allow her to see as much as she needed to build an effective case against Vince Menusco. She was proven wrong almost immediately. The money laundering and drug dealing that went on daily at Angelo's regular stops would be enough to incriminate him. The "family business" ran like a finely oiled machine. Angelo had business lunches daily and was well respected for his age.

Word spread about Mandy like wildfire. Somewhere along the line, rumors of her breaking a finger or two milled in with the truths. She didn't put it past herself to do it if she had to. Despite having to keep a "tough bitch" persona, things really ran smoothly from her standpoint.

She was sure Angelo's tomcat reputation rang true on his nights out, but that was when he was someone else's problem. Going home and getting to play housewife to Gerard was her time. Technically she was still on FBI time, but Gerard never talked about work. That worked out great for her. She couldn't have a case on him if he didn't talk. He would ask about her day, but she usually shrugged it off. "I didn't have to kill anyone. It was a good day."

CHAPTER FOURTEEN

As the weeks passed, Amanda found herself getting close to Angelo. She was having second thoughts about this particular assignment, as if she didn't already worry about things enough. With the time she and Angelo shared together, it was hard to not start to feel "motherly" toward him, despite their ages not being that far apart. She knew that was only going to create problems within the FBI, worse than her being married to Gerard. In him, she saw a misguided boy, not a future mob boss.

It wasn't hard for her to see past what he did and still find the "good kid" that was in there somewhere. Being who he was commanded respect. That left very little 'dirty work' directly placed in his hands. Again Mandy found herself convincing herself of what she wanted to believe. This was not good.

She was told the story of Angelo's mother early on from Gerard. She had died of cancer when he was nine and he had never gotten over it. He tried to hold up a tough exterior, but Mandy saw right through it. His father didn't try to make up for the missing parent. The extent of his consoling was saying, "Suck it up. You're a man. People we love tend to die in this business. You're lucky she went under a doctor's care and in very little pain."

"All my dad's money couldn't do shit for her." Angelo all but cried in his drink. He had gone missing one night. After a search of every possible bar, he was found where he wasn't expected, her apartment.

"I know today is the anniversary of her death, Angelo. I'm sorry, but you can't stay here."

"It was payback. I know it was. For the evil my dad has done. God took it out on my mom to punish him."

"I really think if there's a God, he wouldn't run things that way."

"What do you mean, 'If there's a God?'"

"I'm just saying, I can't believe there is some almighty force out there, whose job it is to punish us or those we love for wrongs we did. I took a lot of classes that covered the crusades and biblical wars. I'm sickened to think of the deaths caused by the hands of man because another man doesn't believe in the same god as he does. I don't tend to do the whole organized religion thing."

Angelo pulled out his cross pendant that was tucked into his shirt and held it up. "I have to believe there is something better after this. I want to know my mom will be at the pearly gates, waiting for me when dad crosses the wrong bastard and I take one to the head."

"You need to believe what will work for you. Whatever it is that helps you sleep at night."

"And what helps you sleep at night, Amanda?" Angelo took a few steps closer to her. She didn't feel threatened. He was humbled by his sadness, not angry with her or even particularly God at the moment.

"For starters, the love of a good man. That and the fact I'm doing my part in my little corner of the world."

He laughed out loud. "Doing your part? You work for the mob. What good are you doing to better this godforsaken planet?"

"I keep you alive for one. There's good in you, Angelo. Even if you don't see it, I do. Maybe your generation will find a better way than the path your fathers have led you down."

He could only scoff as he reached for his drink.

"I don't expect you to understand my thoughts on it." She marched over and took his arm. "We need to get you home. Your father is worried sick."

Violently he pulled his arm free, accidently hitting her in the process. It was then when Gerard walked in. He rushed Angelo and the two of them fell through the coffee table, breaking it and knocking Angelo out.

"What did you do that for?" Mandy screamed.

"He hit you!"

"He didn't mean to. He's drunk and upset."

"Didn't mean to? Holy shit, Mandy. You are the ultimate enabler."

"It was an accident, Gerard. I swear. It's as much my fault as his. Today is—"

"The anniversary of his mother's death. I know. We go through this every year. Just why he came here instead of his usual whores and watering holes is beyond me."

"For some odd reason he likes me. That's why, you asshole." She went to Angelo's side and tried to get him up. Gerard gave in and helped her. The two of them laid him on his back on the couch. Mandy covered him with a blanket after making sure he had no damage done. He was probably more passed out than knocked out.

"Likes you? Like how?" Gerard asked, demanding an answer.

"Like a big sister. Like a mother. Dammit, Gerard. He's my boss's son. You think we're fooling around?"

"No, but I think he wants to."

"It's not like that."

"So he didn't run his arm up your thigh in the limo?"

She was caught off guard for a second. "That was months ago, and I handled it. He has more on his mind than pussy, for crying out loud."

"He's twenty-two. There ain't nothing on his mind but pussy, sweetheart."

Mandy stormed away and picked up the phone.

Gerard took the receiver away.

"Give it back," Mandy said. "I need to call Vince. I need to let him know he's okay. My ass is in a sling because of this little stunt. He snuck away from me. I'll never hear the end of it."

"I'll call him. You go get that little prick's stench off you."

"I beg your pardon?"

"You heard me."

Mandy slapped him and stomped away. She was grateful he knew better than to come after her. Even though he had over a hundred pounds on her, she'd kick his ass just as easily as taking out the trash. Doing a job was one thing. Making her angry was another. None had suffered her wrath so much as those that dared question her integrity.

Mandy didn't bother to come out in her robe at the commotion of Vince's men coming for Angelo. Too upset to really concentrate, she had been staring at the same page of a book for over fifteen minutes. Her mind only went to Angelo, secretly wishing she could send him away from all of this.

Gerard entered the room and she suddenly managed to pull out interest in the pages she held. He tried to pull it away, but she held firmly.

"Come on, Mandy. I'm sorry. He hit you and I went crazy."

"That's why you accused me of sleeping with him?"

"I didn't say that."

"The hell you didn't." She threw the book at the wall. "You honestly think I'm that stupid?"

"No." He took her hands in his and kissed them. "I was an asshole. It's just been a bad day, baby."

"That's no excuse." Sadness was replacing anger and tears were forming in her eyes. She was so hurt by his words, suddenly nothing else mattered. Nothing else that had gone on over the past few months registered at all. The dodging bullets, watching one of Vince's men break a store owner's finger. A dead body left for Angelo to find in a warehouse where a meeting was held. Nothing registered, only the fact that her husband was suspecting her of cheating. Strange how the littlest details brought her to tears.

He held her face and kissed her on the lips hard. "I don't doubt you. I don't. Forgive me." He kissed her lips longer, then kissed her cheeks where the tears fell. Going back to her mouth, he opened it with his tongue. She could no longer fight him.

They made love with a little added aggression that night. Hers was a hint of "I'm still angry, but I want you" while his had the passion of "I'll never suspect you unfairly again." When they were done, Gerard removed a box from his pants pocket.

"I knew I'd need this today," he said as he opened up the box, revealing a two carat weight diamond tennis bracelet.

"Why did you get me a gift?"

"Because I love you. Because you deserve it. And because I don't deserve you."

"It's a bit flashy."

"It suits you. My remarkably gorgeous wife deserves equally beautiful things."

"I don't want things. I want you."

"You'll have both and like it. Say you'll stay with me always, Amanda."

She swallowed hard before saying, "I will." She really meant it. Even if it meant waiting for him while he did jail time...because of her.

The next morning when Mandy went to Vince's apartment to get Angelo, she was escorted into the den.

"What's wrong?" she asked the butler.

"The young master isn't quite... how shall I put it? Up to snuff this morning."

"Has the mother of all hangovers?"

"I've seen worse. He'll be out shortly." He nodded and left. It amazed her a 'gentleman's gentleman' worked for a man like Vince. She guessed if you had enough money, you could get anyone to fetch your bedroom slippers and kiss your ass.

Angelo came out looking like death. He was still in a robe and his hair was untouched. He was drinking what had to be a Bloody Mary.

"Hangover cure?"

"I'll know soon enough."

"I'm sorry about Gerard last night."

"Don't need to apologize. I know what he thought."

"I'm still sorry."

"Because you really are? Or because you're afraid of my father?"

"Dammit, Angelo. I don't give a rat's ass about what your father thinks. Fire me yourself if you want. I'm sorry because you didn't deserve what Gerard did."

"I'm sure I did at some time, on some level."

"Come again?"

"I made a pass at you before. I guess it's catching up with me. That's all."

She took his hand and sat with him on the couch. "I know you didn't mean what you did."

"Why do you think that?"

"We don't have that kind of relationship. I'm not as stupid as you think."

"I don't think you're stupid at all."

"Now who's full of shit? You wanted to see where my loyalties were. You figured if I took you up on your pass, I was yours and not your father's. You didn't want to sleep with me, you just wanted to know if you could."

"Maybe. You didn't sleep with me, but I still want to know."

"Know what?"

"Is your loyalty to me or my father?"

"Aren't you on the same team, Angelo? This is silly."

"You're not answering my question. If both of us were drowning, who would you save?"

Mandy stood in a huff. "What are you? Six? Knock off the shit and get dressed. You have work to do."

Angelo held her by the arm. "I need to know, Amanda. You were right. Okay? I don't want to sleep with you. Not that I'd kick you out of my bed on a cold night or anything. But Gerard has been like a brother to me, and I won't mess with what's his. My dad has half of New York kissing his ass and bending over backward for him. When he says jump they ask—"

"How high."

"Exactly. I want to know—no, I *need* to know who you belong to."

"Who's my daddy?" she asked with a grin.

He smiled back. "Besides Gerard."

She placed a hand on one cheek and kissed the other. "I'd drown saving you both. Now go get dressed."

His smile faded and he left the room. Mandy felt horrible lying to him, but she knew better than to fall for something as simple as that. She knew he meant it with all his heart and that he wasn't setting her up with a bug in the room. This wasn't another test. The kid needed to know. She wished she could tell him. Leaving the room, she returned to the limo to wait for him.

Angelo was downstairs in fifteen minutes. His face didn't look much better, but at least he was dressed. Mandy couldn't tell if he was angry or just sad. He sat next to her and opened up his hand. He picked up the long chain and let the pendant dangle in front of her.

"What's this?"

"A locket."

"I can see that. Why are you giving it to me?"

"Because I want to say thank you."

"Angelo...you don't need to buy me presents for doing my job. As a matter of fact, I'd prefer if you didn't."

"I cleared this with Gerard long ago. I was going to give it to you for your birthday, but I don't want to wait. Open it."

Mandy took the locket from him and opened it. She squealed when a picture of Gerard's niece smiled back at her. "It's Darci!"

"I know how much you love her. You spend more time with her in her room at parties than you do with the adults."

"She's more mature than most of the adults."

"Touché," he said with a laugh. "Are we cool?"

"Of course we're cool. You really shouldn't have done this."

"It was for selfish reasons, too. Look at the design."

She closed the locket and flipped it over. "A cross? Why?"

"Because I think your take on religion sucks. I'd feel better if you at least wore a cross."

"You'd rather me wear a cross and be a hypocrite than voice my opinion?"

"I'd feel better thinking you were looked after. If you don't know any better than to pray for yourself, you'll know I am." Mandy could only stare at the pendant as it dangled in front of her. "If you won't wear it, I'll go buy you a St. Christopher."

"No. This is nice. It has Darci in it. Of course I'll wear it. Thank you, Angelo. I'm just confused. We only had this conversation last night."

"You think my father doesn't have twenty-four hour access to a jewelry store?"

She laughed. "I suppose you're right. I didn't think you were very coherent last night. I never would have thought you paid attention to what I said with such detail."

"I always listen to you, Amanda. I'm beginning to think if it were you and my dad in a pool, I wouldn't have the trouble you would, deciding who to save first."

She placed her hand on his. "You can't ask me to voice what I really feel on this matter again, Angelo. You know I can't."

"I know. I can tell when you're lying too, you know." He grinned.

"Can we get on with this day? People to maim and all."

"Yes, ma'am."

When Gerard arrived at home, Mandy was a little nervous about showing him the necklace. He walked right over to her and gave her a big kiss hello, as if he were still apologizing for last night. After rocking with her for a few moments, he leaned back and picked up the pendant.

Mandy immediately blurted out. "He said he talked to you."

He gave her a kiss on the nose. "He did. No worries, *mi amore*. I like that the little shit put some thought into something for a change."

"He's a better kid than you give him credit for."

"You don't need to defend him. I've been around him since he was in diapers. He'll always be a snot nosed brat to me."

"Even when he's running the show someday?"

"When he earns my respect, he'll have it. I'm really not looking for a fight about Angelo tonight. I know what your relationship is with him and that you can separate personal and business feelings." He grinned as he kissed her again.

"What?"

"I think it's funny the boy got you to wear a cross."

"It happens to be on the back of a locket pendant with a picture of my niece."

"The cross is the front, baby." He chuckled through his words.

"I don't care. I like it this way."

"Can I take you out tonight?"

"I'd rather stay home if you don't mind."

"I sort of do. I promised Eddie we'd hook up at the Black Oyster."

"So, it is work. You don't just want to take me out." She pretended to pout, not really being upset. Mandy didn't mind the fancy dinners. But even if she didn't feel like it, she definitely couldn't pass up a work opportunity to play wife. Work being the FBI. She had to try hard to keep that straight in her head.

Gerard gave her a playful pat. "The limo is waiting. Go get something nice on."

"I know. Underwear optional."

"That's my girl."

"You could have called me," she said as she hurried into her room to change.

"I was just given notice myself. Things are going strange with the Face. Eddie is talking about smokin' him and not waiting for the shipment."

Mandy came out holding her dress. "They're going to kill him? Before you get the goods? Where does that make sense?"

"Vince smells a rat in the organization and wants Willy taken care of."

"Why do you think it's him?"

"We're not sure, but whoever it is needs to get the message."

"This isn't right, Gerard."

"Since when do you give a rip about one of our connections? You don't deal with Willy."

"I do too. Angelo and he seem almost like friends."

"There are no friends in this business. You know better than that."

"I mean it, Gerard. Don't let Eddie jump into this. Willy isn't the rat."

He took a few steps toward her. "You know who it is?"

"No. Of course not. I didn't even know there was one. Are you even sure there is?" She fumbled badly and had to recover fast.

"Been suspecting it for a while."

"But you're not sure."

"Things aren't adding up."

"You can't take it out on Willy!" Mandy dropped her dress and pounded her hands into his chest to make her point be heard.

"Hey. Knock it off, baby," he said as he held her hands. "Why do you care?"

"Because there is no fine line between killing someone to make a point and just plain killing someone innocent. I don't care what Vince thinks about this. I'm not letting you do it."

"I think you have me mistaken with someone who cares."

"Dammit, Gerard. You know we're on the same side, don't you? Willy and Angelo have ties you can't snuff out."

"Says who?"

"Says me, goddammit. Now you're messing with my side of things. We've kind of had this agreement of sticking to our own turf, so to speak. But right now, you're messing around in mine. You can't do this. We need him."

"You want to tell me why?"

"Willy handles the stores on the east. There are punks there I don't even want to deal with. He's proving himself to be invaluable to us. He isn't a rat, Gerard. So help me God I'll drive to Vince right now and shoot him in the leg for even thinking about it."

"You're getting a little emotional here."

"No emotions at all. Just business. Vince put me with Angelo, and I know my boys. You'd be making a mistake."

"And you'll put your ass on the line and say so?"

"To whoever you want. I don't know what you're suspecting, but if you think there is a rat, give me the info. I'll flush it out and take care of it myself if I have to. You can't keep me in the dark about crap like this, Gerard. We're supposed to be a team."

He tucked a strand of hair behind her ear. "My little toughie. You beat up a couple of thugs and now you're ready to kill someone. My little girl is all grown up." He pretended to sniff and she smacked his arm. "Angelo said you kick ass at the range."

"Yeah, well...I'd do even better if there were a set of balls at the crotch of the target."

He laughed. "I can handle the dinner if you want to stay home."

"I really don't feel like it now. If you promise you'll talk him out of it, I'd like to run an errand and maybe go see Darci instead. That sounds like more fun. She'll love my new necklace." She wrapped her arms around his neck. "Is it really all right?"

"Go play with my niece. She'd like that. I'll handle dinner and I promise you, Willy is off limits for now. But if he even sneezes in the wrong direction, I can't make any promises."

"I'll find your rat if one exists. I promise you. You go share the news and bring me back a Bailey's cheesecake."

"Will do." He gave her a kiss and said goodbye. Mandy hurried up and dressed. She knew it was risky, but she had to talk to Abbey about this. Were they on to her? Was this just a setup? Was Gerard telling her this to see if she'd crack? This couldn't be good.

"Are you sure it's safe to be calling?" Abbey asked in response to Mandy's, "Hey, it's me."

"I'm at a payphone at the mall. It's okay."

"What brings you out tonight? Shouldn't you be home sleeping info out of your husband?"

"I acquired info without sleeping with him, you dick. I gave up a meeting with Gerard and Eddie tonight to come talk to you."

"A meeting with Eddie? You should have been there."

"I already know what it's about."

"And..."

"They want to snuff out Willy. They think he's a snitch."

"Willy? Why the Face?"

"I don't know. Is there something you're hiding from me? I haven't done anything to make them suspect a snitch. You have someone else working this from the inside?"

"I don't, Amanda. We're too careful with you to add someone else in the mix. The whole 'too many cooks' thing. I don't like this. Maybe we need to take you out of this until things calm down."

"Take me out of this? How is that possible? You suggesting I leave my husband and tell him I want a divorce because I'm a federal agent, and by the way, watch your ass?"

"You obviously didn't think that one through. Don't go having a hissy fit now. Where do you think this will go?"

"I can't even think of that right now."

"You going double standards on me? When I swore you in, you took an oath to uphold the law."

"When I got married, I took an oath to love, honor and cherish. He's not the monster you think."

"A lawyer is bad enough. A mob lawyer certainly doesn't pull any heart strings with me. Even if he is great in bed."

"Oh shut the fuck up, Abbey. How many times are we going to have this conversation?"

"Look, just watch your back. Do what you need to get in deeper. I want to wrap this up. You need to spend more time with Menusco and less with his son. If we're going to nail him good, you need more one-on-one with him."

"I'm working my way there. It's not easy. Vince keeps Angelo on his own jobs."

"I'm not bringing him in on the pittance you've shared. Your husband will only have him out in no time. There's not enough to hold Angelo either, even to try to cut a deal with Menusco."

"I won't allow you to bring Angelo in, anyway."

"Won't allow? I think you're getting the wrong idea here, Mandy. You work for me. You're getting too close to the situation. You do as you're told and gather info, and we take it from there. If I tell you to shoot Vince's grandmother for jaywalking, you'd better goddamn do it!"

"Don't talk to me like that. I know my job."

"Then start acting like it. I'm the only one pulling for you here. Your ass would have been out for marrying that asshole. I had to convince them it was a good move undercover wise. So far you haven't let me down. But if you continue to make pets out of every member of the family, I can't guarantee your job or your safety, sweetheart."

"Just let me worry about me. I have it covered and I'm making progress. Don't even threaten my job on this. I've gotten more in a matter of months than you've gotten in a year. This was a good step and you know it."

"I worry about when push comes to shove."

"Let me worry about that. I have to go. Darci goes to bed in an hour."

Abbey sighed heavily. "You're getting too close, Amanda."

"I'm the right amount of close. I'll talk to you later." She hung up the phone and regarded the people around her. No one was paying attention. She hadn't been followed. So far she wasn't a suspect. Or at least it still appeared that way. She stepped into a shoe store and bought a pair of shoes she didn't need and a pretty jeweled purse for Darci because she never went over empty-handed. Maybe Abbey was right. Getting attached to the family wasn't a good plan, but she couldn't help it. She had a bond with Gerard's sister that couldn't be explained.

Oddly enough, his sister Sue had no clue what he did. As far as she knew, Gerard was a lawyer and that was the extent of it. Women weren't usually brought into the "family business." Amanda was a great exception. She had earned her way in, then married into it. If things were reversed, she probably wouldn't be where she was now. Some nights, when she couldn't sleep, she lay there wondering if she married Gerard under other circumstances, would she even be aware of what he did? They were discreet if nothing else. No wonder agencies had a hard time locking anyone up.

Mandy longed for a normal life. She really loved Gerard and his sister. Moving away from it was a pipe dream. She knew better than to tease herself to believe it could happen. The exception to the happy family picture was Sue's husband.

Lonny was an active right hand man to Vince and had, since the day she'd met him, always made the hair on her neck stand up. He was nice enough to his family when he was home, but he wouldn't be recognized as the same man at work. She couldn't understand how he shed that man at the door of his home.

He always treated Mandy as if he was suspicious of her, although she gave him no reason to do so. Lonny simply didn't trust women—especially when it came to business.

When she showed up that night, jeweled purse in hand, Lonny wasn't there. Mandy was grateful. Sue allowed Darci to stay up a little late to play with her. After she went to bed, the two women shared a glass of wine and had great conversation. Mandy missed having girlfriends around. Her last real friend was her college roommate. Sadly, they'd parted ways once school was over and never reconnected. Mandy blamed herself. Being a mob-wife left little for lasting friendships. Even with the fancy dinners and dinner parties, it didn't leave much for a social life. While the other wives pampered themselves at spas during their days, she was busy watching fingers be broken, angry disputes over territory, and dirty money exchange hands.

Sue was really the only woman she could relate with. Darci was a bonus and helped keep Mandy in check of what this was all for. Make things better for the next generation. Hugs and cuddle time with her niece helped keep Mandy's thoughts on the right track. *Get the job done. Get out. Save who you can in the process.*

Mandy arrived at home right before Gerard. He did the husbandly eye-roll at the new pair of shoes. There was something oddly normal feeling and comforting at the same time with that little gesture. Mandy allowed herself to feel 'ordinary' for just a while. As they made love, she imagined one day doing it with the hopes of making their own baby. *Someday. When this was just a bad dream.*

CHAPTER FIFTEEN

After stopping to pick up Angelo the next morning, Mandy insisted on going to see Willy before they had even gotten in the car.

"Why?" Angelo asked.

"Does your father tell you anything?"

"Enough. What is it you think I don't know?"

"How much faith do you put in Willy?"

"About as much as I put in anyone."

"Think about it, Angelo. I need to know if you trust him."

"Of course. He's never let me down before. What the hell is up?"

"Someone is complaining about a rat and Gerard mentioned his name last night."

"That's ridiculous. Willy doesn't have the brains to be a fed. Accusing him is like accusing you."

"Excuse me?"

He laughed. "I'm sorry. You know what I meant. I didn't mean it about the brains comment with you. I mean it's ridiculous."

"Well, I put my ass on the line last night, defending him. I wanted to make sure we were on the same page. I still want to go talk to him. Shake him down a little and make sure."

Angelo laughed again. "You sound funny when you try to talk tough, Amanda."

She took his arm and had it stretched behind his back in a flash. Then she pushed him against the car, not so gently. "All right," Angelo said in a half laugh, half in pain. Mandy let go and stepped back.

"Talk tough my ass. I can still whip your punk behind."

"Yeah, yeah," he said as he climbed into the limo.

They met up with Willy at a restaurant on the east side of town. When he requested that for a location, Mandy was worried she had been wrong. There wasn't a lot she could do if things went wrong and he decided to take her on in this neighborhood. But if Craig Abbey didn't claim Willy was working with them, then who was he working for?

Mandy sauntered as sensually as she could over to his table. Willy was obviously surprised at her behavior. "What's up, Mandy? You finally leaving that law book hubby of yours for your favorite boy toy?"

Not caring at all about a scene in a public restaurant, Mandy seized him by his tie and tightened it. She jerked him to his feet, knocked his chair backward, and slammed him at the closest wall. The restaurant fell silent and the owner rushed over. She held her hand at Willy's neck and turned to the owner. "I'll only be a minute. Go tend to your guests if you know what's good for you."

"But miss—"

"Go!" she shouted. She turned back to Willy. "Tell me you're not two-timing me, Willy, or so help me God, I'll kill you right here."

The owner walked away, shaking his head. He mumbled something about a lover's spat as he took the corner.

Willy could barely speak over a whisper. "What are you talking about? You're married, you stupid bitch."

It was her turn to whisper and lean in. "You want me to shout out you're a hit man on the take with the feds right here or would you rather play 'sorry I cheated on you honey?'"

His eyes went wide. "I didn't do anything. I swear!"

She took hold of his crotch. "Make me believe you."

He cried out. "I'm not! I promise!"

"I'm not convinced!"

She released her grip and pulled him by the tie into the men's room. Angelo followed.

"Mandy...I...I swear! I'm not no fed. I have no idea what you are talking about."

"Why are you being fingered?"

"By who?"

"Someone big enough that you'd be dead if the news didn't make it to me."

"I didn't do anything!"

"Who are you talking to?"

"Nobody!" He rushed over to Angelo. "Nobody. I swear! You know me, Angelo. We go too far back for me to do anything to get myself involved anywhere you don't tell me to. It's not me. If there's a rat—it's not me."

"What do you know about a rat?" Angelo asked him.

"I haven't heard anything!"

Mandy shoved him against the wall and pulled a gun out from behind her back. She pointed it at his head. "Not a peep?"

"I swear! Nothing!"

She took a step back and tucked the gun away. "I stuck up for you. I said you couldn't be involved, but I had to be sure. I'm sorry."

Willy doubled over in relief. "Sonofabitch, Mandy. If you trust me, I hate to see how you treat someone you don't."

"Don't ever cross me and you won't ever find out."

Mandy exited the bathroom and over to the table. No one else had moved. Tossing a hundred dollar bill on the table, Mandy said, "You gentlemen go buy yourself some new boxers." She headed toward the door and winked at the owner as she brushed past him. "Sorry. That time of the month, you know."

They climbed in the limo and were silent for a while. Angelo spoke first. "I thought you were going to break something."

"If I didn't believe him, I would have."

"I didn't think he was lying either. You really think there's a snitch?"

"I don't know. I don't have reason to believe there's one, but I'm never too far from you and I really don't think you're it."

Angelo chuckled. "So what now?"

"Business as usual. We keep our eyes open a little better from now on. I know Willy will be looking, too."

When Gerard came home that night, he had already been informed about what Mandy had done. Of course, the story had been exaggerated again a little by the time it reached him.

"I didn't break his nose, Gerard. I hardly touched him. I just needed him to be afraid. I wanted to clear him of suspicion. I knew it couldn't be him."

"Then why did you do it?"

"Because it was my ass if I was wrong." She cuddled up to him as they stood in the doorway. They hadn't gotten past their hello kiss when Gerard drilled her for information. "Do we have to go out tonight?"

"We really should. Vince will be there tonight. You know he likes it when we at least make a showing."

"I suppose it's not good to stand up the boss."

"We can be fashionably late, though."

"There's a thought," Mandy said with a kiss.

"So what happened exactly with Darci?" Hunt asked Craig. They were about a half an hour from their destination.

"You heard that much of the story at the cabin. Gerard accidently killed her."

"Why do I think there is more to the story?"

"You know everything Mandy knows after your last shoot out."

"And what about what she doesn't know?"

Craig glared at Hunt for a long while before he returned his attention back to the road. "I'm not sure you need to know."

"The hell I don't. This is my wife we're talking about!"

"Your wife. Think about that. Wasn't this all just a little sudden?"

"It would have happened a long time ago if I could have found her."

"You don't at all feel like you're another game piece in her big picture?"

"I'm not so sure I appreciate what you are insinuating, Abbey."

"You're a smart guy, Hunt. At least, you seemed like one before she came into your life. You think a big time FBI agent is going to settle for a small town Vermont sheriff?" "She's not FBI anymore, and things have changed. She's a mom. She doesn't want to lose Hannah the way she lost Darci. I'm not even going to sit here and listen to this shit. After she got her revenge, it was over. At least, we thought it was. If you had kept a tighter leash on your men, we wouldn't be having this conversation right now."

"That's right," Abbey said. "If things went the way they were supposed to, she'd be dead."

"What?"

"You dumb asshole. The bullet was meant for her, not the kid. He was ordered to kill her and had no problem following the order. Stupid lawyer bastard was always a lousy shot, lucky for her."

"How could he kill her? Why?"

"They found out what she was. Vince wasn't going to put up with that. He offered the job to Angelo, but the pussy couldn't do it. Gerard ended up killing his niece instead. That pretty little wife of yours is petite, but shouldn't have been mistaken for a three year old. She was too fast on returning fire. He couldn't hit her after that. His brother-in-law was an easy enough target though, the dumb oaf. I hated to lose him with what he knew, but *c'est la vie*. At least we had Mandy for the info."

"This is unbelievable. Why are they bothering kidnapping her? Why not just do a hit?"

"They need the information first."

"What information?"

"That's what we're going to find out."

"I honestly don't think they'd be dumb enough to go back to this same cabin. You have any clues on where to go when this dead ends us?"

Abbey pulled the car over and held his gun up then laughed hard. "I can't do this any longer. This is almost pathetic. You still can't smell a setup, can you?"

"You're on the take, too? What the hell is this?"

"I was almost clean and out of this, but I knew you'd mess it up, so now I'm along for the ride. Thanks a ton, shithead." Craig cracked Hunt in the side of the head with the gun and knocked him out cold.

Mandy woke up when someone brought a tray of food into her room. She recognized him and grew angrier by the second. It was Luke. Pulling at the restraints did no good. "You son of a bitch! You called me in?"

He bowed and made a sweeping motion with this hand. "At your service."

"Don't you have any loyalty to Hunt? To your badge?"

He laughed. "My badge? I'm sorry. Should I be shedding a tear here? The mob pays well, sweetheart. I'm a little surprised you lived in it the way you did and didn't break away from your so called paycheck."

"Being in the FBI wasn't about the money."

"That's right. You were paid at both ends as well as getting this one filled." He placed his hand on her crotch as he said that. She struggled until he removed his hand.

"Don't fucking touch me."

He leaned into her face. "We're more alike than you and Hunt. I like a woman with spunk. Let him keep the kid and you run away with me. I can make us disappear with what they paid me for turning you in. Add that to your stash and we'll be set for life."

"The money they paid me is in the evidence locker. I didn't keep any of it. I took what I had to just to keep my cover."

"I'm not talking about your pay. You know where Lonny has his stash. I know you do. You were the last one to see him before he was killed."

"That's what this is about? You guys captured me because you think I know where Lonny hid some money?"

"That's the rumor, anyway. I'm sure they want to pop you for your treachery 'n shit, too. Come on, Mandy." He placed his hand on her again. "What do you say? You and me. I can get us out of here."

She pretended to consider it and glanced to the door as if she was waiting for someone to walk in. Whispering, "Come here," she motioned with her head that he should come closer. When he leaned down, she head-butted him. His nose heavily streamed blood as he swore loudly. He backhanded her hard before wiping his nose on his sleeve.

"You stupid bitch!" He whipped his belt off and unzipped his pants. He climbed on her and pressed himself hard into her midsection. The door flew open.

"Get off of her!"

"Bitch probably broke my nose," Luke screamed.

"You were warned to keep your distance. Now get the hell out of here!"

Luke climbed off and stormed out the door.

Dan asked, "If I release an arm, are you going to eat or try to kick my ass?"

She didn't care for any food, but she was grateful for his timing. She wasn't about to thank him.

"Shove the plate up your ass."

"Is that any way to treat someone who saved you from being raped?"

"You're going to claim to be my hero? You probably just didn't want him soiling what you're going to do later anyway."

"I was hoping to not have to force it on you." He sat down in a chair next to her bed. "When you finally got

Gerard out of the way, I really thought you'd come to your senses."

"And what? Run to you? I can't believe no matter what line of work a man is in, what position in life he plays, he's still really only interested in one position."

"Don't be silly. I like lots of different positions."

"We worked together, for crying out loud. How was I supposed to form a romantic interest in you? I was practically in lockdown with that job. What kind of relationship do you think we could have had?"

"And when it was over...you found that sheriff."

"And when that was over, I was pregnant with his baby. I love him, Dan. Do what you will to me, but leave him and my baby alone."

"You think I'll buy that you'll pretend to stick around and be my whore? You'd kill me first chance you got."

"I would never make such a claim. You know better. Of course I'd kill you."

"Then what can you offer me?"

"What Luke wanted."

"He was trying to rape you. I thought we just covered this."

"Not that, asshole. Someone told him about Lonny's stash. He promised to set me free if I told him where it was."

"That little prick!" Dan stormed out of the room. Mandy could hear arguing immediately. A shot was fired and she jumped. Dan opened the door after a minute and stood in the doorway.

"We need to talk, Dan. Get me out of here. We can figure this out."

He fell flat to the floor. Luke walked in and stepped on Dan on his way over to her. "Nice try, sweetheart. Who's going to save you now?"

CHAPTER SIXTEEN

As Luke approached Mandy, a car door slammed. "Goddammit! Great timing, Abbey."

"Abbey? Craig is involved in this? I don't believe you."

"Believe it, sweetheart." He placed his hands on her breasts and smiled wide. "Ohhh...that's right. I'll have to come back and sample some of that later." He brushed her nipples with the back of his hands then left the room.

After listening to thuds and muffled voices, Craig's voice was loud and clear. "You what?" Within seconds, he stormed into her room. His face fell to the body on the floor. "Goddammit!" His attention returned to Mandy. "I'm really sorry, Amanda. There could have been an easier way to do this."

"Where's Hunt? What have you done with him and Hannah?"

"Your daughter is safe with Hunt's parents."

"And Hunt?" she said with a hard swallow.

"You're not serious about him, are you? Come on, Amanda. First Gerard, now him? You're an FBI agent for cryin' out loud. You had the makings of something good, and you blew it by ending up playing *woman*."

"I could have had both. If the whole damn department wasn't on the take, this would have worked and you know it. I can't believe you were behind this."

"Really? Because you took your job so seriously? After this case was over then what? Who would you fall for then? The next underdog you're supposed to watch?"

"Gerard wasn't an underdog, and neither is Hunt."

"You're going to talk sweet about the man you murdered in cold blood?"

"I went after him because of Darci, but I didn't expect to kill him. He was going to kill us if I hadn't."

"And you really think you love this sheriff? You're pathetic. I had great expectations for you, and you really let me down."

"Let you down? What were your expectations? To turn crooked like you?"

"Crooked is such a nasty word. I prefer well paid."

"I didn't think men like you could be bought. I thought you had morals."

"And I thought you had nice tits. Now they're wasted on a baby." He sat down next to her. "You should have pulled out when I asked you to. You should have left Gerard and walked away from the case like I told you to."

"You put me there to get them locked up. Did you think I wouldn't find anything out?"

"I thought throwing you in as green as you were would buy me more time. Once you were married, I didn't think you'd be able to separate your love life from your work. I figured you'd solve things and have to play dumb to me. Act like you didn't see what you were seeing to protect your husband and Angelo, who you were getting too close to as well. When you wouldn't, I asked you to walk away. And when you still wouldn't, well...you had to be removed. Unfortunately, hubby screwed that up, too."

"What do you mean?"

"Darci's death wasn't because of Lonny. You were the target, Mandy. Gerard was supposed to kill you."

Her eyes raced between his, searching for the truth. "You're lying. He was taking out Lonny."

"'Fraid not, doll face. You were the mark. I hated that he took Lonny out in the process. Great lawyer, but lousy shot. I miss Lonny."

"So, that's why Lonny always treated me like shit. He knew all along? You're a pig."

"But a rich pig."

"Where's Hunt?"

"Closer than you think. Now rest up, sweetness. I have a hell of a mess to clean up now that the kid blew Dan away."

"I see you're heartbroken over it."

"Horribly. I wanted to do it myself."

"This is unbelievable. Let Hunt go. I'll take you to Lonny's stash. What's left of it, anyway."

"What do you mean 'what's left of it?'"

"I gave some of it to Sue."

"Define 'some of it.'"

"About half."

"Half?" he screamed.

"You killed her husband and daughter. What did you want me to do? Let her sit around and wait to be killed to keep quiet?"

"You should have put her in protective custody."

"Right. So you could have killed her yourself?"

"You didn't doubt me when you were placed in custody, Mandy. Why didn't you turn her in?"

"She deserved to make that decision for herself."

"Where is she?"

"I don't know. I asked her to never let me know. I wouldn't let her life be at risk."

"Now you're lying."

"Why don't you kill me and find out? You'll never find her or the rest of the stash."

"That pleasure is for Menusco himself."

"He's coming here?"

"And your little buddy, Angelo."

"Angelo?"

"I don't think the poor little schmuck ever got over you being a fed. He really liked you. You bone him, too?"

"Our relationship wasn't like that. He's a good kid."

Abbey laughed. "For a mobster."

"He may be in the family business, but he's not the ruthless killer his father is. Or you, for that matter."

"You can paint a bat, Mandy, but it's still a blood sucking creature."

"They also pick off the pests we're better off without."

"You trying to tell me Angelo only has people killed that need killing?"

"I'm just saying...oh, forget it. I'm not getting in a morals argument with you. I wouldn't turn my back if I were you. Especially on Luke."

"I'm not stupid."

"I beg to differ. You were involved with Vince. You're as good as dead anyway. He'd just as soon kill me for being a snitch. You think he gives a shit about a couple million bucks? Get real, Abbey."

He held her face. "Sweetheart, call me Craig. How many times are we going to go over this?"

Luke joined them. "Come on. Help me with this body," he said, kicking Dan's corpse. "The other one is going to wake up soon, too. I'd rather move him while he's out."

"Who?" Mandy asked. "Hunt? Did you bring him here? Dammit, Abbey! You leave him out of this!"

"Too late, doll." They picked up Dan and left, leaving Mandy screaming to let Hunt go.

After the house was quiet, she was left with plenty of time for kicking herself about coming out of protective custody. She never dreamed the missing money of Lonny's would be traced back to her. She often questioned why Craig was kept from her through her wait for the trial. Was there someone even higher up involved in this? If so, why even bother with putting an agent in the mix in the first place? Was there someone even higher than that who could possibly still be in the dark about the double agent crap going on right under their noses?

Mandy wanted to cry at the thought of what would happen to Hunt now because of her, but anger still won the battle. There was no doubt she would be killed once Vince showed up, and she hated herself for letting this happen. She was an idiot. She never should have let herself get involved with Gerard. As much as she hated to admit it, what Craig said was right. It was only a dream and she'd behaved like a silly child. There was no way she could have led a normal life out of the mob with anyone involved. She played a terrible hand and was going to pay for it with her life. Not even Angelo could help her now. Not that he would, anyway.

Her thoughts drifted to Hannah and her tears finally found their way out. Her daughter would be an orphan. She could only hope Hunt's parents would be good to her. Mandy wished she had prayed before. What the hell. There was no better time to start.

After feeling foolish and talking to a God she wasn't sure was listening, her mind once more returned to where she could have gone wrong. Again she beat herself up for what she'd missed.

The weeks turned into months. A snitch was never brought up again. Mandy finally knew she had enough evidence logged of major drug deals, money laundering, and a place or two where a body was buried that she could send Vince Menusco to jail for good. Not even Gerard could get him out of it.

She spent many nights wondering if she could convince Gerard to leave the family. Pipe dream as it was, she wanted to tell him who she was and that she could protect him. Of course, he would have to give up evidence and the two of them would be under witness protection or be running for the rest of their lives, but to keep him, she was willing to do that.

In the back of her mind was the fact that once she told him, it would all be over. He could hate her for what she'd done and want nothing else to do with her. She wouldn't blame him if it came to that, but she couldn't bear it either.

Mandy was surprised when she didn't have to fake a headache to get out of going with Gerard that night. He said he wanted her to stay home.

"I don't like the talk going on out there right now. The streets are kind of getting crazy with the talk of this shipment. Everyone is on edge. I'd really rather you stay home, baby."

"Can't I at least go see Darci?" Talking to Abbey tonight was a must. She had to get out of the house, not being able to trust that they weren't bugged. She'd been told about this shipment today and needed to get him the information right now. This was what she had been waiting for. Mandy turned on her best begging. "I haven't seen Darci in a week. She called today wanting me to come over. Broke my heart, hon."

He sighed. "You can go. Be careful though. Take the limo. I don't want you driving yourself. I want you on full guard tonight."

"Is there something you're not telling me?"

"No. It's a gut feeling. Just for me, baby. Please?"

She gave him a reassuring kiss. "You know I can take care of myself. But I'll be careful."

As soon as Gerard left, Mandy returned to the mall to make her call. She did it from a different phone this time. You could never be too careful.

"I don't like when you have to call me unscheduled like this," Abbey said. "It worries me."

"It couldn't wait. It's going down Friday. Call everyone in."

"What's going down Friday?"

"The mother lode of all mother lode drug shipments, that's what. Vince will be there. Now is your chance. I have a few more leads and a few bodies that will get him put away for sure."

"Will Angelo be there?"

"No. Vince has him somewhere else."

"Maybe we should wait."

"What? No way! I don't have enough on Angelo. It's not going to matter that he's not there. Vince is your man. I'm telling you, Abbey. This is it."

"I just don't feel it, Amanda. I know what you have and I'm telling you, we can't move on this."

"Are you crazy?"

"I mean it. Look...just trust me, all right. Now is not the time."

"It is the perfect time. What the hell is your problem? This is what you had me here for."

Abbey paused for a long time. "I don't know how to tell you this."

"Tell me what?"

"They're...uh...pulling the plug on you."

"They're what?" Mandy screamed so loud, a few women passing quickened their pace. She put on a shy smile. "Darn car repair men trying to rip me off. Sorry." She returned her attention to the phone. "What do you mean 'pulling the plug?'"

"It's been almost a year, Mandy. The brass doesn't feel like we're getting what we need. They have been on my ass about your marriage and don't feel like when push comes to shove, you'll pull through."

"You know that's crap! I've given you everything you've ever asked for. I haven't kept Gerard clean for personal reasons, he's just that good. He's a lawyer for cryin' out loud!"

"And Angelo?"

"What about him?"

"Come on, Mandy. You're attached to the kid. You're not going to turn him in and watch him go to jail."

"I would if there were enough on him. I've given you more on him than you even had on Vince to start off with, and you didn't have enough to do an arrest a year ago. This is horseshit and you know it."

"Cut your losses and come in. You can decide what to do about your marriage, but I'm telling you. Walk now. If things are getting as heavy as you say, I don't think you're safe. Leave. Don't even pack a bag, don't even say goodbye. Just leave and leave now. Work out the details with him later."

"I'm not giving any of this up, goddammit!"

"Get here and get safe. We'll bring Gerard in and you can explain it to him. He can leave the Menuscos and stay with you and we can give him some kind of protection. If he chooses to stay...I can't make any promises."

"You can't do this to me now, Abbey! I'm telling you—this will put Vince away for good this time. You have to intercept this shipment, if nothing else. You have no idea what this is going to do to the streets. I know at least twenty—"

Abbey cut her off. "No. You listen to me. Get the hell away from there. You're done. If you are not at my office in twenty-four hours, you'll be considered rogue and placed under arrest on sight. This case is over, Mandy. Come in, dammit."

"Fuck you, Abbey." She hung up.

Mandy was too upset to see Darci, but she had already told Gerard she would be there. She picked up a pretty dress for her at her favorite toddler shop at the mall and had the driver take her to Sue and Lonny's house. Mandy was less than thrilled to see Lonny home. She'd hoped he was at the meeting with Gerard.

"Why are you here?" he barked at her.

"I thought you'd be with Gerard tonight at the meeting. I came to see Darci. She called me the other day."

He motioned to the bag she carried. "You have to bring something every time you show up?"

"I like to."

"You're turning her into a spoiled brat."

"What the hell is wrong with you?"

"Come here," he said as he pulled her into his office. He looked out to the hall one last time before he closed the door.

"What gives, Lonny?" Amanda said with a huff. She didn't appreciate the manhandling.

"I didn't know you were showing up."

"I don't usually need an invitation." She tried to walk away but he stopped her, taking hold of her arm.

"If I tell you something, you have to promise not to run to your husband about it."

"You know I can't do that. What the hell is going on?"

He ran his hand down his face in frustration. "Just keep it on the down low. Please? Give me a day. That's all I'm asking." She was skeptical and it showed. "Sue and Darci's safety depends on it."

"Now you have me worried. What the hell is going on?"

"I have them packing a bag, Mandy. We're slipping out of here tonight."

"You're leaving? Are you crazy? You're going to try to run away with the shipment money?"

"I'm not stupid. I'm not stealing anything. Things have gotten out of hand..." He nervously glanced around again. "There's talk again of an informant."

"Again? I thought we killed that rumor off long ago."

"Well...it's still there. I'm not sitting around, waiting to go to jail. I have a family to think about."

Mandy was getting more nervous by the minute. She had to play cool. "How very un-mobster of you, Lonny."

"This is no joke. You know Sue doesn't know anything. I can't let something happen to them."

"I'll keep quiet. I've got your back. I'm all for keeping them safe, I just hope I can successfully lie to my husband. I haven't done it before, and I don't want to start now. But for Sue and Darci, I'll do it."

"Thanks." Mandy was surprised when he gave her a kiss on the cheek and a big hug. "You know where my safe is. Give me twenty-four hours and tell them I called you and told you where it was. We should be deep enough in Mexico or Canada by then. From there...I don't know where we'll go."

"It'll be best if I don't know anyway. I'm going to miss the hell out of Darci though."

"Yeah well, you'd miss her more if she were dead." Lonny opened the office door and they walked out into the living room. Mandy managed a smile at Darci standing on the couch with her arms spread wide, eager to greet her.

"Auntie Mandy! You came!" Before Mandy could take a step toward her, the window shattered and Darci fell forward.

"No!" Mandy screamed and ran to her side. As she ducked down to get Darci, the window shattered again. This time, the bullets found Lonny and he dropped hard to the ground.

Sue screamed from the top of the stairs. Mandy hollered for her to get back as she rushed to the window and returned fire. She had no idea where to shoot, she knew she had to give Sue some cover.

Mandy screamed. "Get back! Sue, get back!" When the firing ceased, Mandy scooped up Darci and ran up the stairs to join her. A few shots flew in again, but Mandy escaped being hit.

After Mandy reached the second floor, hysterical tears came from Sue as she clutched her unbreathing daughter. Mandy called Gerard, more than slightly hysterical herself.

"What do you mean Darci's been hit? Calm down, baby. Tell me what's going on!"

"Darci and Lonny were shot. Someone was outside. I'm afraid to leave Sue and go check."

"I told you something was going down and you should have stayed home! Dammit! Don't you dare go outside!"

"Then hurry up!"

"Give me fifteen minutes. Shoot anyone who walks in there between now and then."

"I'm sure the driver was killed, too, or he would have come in at the commotion. There was no silencer. Aw shit..."

"What?"

"I hear the cops."

"Just sit tight. You can talk your way through this."

"I know but, dammit. Just hurry."

"I will, baby."

Gerard slid his phone in his pocket as he ran back to the car. Vince was waiting inside. "Well, fuck me."

"What?"

"I just killed Darci."

"You what?"

"Shit! I thought it was Mandy. Took out Lonny, too. Bitch was too fast. He had it coming for wanting to split, anyway."

"You stupid sonofabitch. He has the drop money!"

"Why does he have it?"

"He set it up. Dammit! You'd better find it now, or I'll have you buried next to him."

Gerard started the car. "Don't worry about it. We have to do a few loops. I told her I'd be there in fifteen minutes." The police car screeched to a halt at the house as he pulled away.

He pulled up after exactly fifteen minutes. They figured it was best if Vince wasn't with him with the cops there. He tried to act frantic as he ran up to the house. "Let me in! My wife is in there!"

"There's no one in there but a dead man and toddler."

"What do you mean? My wife called me from here a few minutes ago. Told me there were shots being fired."

"Well she's not in there now."

"Let me in. I'm—"

"I know who you are, and I don't give a shit. No one comes in until the chief gets here. You want to tell me this Lonny worked for your boss?"

"All I'm telling you is my wife was here and called, frantic, because she heard shots."

"Why was she here?"

"This is my sister's house."

"Was she here, too?"

"As far as I know, yes."

"Well...no one is here now. Just sit tight and wait for the chief."

"I need to go look for my wife."

"That wasn't really a suggestion, sir."

Mandy lowered her phone after hanging up with Gerard. Sirens blared loudly as emergency vehicles approached. What bothered her was that she heard the same thing through Gerard's phone. It couldn't have been a coincidence where he was, he was hearing the exact same sirens, too.

"We have to go," she said to Sue.

Sue had gone from hysterical to shock. She was still cradling Darci. All she could do was shake her head no.

"Now, Sue!" Mandy took Darci from her. She went over to the bed and laid her down on it. She kissed her cheek then went back over to Sue, who was still sitting on the floor. "She's gone. There's nothing we can do, but I need to get you out of here. I can't explain it now, you're going to have to trust me."

Sue nodded and Mandy helped her to her feet. Pulling Sue along, Mandy carefully went down the back stairs to the kitchen, then through the adjoining garage door. Lonny's garage had six stalls. He loved his cars as well as his motorcycles. Mandy was able to walk one of the motorcycles through the regular door and down the sidewalk. She climbed on and ordered Sue to get on with her. They took off in the direction opposite of the sirens.

Mandy parked the bike at her apartment and ran with Sue upstairs. They both hurried to change out of their bloody clothes then took off in Mandy's car.

Sue finally spoke. "Why are we running?"

"Because I need to keep you safe. I don't know what is going on, but I'm afraid Gerard was in on this somehow."

"He wouldn't kill his own niece!"

"No. I'm not saying that. I'm sure it was an accident, but I know he's involved. Look, Sue. I don't know what you think Lonny did, but he worked with some shady people. I'm afraid Darci took a bullet meant for him."

"What do you mean 'shady' people?"

"The mob."

"You're insane!"

"Just trust me. Your brother is involved, too."

"I'm not listening to this shit. Get me back to my husband and daughter." Sue reached for the door handle and Mandy pulled her hand back.

"Dammit, Sue! I'm FBI. I know what I'm saying. You're not safe."

A look of pure fear was once again on Sue's face. She was quiet until Mandy pulled up to a small convenience store. "Why are we here?"

"Because you're going to disappear and I'm getting you some traveling money."

"Why don't I go into protective custody?"

"Because I don't know who I can trust right now."

Mandy used her old key to get in. They never bothered changing the locks or the alarm code on the store. *Guess the mob doesn't worry about break-ins.* She hoped Angelo wasn't home or anyone else that might have heard her. She got in and out without any problems and was on her way to the airport within a few minutes.

"I'm sorry. I know this is too much to handle. I know leaving Darci like that has to be the worst part, but you can't come back for her funeral and you can't contact me ever again. Change your name, change your hair. Move often. You should have enough money to last your lifetime if you manage yourself."

Sue was still unmoving. Finally tears welled in her eyes. "I don't understand."

Mandy put her hand on Sue's. "I don't either but I promise you, whoever did this is going to pay."

"Why can't I contact you?"

"Because any contact with anyone could lead whoever this is to you." She held Sue tight. "When it's safe, I'll find you."

Mandy accompanied her to security after buying her ticket. They bought the first available flight out. By chance, it went to Texas. Mandy bought two others. One going to Maine and one going to California, just to give Sue a chance in case someone really was after her as well.

"Stay in crappy motels for a few days. They take cash and won't ask questions. No more than two nights at a time. Your chances of getting into Mexico without your passport are good in the smaller border towns. If Mexico doesn't interest you, go to Paris. Go to Italy. Find a way to get a passport and get the hell out of here." Mandy held her hands tight again. "If you think I'm trying to scare you, you're right. I want you to stay alive." Mandy gave her a tight hug. "I'm so sorry. If I could have done anything at all..."

"I know," Sue said as she broke the hug and gave her ID to the security guard. Mandy walked away and didn't look back.

Mandy had been ignoring her phone all night. She finally picked it up when it rang once she was back in her car.

"Gerard."

"Why the hell haven't you been answering your phone? I've been worried to death about you!"

"I'm fine."

"Where's Sue?"

"I made her disappear."

"You what? Why? She needs family! Her husband and daughter were just killed. Tell me how to get ahold of my sister, dammit!"

"I don't believe she's safe."

"And you're going to keep her safe by sending her out here in the world alone? She's not like you, Mandy."

"She's stronger than you think. Your sister will be fine. It's not really her I'm worried about right now."

"Darci is dead."

"I know that."

"Why did you leave the house?"

"Because I didn't want to be there when this thing played out."

"Talk to me, baby. Come home. We can talk through this."

"Why was Lonny killed, Gerard?"

He let out a heavy breath. "Sonofabitch was going to run."

"How do you know?"

"How do we know anything? I didn't know they were going to kill him. I would never have allowed you to go over there if I knew. Somebody is going to pay for this. You have my word. I know what Darci meant to you."

"She was your niece, Gerard. Don't you even feel anything?"

"Of course. What am I? Heartless?"

"I wonder sometimes."

"What the hell is that supposed to mean?"

"It means...I wonder if you would have shot your own sister if you suspected she was the rat."

"What are you talking about? You know she wasn't involved."

"Could you, though?"

"Come on, baby. Seriously? You know it's family first."

"I do. The question is which family, Gerard?"

CHAPTER SEVENTEEN

Mandy never returned to her apartment. She was in Abbey's office when he showed up for work the next morning.

Craig pointed at his watch. "Lucky you. Your twenty-four hours isn't quite up." His grin faded when he got a good look at her. "You look like shit, Mandy. What the hell happened?"

Mandy charged him and punched him so hard in the chin he stumbled back into his desk. When he stood upright, she tried punching him again, but he held her wrists. She shouted at him. "You sonofabitch!"

"What the hell are you going on about?"

"Oh please. Don't insult me, Abbey. You had to have received the news about Lonny."

"I don't know what you're talking about! You're my man on the inside. What is going on?"

Mandy collapsed in tears and into his arms. "You fucking son of a bitch. They killed Darci before they shot Lonny."

"Who?"

"I don't know who! Gerard was involved. I know he was."

"How?"

"I just know." She pushed herself off of him and harshly wiped the tears rolling down her cheeks. "Why did you call me off this thing? Why?" she screamed.

"Because it was getting nowhere! Don't you see? That could have been you last night. Things are getting out of hand fast and you're not safe."

She stared at him blankly for a few seconds. "What did you say?"

"You're not safe."

"Before that."

"It could have been you."

She dropped down on the couch. "Sonofabitch. They knew it was me. That bullet was meant for me." Two men stormed in the room and Mandy stood. "Who are you?"

"You're coming with us, Agent Smith."

"Why?"

"We want to know what you know, and I think you have a year's worth of explaining to do."

"Wait a second!" Abbey protested. "She's my agent."

"Not anymore. You no longer have privileges on this case, Abbey."

Mandy left without a fight. She didn't particularly care what happened to her right now.

She was taken down to the same room she'd first entered almost a year ago where she bullied the information out of Melvin the drug dealer. She never gave him a second thought after that day. It hadn't even occurred to her to ask. Now was not the time to care. In a matter of one evening, she no longer had any respect for the agency. When this was over, she was out.

Her attitude was starting to kick in after sitting alone for twenty minutes. One of the men who brought her here from Abbey's office came walking through the door with coffee and rolls.

Before he spoke she complained. "Don't I get to make a phone call?"

"You're not under arrest."

"Feels like it to me."

"We need to ask you a few questions first, then you are free to leave. However—"

"I knew there was going to be a however."

"However," he said again, "We suggest you don't."

"Why not?"

"We're concerned for your safety. Your cover was blown and you need to be placed in protective custody."

"You mean jail."

"No. I mean in hiding."

"Witness protection? You can't be serious."

"I'm afraid we are. We're cutting ties with everyone here at the agency as well. Only a few will know of your whereabouts."

"Even Craig Abbey?"

"I'm afraid so. This has gotten out of hand. You should have been pulled in long ago."

"I want to call Gerard."

"That is absolutely out of the question."

"He's my husband, dammit."

"Not technically. You used your assigned name on the license. It's a voided contract. Besides, you really want something to do with the one responsible for killing your niece?"

"That was just my speculation. And how did you hear already?"

"How do you think? It's what we do, Agent Smith. We don't like what's going on. We've been studying the transcripts of your last year. We need to sit down with

Abbey and find out exactly where this all became screwed up."

"It's not screwed up! You can still get Menusco. That Friday drop—"

"Is no longer happening. Lonny was killed and he was the key player—not Menusco."

"You're wrong! He had the money, but Vince—"

"Has called it off. No money—no drop."

"Goddammit!" Mandy slumped into a chair and reached for a cigarette. There was a pack on the table, same as there was the last time she was there. She didn't care if it was the same one and a year old.

"I didn't take you for a smoker."

"Well...I didn't take the FBI for pussies either."

"It's done. Let it go. Your cooperation will be better accepted than your attitude. There's nothing you can do. Abbey is on suspension until further investigation."

"Why take it out on him?"

"Chain of command. If your stories jibe then you have nothing to worry about. For now, we worry about your safety. If we find out otherwise, you will go to jail, Agent Smith."

Again she shot to her feet. "I didn't do anything wrong!"

"I guess we'll find out, won't we?"

Mandy had drifted off while reliving her story. Her last thoughts were of why Lonny told her he was leaving and let her know about the drop money if he knew she was an agent. Maybe she did wear her love of his family too much on her sleeve and he knew she wasn't a threat. Maybe he thought she'd go easy on him for his participation or leave him alone altogether because of her love of Sue and Darci.

Abbey was right. She was too involved and did make a hell of a mess out of things.

If she hadn't gone to visit them that night, she'd be the one dead now instead. At least Hunt wouldn't be in trouble now. And Hannah...

She woke up with a start when Luke staggered into her room with a half a bottle of Jack Daniels in his hand. She feared what was coming, but had to remain tough.

"Where's my husband?"

"Never said I had him, did I?"

"You're such a fool. They're going to kill you. You have to know that. Do you really think a small town deputy is worth keeping around for any reason?"

"I don't want to stick around. I'll get my money and go."

He wasn't worth arguing with sober—let alone drunk. Mandy opted for silence. *Think, Mandy. Think.* She finally blurted out. "I gotta pee."

"Like I'm falling for that."

"I mean it. You've had me tied up for almost a whole day. What am I supposed to do? Pee the bed?"

He ran his hands down the neckline of her blouse. "No can do, babe. Can't make love to you in a puddle of piss now, can I? Can't let you go, either. You're going to try to take me and I'm going to have to kill you. This Menusco fellow is going to be ticked off if that happens, and I don't want that."

"Look, dipshit. I need to use the bathroom. If you're too chicken to help me, then go get Detective Abbey. He'll be more than happy to babysit your punk ass while you watch me pee."

She could tell her words worked. He was starting to get angry. After another swig, he backhanded her. "You and Hunt think you're such tough shit. Hunt and Roy always talked to me like I was a piece of shit, too. Well, look who's on top now? I'm not afraid of you or this Vince!"

"Point taken, tough guy. So, let a girl pee."

"I let you pee, you promise to at least struggle a little when I do you so I really enjoy it?"

"You'll get your struggle, asshole. But if you don't let me pee, my bladder will explode if you so much as look at my stomach right now."

He took another long draw of Jack, seeming to contemplate his choices.

"I have to go, Luke. Look, I know you're not stupid and neither am I. You experienced my best moves back at the station. I just had a kid and I haven't worked out in over a year. I haven't eaten all day either. You think I'm in any shape to try to take you?"

"You acted helpless enough last time, too."

"Go get Craig then, dammit. I gotta go!"

"Shit!" He slammed the bottle down and took out a pocket knife. He held the point tight to her neck.

Mandy was sure he poked through her skin.

"You try anything and I swear to God I'll gut you."

"I got it," she said, feigning fear in her eyes. She tried to muster a tear as well. "You're hurting me."

"Good." He cut through the bindings on her legs then her hands. She sat up and rubbed her wrists.

"Can I get up?"

"Slowly." He took a step back and motioned with the knife toward the door. Mandy carefully stood then dropped to her knees and cried out. "I'm not falling for it," Luke said as he kept his distance.

"I'm not faking it. My legs fell asleep. Just bring me a bucket already."

"Bullshit. Get up!"

She put her hands on the bed and sluggishly pulled herself up. "I need a second. I have pins and needles going on here."

"Oh, do take your time. I'm getting a boner just watching you struggle." He picked up the bottle of Jack and went for a swig. That's when Mandy made her move. She seized it and shoved the bottle into his nose, sending him backward. In his stumbling, she was able to take control of his knife and plunge it into his heart. Her free hand covered his mouth as they fell to the floor. Luke only struggled for a second.

"You stupid little shit," Mandy said as she stood up. She wiped the knife on his pants and went over to listen by the door. Hopefully the fall hadn't woken up Craig. After waiting for a few minutes and hearing nothing, she thought the coast was clear and headed out of room.

She walked cautiously down the long hallway and toward the kitchen. She could tell they weren't in the same cabin, but it was close to the same layout. She stuck close to the walls, trying to keep any floor squeaks from giving her away. When she reached the kitchen, she could make out a figure past the counter in an overstuffed chair in a sitting room. He was hunched over; either sleeping or knocked out. It had to be Hunt. Mandy had to resist the urge to run to him. Craig was still around somewhere.

She tiptoed through the kitchen and over to the chair. She was surprised when she found it wasn't Hunt. It was Roy. Just as she gasped, an overhead light came on. Jumping upright and holding the knife in front of her, she spun around to Craig standing there, holding a gun to Hunt's side. He was gagged and his hands were bound behind his back.

"Let him go," Mandy demanded. "I'm who you want. Just let him go. I don't want my daughter raised an orphan."

Craig laughed. "You think I give a rat's ass about your kid? Only you could manage to get knocked up while you're on your way to a murder. You really are something else. Sit down, Amanda. Your old boss will be here soon enough to take care of things."

Hunt shoved against Craig with all his might and sent them both to the ground. Mandy seized Craig's gun and aimed it at him.

Craig lay flat on the ground with his hands at his side.

Keeping the gun pointed at him, Mandy hurried to Hunt and cut through the zip ties that bound his hands. As much as Mandy wanted to hug him, she resisted to keep an eye on Craig. Hunt took care of his gag.

"Keep him covered." Hunt said as he went over to check on Roy.

"How is he?" Mandy asked.

"Just knocked out. He'll be okay." Hunt took the knife from Mandy and cut him free. Roy didn't even blink as Hunt laid him back in the chair again.

"How did he get here?" Mandy asked.

"We were supposed to meet in town and start searching the homes around the lake for starters. I guess he found this place—"

"And I found him," Craig said, interrupting. "Not bad for a hick town cop. I wonder if he could be bought."

"Don't bet on it," Hunt growled.

"Where's Hannah?" Mandy asked.

"She's safe. She's with my parents. Keep the gun on him. I'm going to call the local PD."

"I don't think so."

They spun at the sound of the voice Mandy recognized well. She refused to drop her gun.

"Drop it, Amanda," Vince demanded. "I don't appreciate having to take care of my own dirty work."

"Don't I know it," she said, cocking back the hammer on the gun.

"Mandy, don't," Hunt pleaded.

"Is this him?" Vince asked Craig, who was getting to his feet.

"That's him. Don't look like much, does he?"

"Enough that it appears he pulled one over on your sorry ass. Did you fail everything in FBI school?"

"I brought her here. That's more than I can say for your boys over the past year."

The gun was still pointed at Vince, but she was looking at Angelo.

"You really do fall for every sucker, don't you?" Vince said. "Drop it or I'll shoot him."

Mandy aimed the gun at Angelo. "You kill Hunt and I'll shoot your son."

"We know you won't. Drop it, Amanda."

She couldn't even pull off a bluff. She dropped the gun to her side. Craig quickly took it from her. "Pussy."

She punched him, sending him backward. Hunt rushed over but Vince yelled, "Stop!" and Hunt froze. "Both of you sit." He pointed to the dining room chair. "Angelo. Bind their hands."

"Yes, father." He ran to the kitchen closet and came back with a container of zip ties.

"You like to keep stocked up I see," Hunt said sarcastically. That earned him a smack on the back of the head with the butt of Craig's gun.

"Stop it!" Mandy cried. "You kill him and I'll never tell you what you want to know."

"So, you do know something," Angelo said as he stepped forward. "I never would have thought you would have stooped to stealing, Mandy."

"I didn't steal anything. It's right where Lonny left it. If I wanted it, I would have gotten it long ago. I wasn't even aware it was still an issue until Dan told me about it."

"And I'm supposed to believe this?"

"Why would I lie? You're only going to kill me, anyway."

"I don't want to, but I'm sure you're more than aware of our rules by now."

Hunt groaned. "Can I go to him?" Mandy asked.

Angelo motioned the gun toward Hunt. She took that as a yes and went to his side.

"So, what do you want to do with your friend now, Angelo?" his father asked.

"Let me take her to go get the money. I'll come back and we'll do what we need to do."

Vince held the gun toward Hunt. "No sense waiting to shoot anyone until later."

"No!" Mandy bolted to her feet and spun around, blocking Hunt. "He comes with me or I don't go. The second I'm out that door you'll kill him."

"We don't barter, Amanda," Vince said. "You've learned that if nothing else by now."

"You also learned even though I was undercover, I still had a certain amount of loyalty to you. Especially to your son. You treated me like family and don't think I forgot it. I didn't want your money then and I don't want it now. Leave Hunt out of this. I'm who you want. Just let him go. I'll tell you where the money is." She turned to his son. "We don't need to drive there, Angelo. You can have one of the guys go get it. Should be easy enough to bust into his safe."

"We're not that stupid," Vince said. "You think we wouldn't have searched his home?"

"It's not at his home. It's at the store. He had his own put in. Not even Joey knew about it."

"How did he manage that?"

She shrugged. "I don't know. Maybe it has been there since before Joey owned the place. I walked in on Lonny one day. He threatened me to never tell anyone about it."

"I thought your loyalty was to me?" Vince said.

"I didn't want you killing Darci's father. It wasn't my business where he kept his stash. He swore it was his money and not yours."

"I don't believe you."

"Believe what you want. You want to know where it is or you want to just kill me and never find it?"

"You've already told me where it was. Not too smart on your part, Agent Smith." Vince pointed his gun at her head.

Angelo cried out, "No!" as he shoved his father against the wall. Vince's gun went off, waking Roy out of his drugged stupor as the bullet grazed his left arm. Roy instinctively reached toward his calf in all the commotion. Mandy couldn't imagine them not searching him well, but when his hand came up, it held a small revolver. He aimed it at Angelo and it was Mandy's turn to cry out. Diving on Roy before he got a shot off, the bullet went wild and hit Vince high in his chest.

Hunt stood and tried rushing Vince, but he was hit in the shoulder by a bullet from Craig's gun. He was slammed into the wall and slid to the floor.

"No!" Mandy shouted. Things were falling apart fast. She took Roy's gun and spun around, sinking three bullets into Abbey's chest before he could blink. Angelo was no threat. He held his hand against his father's wound and repeatedly apologized.

Mandy rushed over to Hunt.

"I'm fine," he said with a wince. "You agents use pussy guns, just like the bad guys." He tried to laugh, but a cough came out instead. "Go get his gun. Bastard probably has Kevlar on."

Mandy went over to Craig and rolled him over. She took his wrist to check for a pulse. It was there, but faint. She ripped his shirt open. He had lightweight body armor on, but one of her bullets had gone right below his neck. He wasn't going to last.

"Why, Abbey?"

"On my deathbed you can't call me Craig, sweetheart?"

Mandy couldn't explain the tears she was fighting. She respected Abbey with everything she had. She'd almost had a school teacher crush on him in the beginning, but he always kept it professional. There was no one better in her eyes than him until Hunt came along. Even then, she thought the scales were hard to tip to who was a better cop.

"Why?" she said again.

"Why else?"

"Money? You sold your soul for money?"

He reached up and held her face with his blood soaked hand. "I'm sorry I got you involved in all of this. I needed to stall the high ups on this case. I figured I'd throw you in and keep them at bay with bullshit reports."

"You never thought I'd succeed?"

"I thought you were good enough to think you were getting somewhere, but not really become anything. Especially after marrying Gerard. I didn't think you had it in you, kid." Abbey winced in pain. "I...I never wanted you killed. I'm sorry."

"I'm sorry too...Craig," Mandy said before he faded away. She allowed a tear to fall for him before she returned to Hunt.

He again reassured her he was fine. Mandy hurried over to Angelo and Vince.

"How is he?"

"He'll be all right," Angelo said. He gently stroked his father's cheek with one hand while he held pressure to his wound with the other. Mandy called 9—1—1 then returned to the room. Hunt and Roy were sitting up and fine, except for their bruised egos. Angelo stayed at his father's side. He couldn't meet Mandy's gaze. "I couldn't let him shoot you."

Mandy placed her hand on his shoulder. "I had to save you from drowning first, too. You always knew I would."

He finally smiled. "I've loved you like no one I ever have loved, Mandy. Not a lover or a best friend, not a sister or even a mother. It was so much more. I hate what you are."

"And I hate what you are. I wanted so much more for you. You don't have to stay where you are, you know. I can help you."

Again his gaze lowered to his father. "You know that's not true. I can't change who I am."

"But you can change what you choose to be."

He could only shake his head and glance down at her pendant. "Just pray for me, Mandy. I'll keep praying for you."

Mandy returned to Hunt. Within a few minutes the police, EMTs, and fire department stormed the cabin. Even wounded, Hunt took charge of the situation and filled in the town sheriff on what went down and who the men were. As Angelo was cuffed, Hunt added, "He's been nothing but cooperative and saved my wife's ass. Go easy on him."

The scene was too familiar. Mandy was covered in a blanket by the fireplace while the county police swarmed around the mass of bodies. Roy was on his way to the hospital, but Hunt refused to go right away. After giving the story over and over, he finally settled by his wife and let an

EMT tend to his wound. He placed his good arm around Mandy. "You okay, babe?"

"I want to get out of here. I want Hannah," she said, not looking away from the fire.

"She's safe. We'll go straight to her."

"No. You're going to the hospital."

"And risk you taking off? Not on your life." He took her chin in his hand and gave her a kiss.

"My boobs are killing me."

"Full?"

"And then some."

"Want me to help with that?"

"If we could be alone for two minutes, I'd consider the shit out of it."

He chuckled. "We really need to cut the drama. Maybe I need to accept a nice meter maid position."

"Maybe we ought to move to Florida."

"Hang out with retired folk and live humbly on a fixed income? Sounds good to me."

"Could you give us a second?" Mandy asked the EMT.

He closed his case and joined his teammate.

"Let's just say, I could have us covered," she said to Hunt when they were alone.

He took her by the biceps. "You have mob money?"

"I know where I can get my hands on it. Yes."

"Don't even do this to me, babe. You were so not on the take, too."

"Of course not, you jackass. I know of a big deal that didn't go down thanks to Gerard trying to kill me, and I know where the stash is."

"That's what this was about?"

"Parts of it. The rest was plain old revenge. They found me out and I had to get taken care of. I don't know if this is it, Hunt. I never would have suspected Abbey as crooked."

Hunt took a step closer to her. "Did it bother you what he said about Gerard? About him truly loving you?"

"I knew he loved me, Hunt. You know I loved him. But it was never going to last. I only fooled myself, and I'm not so sure I ever did it that convincingly."

"Did you know a bullet would end it?"

"For either one of us. Yes."

Hunt closed the gap between them and wrapped his hand around the back of her neck. "You know I'd kill for you."

"You've proved that. You know I'd kill for you."

"You've proved that, too. What I can't do is run away with mob money. I can't live with that, Mandy. If you don't want to stay in Vermont, we can move. But I won't do it that way."

A smile broke out over Mandy's face. She tiptoed up and kissed Hunt. "That is so the right answer, my love. There is no money. I gave it all to Sue." She took her index finger and poked by his wound.

"Ow!"

"Now get your ass to the hospital. I'll get our daughter and see you there, hot shot." She turned to the EMT. "The oaf is ready now. Take his ass in before I kick it all the way there."

The EMT hurried over. "You two act like you're married or something."

They both replied. "We are."

"FBI meets small town Sheriff? This ought to be a good story."

"Oh, it is. Trust me. It is," Hunt said before kissing Mandy goodbye.

EPILOGUE

A year later, Mandy delivered Hunt a beer, then sat next to him with her iced tea. They were spending a relaxing day, poolside, at their Florida home. She placed her cell phone on the small table between them.

"How is Sue doing?" Hunt asked.

"We didn't get to talk for long. She was on a gondola."

"She's still in Venice? I thought she would have had enough of the Italians."

Mandy laughed. "She loves it there. Paulo is still in the picture. I think she finally found love again."

"Good for her." Hunt joined Mandy on her reclining chair. "We really have to go eat on Main Street again?"

"Hunt, half the fun of living in Celebration is being so close to Disneyworld."

"Hannah is too young for a vote in this. I know it's your doing."

"You see how she lights up at the characters."

"You think she'd be afraid of the six foot rat."

Mandy playfully crossed her arms as if in a pout. "If you don't want to take us, I'll just go without you."

"Oh, no you don't. I didn't take a transfer and a pay cut to play bachelor."

"You took a transfer because you were as sick of the winters as I was."

Hunt leaned in closer. "Come on, babe. Do me."

"My pleasure, dearest. It will have to be quick though. Your parents will be here in an hour."

"Again?"

"You know I can't tell your mother no. They're great grandparents to Hannah."

"When I agreed to move here, I didn't realize it would be like moving back into my parents' house."

"Come on, you big baby. It's not that bad." They stood and she wrapped her arms around his neck. "You're down to fifty-eight minutes."

He placed his hand on her stomach. "Let's work on having to extend our family pass by one member."

She smiled at him. "Really? Already?"

"Really. I missed out on the first time. I want to be there for you every step of the way this time."

Mandy took his watch and tapped at the date. "The timing is actually pretty good."

"If it isn't, we'll have fun trying again."

She pointed to his watch again. "Fifty-six minutes."

ABOUT THE AUTHOR

June, who prefers to go by Bug, was born in Philadelphia but moved to Maui, Hawaii, when she was four. She met her "Prince Charming" on Kauai and is currently living "Happily Ever After" in Minnesota. Her son and daughter are her greatest accomplishments. She takes pride in embarrassing them every chance she gets.

Visit www.junekramin.com for more releases.

Time Travel Series:
Dustin Time
Dustin's Turn
Dustin's Novel

Romantic Suspense/Thriller:
Double Mocha, Heavy on Your Phone Number
Hunter's Find
Amanda's Return (Hunter's Find II)
I Got Your Back, Hailey
I've Also Got Your Front (I Got Your Back, Hailey II)
Amanda's Got This, Hailey – I Got Your Back Hailey III
Here Today, Gone to Maui, Hailey - I Got Your Back Hailey IV
I'm on Your Side, Hailey - I Got Your Back Hailey V
Before Parker Met Hailey - I Got Your Back Hailey Prequel
Romance:
Come and Talk to Me
Money Didn't Buy Her Love
Devon's Change of Heart (Money Didn't Buy Her Love II)
I'll Try to Behave Myself
88s, Baby & 88s, Lady
Contemporary Fiction
The Green Flash at Sunset
Baby, Just Say Yes
New Adult
Let's Start With Forever

Visit www.beforehappilyeverafter.com for her middle grade fantasy series written under the pseudonym of Ann T. Bugg.

If you've enjoyed this novel, a review would be appreciated!